Women and Relationships
in
Contemporary Irish Women's
Short Stories

張婉麗 著

出 版 心 語

　　十多年前，全球數位出版蓄勢待發，美國從事數位
出版的業者超過百家，亞洲數位出版的新勢力也正在起
飛，諸如日本、中國大陸都方興未艾，而臺灣卻被視為數
位出版的處女地，有極大的開發拓展空間。植基於此，本
組自 2004 年 9 月起，即醞釀規劃以數位出版模式，協助
本校專任教師致力於學術出版，以激勵本校研究風氣，
提升教學品質及學術水準。

　　在規劃初期，調查得知秀威資訊科技股份有限公司
是採行數位印刷模式並做數位少量隨需出版（POD＝
Print On Demand）（含編印銷售發行）的科技公司，亦為
中華民國政府出版品正式授權的 POD 數位處理中心，尤
其該公司可提供「免費學術出版」形式，相當符合本組推
展數位出版的立意。隨即與秀威公司密集接洽，雙方就
數位出版服務要點、數位出版申請作業流程、出版發行
合約書以及出版合作備忘錄等相關事宜逐一審慎研擬，
歷時 9 個月，至 2005 年 6 月始告順利簽核公布。

執行迄今，承蒙本校謝孟雄董事長、歷任校長、教務長、圖資長、法律顧問以及秀威公司宋政坤總經理等多位長官給予本組全力的支持與指導，本校諸多教師亦身體力行，主動提供學術專著委由本組協助數位出版，數量逾 80 本，在此一併致上最誠摯的謝意。諸般溫馨滿溢，將是挹注本組持續推展數位出版的最大動力。

　　本出版團隊現由錢中媛組長、王雯珊老師以及秀威公司出版部編輯群為組合，以極其有限的人力，充分發揮高效能的團隊精神，合作無間，各司統籌策劃、協商研擬、視覺設計等職掌，在精益求精的前提下，至望弘揚本校實踐大學的辦學精神，具體落實出版機能。

實踐大學圖書暨資訊處採編暨出版組　謹識

2021 年 3 月

Contents

Acknowledgements

I acknowledge my appreciation of my partner Michael, for being supportive and his hard work in proofreading my chapters as well as his precious advice on the book. This book would not be complete without his efforts and encouragement. I am greatly indebted to the library of the University of Ulster and the interlibrary loan service, from which I have gained the firsthand sources which are essential to the core of writing this book. I thank my father, who had supported me financially and emotionally, so I was able to concentrate on my PhD and research in the UK. Besides, I would like to express my thanks to friends for their support: Mika, Machiko, Norie, Gemma, Andy, Tiffany, Daphne, Sandy, Kathy, Chien-shiu, Connie, En-ju, Susan, and also to my colleague Tseng Ching-yi.

Abbreviations

The abbreviations used for anthologies and individual story collections in this book are here listed alphabetically:

Abbrev.	Title of Story Collection or Anthology with Publication Dates/Name(s) of Author(s) or Editor(s)
AN	Antarctica (1999), Claire Keegan
BF	A Bona Fide Husband (1991), Lilian R. Finlay
BM	Big Mouth (2000), Blánaid McKinney
BS	By Salt Water (1996), Angela Bourke
BT	Blood and Water (1988), Éilís Ní Dhuibhne
BW	A Belfast Woman (1980), Mary Beckett
CN	Cutting the Night in Two (2001), Conlon and Oeser (eds)
CS	Collected Short Stories (2000), Clare Boylan
DK	Different Kinds of Love (1987), Leland Bardwell
DW	A Dream Woke Me (1999), Marilyn McLaughlin
EW	Eating Women is Not Recommended (1991), Éilís Ní Dhuibhne
FD4	Field Day Anthology Vol. IV (2002), Angela Bourke, et al (eds)
FH	A Fanatic Heart (1984), Edna O'Brien
FL	The Female Line (1985), Ruth Hooley (ed).
FLI	A Family Likeness (1985), Mary Lavin
GH	A Gift Horse and Other Stories (1978), Kate Cruise O'Brien

GM	A Green and Mortal Sound (1999), DeSalvo, D'Arcy and Hogan (eds)
II	The Inland Ice (1997), Éilís Ní Dhuibhne
IO	If Only (1997), Kate Cruise O'Brien and Mary Maher (eds)
LE	A Lazy Eye (1993), Mary Morrissy
LG	The Little Galloway Girls (1997), Mary Leland
LH	A Life of Her Own (1976), Maeve Kelly
LO	The Love Object (1968), Edna O'Brien
LR	The Lady with the Red Shoes (1980), Ita Daly
LS	Lantern Slides (1988), Edna O'Brien
LW	A Literary Woman (1990), Mary Beckett
MC	Man in the Cellar (1974), Julia O'Faolain
ME	A Memory and Other Stories (1972), Mary Lavin
MF	Midwife to the Fairies (2003), Éilís Ní Dhuibhne
ML1	The Stories of Mary Lavin Vol.1 (1964), Mary Lavin
ML2	The Stories of Mary Lavin Vol.2 (1974), Mary Lavin
ML3	The Stories of Mary Lavin Vol.3 (1985), Mary Lavin
MO	Magician and Other Stories (1996), Ivy Bannister
NW	A Noise from the Woodshed (1989), Mary Dorcey
OH	Orange Horses (1990), Maeve Kelly
PG	The Pale Gold of Alaska (2001), Éilís Ní Dhuibhne
PV	The Portable Virgin (1992), Anne Enright
RH	A Rose in the Heart (1979), Edna O'Brien
RN	Returning (1983), Edna O'Brien
SC	Stories by Contemporary Irish Women (1990), Casey and Casey (eds)
SM	A Season for Mothers (1980), Helen Lucy Burke

SO	The Shrine and Other Stories (1977), Mary Lavin
SP	Strong Pagans (1991), Mary O'Donnell
SS	Sisters (1980), Barr, Walsh and Mahon (eds)
SW	A Scandalous Woman (1974), Edna O'Brien
TB	Tales from Bective Bridge (1978), Mary Lavin
TL	Telling (2000), Evelyn Conlon
TV	Territories of the Voice (1989), DeSalvo, D'Arcy, Hogan (eds)
VH	Virgins and Hyacinths (1993), Caroline Walsh (ed)
WB	Who Breaks Up the Old Moons to Make New Stars (1978), L. Redmond
WP	The Way-Paver (1986), Anne Devlin
WS	Women Are the Scourge of the Earth (1998), Frances Molloy
WT	Wildish Things (1989), Ailbhe Smyth (ed)

Prologue

Since the advent of second wave feminism in the 1960s contemporary Irish women's writing has become an increasingly vivid and important facet of Irish literature. Many Irish women have chosen to write for the modern media in the form of journalism, magazine articles, television drama or radio broadcasts, in order to reach a broad readership and gain publicity.[1] They also have chosen to work in a variety of literary genres, particularly the novel and the short story. There have been some notable, if gradual, changes in many aspects of Irish women's roles and lives in general since 'the other voice' emerged in Irish society in the aftermath of the Eamon De Valera period in the 1960s. It is evident that many contemporary Irish women's short stories reflect some of these changes in Irish women's lives. It is also the case that some Irish female writers are active feminists or have been engaged with the women's movement; consequently, their literary works tend to be 'gynocentric' and consciously concerned with feminist issues. For example, one of the foremost activists of the women's movements among Irish female writers is Mary Dorcey. Dorcey is also one of the founder members of Irish women's organisations such as the Irish Gay Rights Movement (founded in 1974) and Irish Women United (founded in 1975). Other Irish female writers such as Maeve Kelly and Evelyn Conlon are also feminist-conscious as regards women's rights. Their short stories explicitly uncover female unrest in the face of prejudice as well as giving voice to the feminist outcry for justice. Generally speaking, there is a wide range of writing styles as well as choice of topics and representations of Irish women in short stories by contemporary Irish female writers. Some Irish women's stories, such as those by Éilís Ní Dhuibhne and Marilyn McLaughlin, appeared in the late 1990s and after the millennium, and consequently present assertive and independent female characters. The characterisation in these stories is in many ways in stark contrast to that in stories by earlier generations of writers in the 1980s and before like Edna O'Brien, Mary Lavin or Clare Boylan, which tend to unveil critical perspectives on women's issues through portraits of victimised women who are usually shown as powerless and tragic. [2] There appears a noticeable difference in the ways in which different generations of Irish female writers have represented Irish women, from women who were portrayed as being victimised to those who have gained their self-esteem and independence in different Irish social and historical contexts. Thus, contemporary Irish women's short stories appear to encourage a critical or feminist reading so as to challenge or subvert traditional patriarchal values and views regarding Irish women, as well as various related gender issues. It is therefore important to contextualise the effects of women's movements upon the depiction of Irish women in Irish women's writing during the past four decades.

The focus of this book is the short story form as written by Irish women during the period from the late 1960s to the present, concentrating on the representation of women's relationships, between lovers, mothers and daughters, among sisters, and the dilemmas that arise within these relationships. It is evident that many Irish women's short stories prominently focus on human relationships. Human relationships obviously play a central role in humans' lives. Human beings are associated with or identified by a variety of forms of social relationships between them in societies. 'The woman question' is also largely associated with human relationships because any form of relationship, separate from the biological imperative of reproduction, is socially constructed to designate roles for people according to the structure and the system of the particular society. Irish female writers tend to reflect, in a realistic way, 'flesh and blood' issues (even when they rely on traditional romance themes) which link people in a social network of interactions during a period of economic, as well as social, upheaval in Ireland. The core of this book aims to analyse those relationships which are presented through 'archetypal' motifs, which reflect overtones of feminist awareness within the patriarchal contexts of contemporary Irish women's short stories. Here the term 'archetypal' refers to a broad recognition of recurrent patterns in literature as theorised by feminist scholars such as Estella Lauter and Carol Schreier Rupprecht or Annis Pratt, and to those patterns which have been studied to reveal a particular phenomenon in certain cultural contexts, namely, for the purpose of this book, the context of sexual politics. The definition of 'archetypal,' which originates from the term 'archetype' as conceived by Carl Jung, will be elaborated upon in a later section of this chapter. Firstly, however, it is essential to understand the role of women's writings in the Irish contexts.

Irish Contexts

The second half of the twentieth century brought tremendous social change in Ireland, especially for Irish women. Since the late 1960s, when

Ireland gained membership of the European community and women's liberation movements began to emerge, Irish women's status has radically altered. It is important at this point to consider the position of female writers in Ireland. Traditionally, the Irish literary canon has been predominantly male, with highly acclaimed writers such as W. B. Yeats, John M. Synge, James Joyce or Samuel Beckett holding court. Frank O'Connor even remarks that the Irish Literary Renaissance is a 'peculiarly masculine affair' although Irish female writers have always existed, but simply remained invisible and silenced in the critical arena.[3] Despite the exclusion of female writers from the canon, things have gradually changed in Ireland, especially since the second half of the twentieth century. Many more female writers have emerged and works by Irish women have been studied, re-discovered and researched by critics. This flourishing female literary phenomenon has aroused a great deal of interest in Irish women's writing and critical studies and vice versa. For example, editors of *The Field Day Anthology of Irish Writing*, which plays an eminent role in Irish studies, also felt compelled to publish two new volumes wholly dedicated to Irish women's writing in September 2002. Volumes IV and V of *The Field Day Anthology* show that by the second half of the twentieth century there were a large number of female writers in Ireland, but that not many of them were recognized by the Irish 'male' literary canon, epitomised by 'intentionally selected' excerpts in the first three volumes of *the Field Day Anthology* (1991). These two latest volumes of *the Field Day Anthology of Irish Women's Writing*, with over 3000 pages covering various genres and subjects, may be the first two substantial collections of Irish women's writing ever published in Ireland or in the arena of Irish studies elsewhere. They collect works by

Irish female writers dating from the 6th century to the present, and they also uncover a comprehensive picture of the presence of women in Irish literature. In a way this female literary phenomenon, as well as the tendency to publish female literary output as shown in *The Field Day Anthology* Volumes IV and V, has also encouraged more work to be produced and published by Irish women.

Although Irish women have experienced unfair treatment in various aspects of Irish society, it would be simplistic and arbitrary to describe them exclusively as powerless, downtrodden victims or helpless 'maidens in distress.' Irish women may have been marginalised in general, but this single dimension simply does not visualise a broader, multifaceted picture of women in Irish society. As a matter of fact, the roles and status of Irish women have been paradoxical and problematic. Traditionally, especially in the private sphere of the family, Irish women appear to have had a powerful role, both historically and in the contemporary period. However, Irish women's status has also been shaped by the cult of the Virgin Mary, which was particularly emphasised in the nineteenth and early twentieth centuries. The Virgin Mary, an iconic figure of an asexual, suffering mother, has endorsed an idealised role for Irish women as mothers as well as an image of passive and obedient women who rely on their children to make them 'whole and glorious.'[4] Conformity to this ideal marginalised and silenced Irish women in the private as well as the public sphere. Ironically, the periods of the nineteenth and early twentieth centuries also saw some outstanding women who played active roles in the Irish Suffrage Movements, as well as those who made remarkable contributions to the state in terms of culture, education and politics. These famous women include Anna Parnell (1852-1911), the founder of the

Ladies Land League (1881), Maud Gonne (1865-1953) of the Irish Suffrage Movement and Lady Augusta Gregory (1852-1932) of the Irish Literary Renaissance. Thus, on the one hand, powerful Irish women have achieved much in society, while on the other hand, the social consciousness that reflects the male-dominated culture in organized politics in Ireland locates Irish women as objects of dependence within a patriarchal framework. Generally speaking, from the 1920s to the 1950s Irish women were entitled to very little from the government in terms of social or financial support, and often they were only considered dependents of their husbands, rather than individuals. There was virtually no support for single mothers or battered wives at that time. In the civil service, women could work only before they got married due to the marriage bar, and in other occupations women had to endure discrimination in terms of unequal pay in comparison with their married male co-workers. Women's under-representation at parliamentary level or at senior positions in the civil service was sustained until the 1980s.[5]

There were some changes introduced in the late 1960s and 1970s. With the establishment of the Commission on the Status of Women in 1972, there were reforms of the discrimination against career women in terms of the marriage bar or inequality of pay as well as limited support for single or married women when they were in crisis or difficulties. Even then, many Irish women still thought of themselves as primarily homemakers or caretakers rather than envisaging the same career opportunities as their male counterparts. One of the main reasons for this conservatism may have been the fact that the primary and second-level systems of education were still denominational and largely controlled by the Catholic church, and so teaching was heavily influenced by religious doctrines that tended to encourage women to sacrifice their individuality for their families. This 'bias' had of course previously been enshrined in the Constitution of Ireland. It is conveyed clearly in subsections 1 and 2 of section 2, Article 41 of the Irish Constitution as the following:

> In particular, the State recognizes that by her [woman's] life within the home, woman gives to the State a support without which the common good cannot be achieved. The State shall, therefore, endeavour to ensure that mothers shall not be obliged by economic necessity to engage in labour to the neglect of their duties in the home.[6]

It is hardly surprising, then, that within such a framework, which presumably imposes domestic duties upon Irish women as their primary or sole responsibility, human relationships between men (as husbands) and women (as wives) were still based on power (dominant) and subservience (dominated). However, with the emergence of feminism in the late 1960s, the authority of male dominance began to be questioned and the old value system gradually began to crumble. This process was helped along in various ways by the impact of new insights obtained from the outside world through the mass media, especially television and radio. Increasingly Irish women began seeking more authentic representations of themselves as women in modern and post-modern Ireland. By the mid-1990s a new milestone was reached when divorce was finally legalised in Ireland.

The social problems in Northern Ireland arising from the 'Troubles' which broke out in the late 1960s and brought the recurrent threat of violence, created a traumatic sense of anxiety and insecurity in people's mentality and their behaviour and this is depicted in some stories by Northern Irish female writers. Characters are drawn against a background of a conflicting battle of communities divided between Catholics and Protestants, of hatred and suspicion as well as crisis in trust and love for humanity such as in Fiona Barr's, Anne Devlin's or Blánaid McKinney's stories. In the southern part of Ireland, now an independent republic state and comparatively politically stable, Irish female writers explore the problematic moral hypocrisy underlying Catholicism and a scandalous priesthood. Their work challenges traditional values, unmasking the paradox between different values. In some stories, when the old certainties have collapsed, people seek to negotiate the powerlessness and emptiness within themselves so as to establish a new order. Hence, Irish women's aspirations for a place and a meaning of their own has resulted in stories questioning the absurdity of women's existence in a world which devalues and denies them as individuals. This quest often surfaces as rebellious unrest disguised by indulgence and obsession, or turns to escape and exile. Take some of Edna O'Brien's stories about disorientated women, for example. These women are often portrayed as suicidal or as suffering from some mental and physical symptoms of disorder such as sleepwalking, vomiting, paranoia, depression or schizophrenia. The explicit exploration of sexuality and passion in the short stories sometimes serves as another indicator symbolising women's struggle for freedom, as in Mary Dorcey's, Ivy Bannister's, Éilís Ní Dhuibhne's and Evelyn Conlon's stories. Irish women have usually been the 'objects,' or the muses, in the literature that forms the predominately male 'Irish canon.' Not inspired by unrealistic, idealised female images from male fantasy, Irish women's stories, which are normally conveyed by a female narrator, reflect and express a female way of thinking and behaving as well as reveal a female vision of the world which takes account of the society Irish women also inhabit. Irish female writers have also experimented with a variety of new forms and styles in their stories. Irish women are no longer presented only through a male lens.

Although things have begun to change widely if gradually in Ireland, conservative, biased perceptions of women still persist. Some stories are inspired by real social tragedies, and they reflect a clash between old and new values in Ireland. For example, there is the verbal and physical harassment of women by men in Clare Boylan's 'Concerning Virgins' and 'Confession,' or more disturbingly the sexual abuse encountered in Leland Bardwell's 'The Dove of Peace,' Mary Dorcey's 'The Orphan' and 'A Sense of Humour.'[7] The ghosts from the past which haunted Irish women's short stories in the 1980s echo some of the social inequalities and challenges of earlier periods in the 1960s and 1970s. However, when we approach the late twentieth century and the twentieth-first century, other new stories from a younger generation have emerged in varied forms and styles. These younger female writers set their characters and stories not only in Ireland, but also in the wider contexts of Europe or America. So, in a world of varied cultures, values and experiences have been represented in the stories by these new authors of 'post-modern' Irish literature. This tendency to embrace a more open, diverse world beyond the island of Ireland in contemporary Irish women's stories may also reflect Ireland's recent social and economic development and confidence as a 'Celtic Tiger' in the European Union which has replaced the self-image of a backward, miserable, shattered world of poverty, despair and self-pity.

It is believed by some critics that literature can be viewed as a literary reproduction reflecting or even constructing human experiences in a given cultural context. Critics such as Northrop Frye think that 'literature as a unity in itself does not withdraw it from a social context…it becomes far easier to see what its place in civilization is.'[8] In Frye's view, literature is not purely a product of fantasy; there is, he argues, something else to be gained from literature interacting with the society. Like Frye, feminists including Elaine Showalter, Sandra M. Gilbert, Susan Gubar, Patricia Stubbs or Rachel Brownstein also see literature as representing some women's experiences, which can be evaluated against reality.[9] Thus, a close examination of recent stories by Irish female writers may help us to evaluate how literary representations reflect and respond to the impact made by some changes which have occurred in Irish society. It may also help us to understand the impact of these social changes on human experience and culture in Irish society.

As stated above, the aim of this book is to explore the 'archetypal motifs' within the human relationships depicted in contemporary Irish women's short stories from the late 1960s to the present. These motifs are archetypal not only because they emerge in strikingly recurrent patterns but also because they describe relationships adulterated by an ideology which aims to shape human relationships and behaviour in a particular (patriarchal) context. These stories disclose some Irish women's attempts to subvert established forms of relationships with men and with other women, or Irish women's efforts to try to negotiate a new interface with the changing society and within women themselves. Certainly, this is not to suggest one single simplistic explanation for the complex dimensions of varied human relations in Irish women's stories; rather, the aim is to let the stories speak for themselves. Moreover, it is notable that a female outcry of rage due to inequality of gender roles in Irish society surfaces in many stories as a challenge to existing perceptions and a system which favours men as well as to encourage (if not demand) stronger female aspiration towards women's development and freedom in their own right.

Inevitably, the term 'archetypal' may appear ambiguous and problematic here as the terminology originating from 'archetypes' seems 'out-dated' from today's critical points of view. Archetypes are often associated with oversimplified generalisation, contributing to reinforcing 'stereotypes' at the expense of variation on an individual basis, which is especially unfair to women. 'Archetype' is sometimes treated as the synonym of 'stereotype,' which concept is strongly questioned and opposed by modern theorists and feminists. Therefore, it is essential to clarify the confusion as well as dispel the skepticism before beginning to evaluate recurrent motifs as 'archetypal' in contemporary Irish women's stories.

Archetypal Motifs and Patterns

The term 'archetype' can be traced back to its Greek origin 'arkhe,' which means primitive or beginning, and 'tupos,' a model, referring to an original form from which diverse variations can be made.[10] While the term 'stereotype,' meaning rigid generalisation, denotes the original plate from which subsequent imprints are made, 'archetype' seems to embrace a more fluid quality in setting such forms. One of the most renowned scholars in the development of the concept of the archetype is the psychologist Carl Jung (1875-1961). Having studied many schizophrenic patients and having experienced the horrendous human catastrophe of the

Great War, Jung was overwhelmed by how some patterns manifested themselves through various recognised symbols and images in human culture. Jung was enormously interested in these patterns, originating from what he terms archetypes, and developed his ideas on how archetypes take shape across cultures and decades. Archetypes, as Jung describes them, are patterns of psychic energy originating in the collective unconscious and commonly finding their manifestation in dreams, fairy tales, religious beliefs, fantasies or mythologies.[11] An archetype, in Jung's recognition, can be a process, a perspective or a form but not the content itself, as it is 'directly from the unconscious predisposition.'[12] Here Jung's definition of 'archetype' seems flexible:

> With regard to the definiteness of the form, our comparison with the crystal is illuminating inasmuch as the axial system determines only the stereometric structure but not the concrete form of the individual crystal. The same is true of the archetype. In principle, it can be named and has an invariable nucleus of meaning—but always only in principle, never as regards its concrete manifestation.[13]

Jung suggests that archetypes are 'universally' inherited from the unconscious of humankind, therefore there may be some common ground that human beings will share across varied cultures.[14]

However, Jung's perception of the 'universality' of archetypes, and especially those of anima and animus understood as the so-called 'masculine' and 'feminine' qualities, have been severely criticised by feminists as absolutes which reinforce gender stereotypes based on bipolarity.[15] Nevertheless, Jung's groundbreaking ideas on archetypes opened a window for later generations to investigate further how the tendency of the human mind to make patterns actually manifests itself in the complexity of human societies and through cultural production, and whether this tendency may or may not have made some impact on culture and society in the form of a kind of 'ideology.' Archetypal theories since Jung have become more than a simplistic study attempting to search for symbols and images through mythologies or fairy tales in order to apply these to literary texts, but have evolved into a way of examining recognisable patterns in literary texts in an inductive manner as well as evaluating how these patterns recur and in which contexts. Thus, some feminist theorists discard in part Jung's ambiguous implications of rigid attributes such as his ideas on gender qualities or the application of certain symbols to fixed meanings in interpretations of dreams. They tend to evaluate mythologies and fairy tales as cultural products constructed in particular contexts under male-dominated ideology. This way feminist theorists view archetypes as a principle in identifying recurrent patterns of representations in art and literature. Christine Downing recognises the archetypal dimensions of human experience in the following:

> [W]hen I say 'archetypal' I do not mean to approve the essentialism or the universalism implied by some of Jung's own writing about archetypes. I mean simply the valuation of the imaginal and metaphorical 'depth' of experience and the recognition that at that 'depth' level our experience reveals typical, transpersonal features that connects us to other humans, both those

we know only through myth and art and those we know directly, in a way that feels transformative.[16]

Estella Lauter and Carol Schreier Rupprecht, in a feminist archetypal theory-based study, give their definition of archetype as 'a process of valuing an image,' of which the forms may vary according to 'the personal and social history of the person who manifests it.'[17] It is, as Lauter and Rupprecht point out, 'a process, a tendency to form and re-form images in relation to certain kinds of repeated experience.'[18] That is, a tendency to form or re-form symbols and images either in culture, media, art or literature, manifests as so-called 'archetypes' which create recurrent models of image, symbol or narrative in literary texts, art or culture which can be recognised as 'archetypal' images or patterns. These archetypal patterns may vary and be tempered by different ideological and cultural backgrounds, as well as understandings, depending on the individual case.

In the light of Lauter's and Rupprecht's approach, this book follows Professor Annis Pratt's conception of archetypal analysis as inductive rather than deductive so as to avoid absolute, universal generalisations about certain findings. Therefore, the objective of this book is to examine such recurrent thematic aspects through representations in Irish women's short stories and to evaluate how and why such a process is constructed in a certain way rather than simply to impose fixed forms of symbols or images upon the texts and look for rigid explanations valued as 'truth.' The key objective is not to assert any discovery as 'absolute truth' but to uncover what Irish female writers seek to subvert or to construct through their representations of women and how those representations are constructed in their stories. Representation is a continuous process and

Irish female writers have been engaged with the process of representing Irish women through certain themes and characterisation in their stories against the backdrop of contemporary Ireland, which has also registered the impact of feminism since the late sixties. Do contemporary Irish women's short stories express feminist viewpoints or simply convey stories about female experience? If they do appear feminist, to what extent is this purpose served and in what ways? These questions need to be addressed and readdressed as they inform the recurrent motifs and themes examined in this book. As a result, the study of literary representations of women in Irish women's short stories may provide a partial understanding of Irish women and their lives as constructed and represented in this field of cultural production and prove useful for research in other fields of study concerned with women in a changing Irish society. It is the goal of this book to study collectively representations of Irish women under the impact of Irish women's movements so as to decode those patriarchal ideologies which underlie gender relations and form the root of gender bias and inequality, as well as to provide useful sources for interdisciplinary research.

Breaking the Ice: Landmarks of Irish Women's Short Stories

In the course of Irish women's history, the backlash against women's liberation in the 1980s was the catalyst for repression and frustration. This period, highlighting the passing of an amendment to the wording of the Constitution which favours the pro-life lobby on the abortion issue, is generally considered as a time when the revolutionary ardour of the women's movement from the earlier years waned due to the economic recession and the fundamentalist repression of the mid-1980s. In 1983, the anti-abortion campaign won the referendum of wording amendment in the Constitution by 841,223 to 416,136 votes.[19] The amendment was then placed in Article 40.3.3:

> The State acknowledges the right to life of the unborn, and with due regard to the equal right to life of the mother, guarantees in its laws to respect, and as far as is practicable, by its laws to defend and vindicate that right.[20]

This amendment once again was placed as another obstacle for legality of abortion in Ireland. However, this was also a period of transition, during which a new direction in the Irish women's movement diverted energies from social and political concerns to educational, cultural and creative arts pursuits. All of this, Ailbhe Smyth suggests, certainly aroused public awareness of the women's movement in Ireland and eventually contributed to the victory of Mary Robinson's presidency campaign in 1990.[21] In this period, Irish female writers gradually surfaced and their stories began appearing in more publications. Among them, two major collections of Irish women's writing published in Ireland are worth a mention—*The Female Line: Northern Irish Women Writers* (1985) edited by Ruth Hooley and *Wildish Things: An Anthology of New Irish Women's Writing* (1989) edited by Ailbhe Smyth.

Both collections were published in the second half of the 1980s and brought together a variety of genres from poetry and drama to prose and short stories written by Irish women. *The Female Line* served as the first collection of Northern Irish women's writing at that time, while *Wildish Things* collected works by Irish women both from the North and the South. *Wildish Things* brought to the fore a certain degree of the submerged anger of women's silenced consciousness and attempted to challenge the injustice endured by women in a direct tone laced with bitter sarcasm. The difficulties women have coped with in Irish society over the years eventually forced them to gaze into 'the forbidden well' and to demand fair play.[22] The groundbreaking collection *The Female Line* portrayed the bitter hardship of women's lives in the shadow of the social turbulence of the 'Troubles' in the North.

Territories of the Voice: Contemporary Stories by Irish Women Writers (1989), edited by Louise DeSalvo, Kathleen Walsh D'Arcy and Katherine Hogan and published in London and Boston, covered controversial issues such as abortion and sexual abuse in Ireland in the 1980s.[23] Another collection of Irish women's short stories appeared in the U.S.A.—*Stories by Contemporary Irish Women* (1990), edited by Daniel Casey and Linda M. Casey—who compiled the works of different generations from the 1970s to the mid 1980s, and demonstrated a troubled and torn parochial rural world of hypocrisy. *Store of My Heart: Contemporary Irish Short Stories* (1991), edited by Bernadette Halpin, was published in London by an independent feminist publisher, the Sheba Feminist.[24] In Ireland, *Virgins and Hyacinths* (1993) echoed the chaotic background of the 1980s and the early 1990s, and provided more views from younger writers such as Anne Enright and Mary Morrissy, who deployed a cosmopolitan atmosphere of absurdity and powerlessness in a modern society, sometimes through humour laced with harsh bitterness. *If Only* (1997), a collection of stories by Irish women on the motifs of

love and divorce, marked the legalisation of divorce in Ireland in 1995.[25]
Cutting the Night in Two (2001) is a recent collection of Irish women's
short stories which gathers works from the previous half century,
including writers from the earlier generation such as Elizabeth Bowen in
the post-independence period to the younger emigrant generation of
Bridget O'Connor and Sara Berkeley in the post-Eamon De Valera era.
The thirty-four stories in the collection represent a chronological tableau
of Irish women and their relationships with others from the past to the
present, from the earlier awakening of the Irish women's liberation
movement to the post-colonial, post-modern mosaic of the new century.

The Speaking Voice in Irish Women's Short Stories

Dermot Bolger states in the introduction to his edited anthology of
contemporary Irish fiction that recent generations of writers have
reinvented a new diversity of 'Irishness' in contemporary Irish fiction
beyond the established traditional themes and styles, so even defining
Irish contexts has become increasingly multi-dimensional, and sometimes
problematic. [26] The choice of setting in the stories ranges from a
conventional rural village to a modern cosmopolitan city; from local
Ireland to a territory with more international atmosphere such as London,
or other countries in Europe or the U.S.A. Countries such as France or
Italy, both also Catholic, are sometimes treated as utopias in a quest for
freedom by female characters in Irish women's stories. The switch to an
exotic setting recalls to readers the characteristic motifs in E. M. Forster's
novels *Where Angels Fear to Tread* (1905) or *A Room with a View* (1908),

where the repressed English female characters experience a journey of freedom and passion in Italy.

The motifs and themes in Irish women's short stories generally focus on an exploration of the inner and outer worlds of the central (usually female) character. It is important to note that the focus is also on the way the woman manages to negotiate with society or, alternatively, on an 'awakening' of the female character to her self. The narrative is frequently a self-discovery journey fuelled by the female aspiration for individuality. Some stories focus on the 'stream-of-consciousness' of the main character(s), such as the explicit female sexual confessions in Evelyn Conlon's 'Taking Scarlet as a Real Colour.' Some stories are narrated by an authoritative speaking voice with a wit and humour which recalls the Irish storytelling tradition, such as Éilís Ní Dhuibhne's 'Midwife to the Fairies' or Juanita Casey's stories. Yet other stories are treated in a more complicated way, introducing fragmentation and dislocation of time and space, such as Mary Dorcey's title story in her renowned lesbian story collection *A Noise from the Woodshed* (1989). Dorcey in this story displaces the boundaries of time and space, the central self and others ('you' and 'she' and 'they'), through her fluid verbal expression.

Forms and styles in contemporary Irish women's short stories are varied, and stories are sometimes not presented in a traditional manner. For example, a story may not be presented in a linear way, either chronically or retrospectively. In Irish women's stories the central character is often a woman. It is also interesting to note the absence of male characters in some stories in which the father or husband is either dead or away. The frequent use of first-person narrators in Irish women's stories serves to evoke the central characters both in mental and physical contexts. Surroundings too are closely associated with the mental response as well as physical activities by the juxtaposition of the inner and outer worlds of the character(s). The physical context is sometimes twisted, reflecting the divided mental world of the character, as in Lucile Redmond's 'The Shaking Tree,' F. D. Sheridan's 'The Empty Ceiling' or Clare Boylan's 'Life on Mars.' Anne Devlin weaves a story about obsessive love associated with the metaphor of the snake's poison in 'First Bite.' In Shirley Bork's 'The Palm House,' a juxtaposition is created between the environment and a helpless woman's chaotic anxiety about her handicapped baby and her lover. In these cases, the imagery has a cinematic quality while the tone and style of the narration vary to a wide degree. Irish female writers appear experimental in terms of their style of weaving and 'telling' a story.

'Was marriage for two people or only for a woman? The two people entering into the holy bond of matrimony, did that not set them apart? Both of them or only the woman? Did the man lay himself open to ribaldry, exposing himself for the gratification of fun-makers?…She wondered if marriage could be a trap with steel teeth, ready to snap on her.'

from Lilian Roberts Finlay, 'In the Beginning,'
A Bona Fide Husband (1991)

1. Pursuit, Submission and Subversion in Love and Marriage

This chapter evaluates the archetypal motifs of pursuit, submission and subversion of the primordial relationship between men and women as lovers in contemporary Irish women's short stories. It is notable that themes of love and marriage dominate in Irish female writers' explorations of the human condition. The relationships, which Irish female writers depict in recurrent patterns of motif (identified as 'archetypal motifs') in their stories, illustrate the paradoxical and complex dimensions of fundamental societal forces and their impact on human interactions in Irish society. The stories about heterosexual relationships generated by the Irish female literary imagination serve as a prominent arena in which to evaluate the way gender relations and roles are constituted as well as constructed so as to create and/or maintain a social framework under patriarchy in Irish contexts.

It is clear that themes of love and marriage have been popular amongst writers of women's fiction in English, both American and British, since the emergence of female novelists during the eighteenth century. Until relatively recently, that women's fiction tended to be marginalised as tedious, second-rate and beyond serious academic consideration or worthy of a place within the literary canon is perhaps due to a perception which tends to generalise that women's fiction is preoccupied with the sentimental and the sensational (in terms of love and marriage). In her major study of nineteenth and twentieth-century women's literature in English, entitled *A Literature of Their Own* (1982), Elaine Showalter examines women's fiction and seeks to defend female writers in this respect. Showalter does point out that women's fiction, particularly from the late eighteenth- and nineteenth centuries, seems frequently to be associated with sentiment and romance. The pursuit of marriage, the ecstasy of love and domestic descriptions are made impressive by female writers such as Aphra Behn, Frances Burney, Ann Radcliffe, Jane Austen or Charlotte Brontë. Gothic romances prefigured the popularity of the so-called 'sensation novel' in the late Victorian period, which was a popular genre of fiction featuring a plot of suspense that revolves around crimes and mysteries in wealthy families. Apart from what Showalter has argued about love and marriage as the dominant themes in women's fiction in the eighteenth and nineteenth centuries, there are also popular novels such as the Mills and Boon or the Harlequin romances which are worldwide bestsellers written by, read by, and marketed for and about women in the twentieth and twentieth-first centuries.[27] These romance paperbacks seem to retain a certain degree of popularity among teenage or adult female as well as some male readers, and many of these novels have also been translated into various languages as one of the largest sources of pulp fiction entertainment among the general reading public.

Notwithstanding all of this, is it fair to judge women's fiction as of no more worth than superficial sensation and, therefore, lacking in-depth subtlety and a broader vision of the world? It would be arbitrary and simplistic to draw any conclusion at this point because, as Elaine Showalter has suggested in *A Literature of Their Own*, the phenomenon that women's fiction was largely centred around domestic affairs and personal relationships involves a much more complicated context in which women struggled to write in their difficult roles as both women and writers. Furthermore, they had to face harsh attitudes from the existing male literary canon. Having taken examples from the nineteenth and early twentieth centuries, Elaine Showalter argues that women's fiction was considered inferior to men's works by male literary critics also due to a (male) perception of so-called 'women's natural taste' for the trivial.[28] This particular point of view seems to assume women '[always] enjoy getting involved in other people's affairs.' [29] These speculations, according to Showalter, seem to echo claims of some physicians and anthropologists in the Victorian period regarding inherent physical weaknesses in females due to their smaller and less efficient brains. Such pseudo-science contributed to a (male) belief that women are unable to produce masterpieces and are simply engaged in a 'self-destructive imitation of a male skill.'[30] This belief in women's inability to be 'good' writers is epitomised by a Victorian scholar, R. H. Hutton, who claimed, perhaps with negative intent, that women's fiction is influenced by the fact that women respond from the heart instead of the head; women's perceptions are 'finer, subtler, quicker than [men's]' with 'delicacy and skill in delineation' but it is difficult for women when they come to reason abstractly.[31] Hutton then continued to draw his conclusion, saying that 'what they [women] lack is an eye for universality, a power of seeing the broad and representative element.' [32] Another commentator from the same period even classified women's fiction as a distinctive 'genre,' saying that it is so 'exclusively dedicated to the passion of love' that the very word 'Romance' has been 'engrossed' by the term novel.[33]

However, this is not to say that there were no male writers in the Victorian period who were also preoccupied with the theme of love, nor to claim that the theme of love is all that women write about in fiction. Literary critics (perhaps mostly male) tended to generalise this theme in women's writing, reinforcing theories that women's craft can only be presented in a 'petty' way. Hence, Elaine Showalter has attempted to provide some possible reasons why female writers have been 'mistakenly' classified by critics as only good at describing personal relationships and romance in their writings, which are generally dismissed as 'pettiness' by such critics. Showalter thinks it can be associated with the limited scope of experiences which women were allowed in the Victorian period, as well as the kind of subject a female would be expected to select in her work if she did dare to pick up the pen to write as her male peers. Furthermore, female writers were under pressure from the double critical standard of a male literary tradition.[34] The implicit and devaluing implication of such judgment on women's writing due to this double critical standard in the male literary tradition, exemplified by the comment made by R. H. Hutton, is that women's writing is inherently different from and inferior to that of men. The consequence of this kind of literary judgment has been a longstanding neglect of the distinctive achievements of female writers.

This tendency to devalue women's writing may also underlie the bizarre phenomenon that a large number of Irish male writers are contrasted with a small group of Irish female writers as representatives of the history of Irish literature over one thousand years in the first three volumes of the 'authoritative' anthologies of Irish writing edited by *Field Day*. For example, the first volume lists only a few female writers such as

Mary Barber (Anglo-Irish verse), Charlotte Brooke (Gaelic classics translation), Mary Delany (letter writing on Irish life) and Maria Edgeworth (fiction). In similar fashion, there is a sparse number of Irish female writers collected from the early nineteenth century to the first half of the twentieth century over the 1200 pages of the second volume—Mary Balfour (poetry), Lady Dufferin (songs and ballads), Lady Gregory (drama), and (fiction) Elizabeth Bowen, Emily Lawless, Edith Somerville and Martin Ross, Kate O'Brien, Mary Lavin. What *Field Day* presents in these three volumes of the Anthology is an overall picture of the Irish literary 'canon' in which Irish women's writing appears scarcely to exist. Seamus Deane, the editor of *The Field Day Anthology of Irish Writing* (1991), denies that the Anthology is an attempt at a canon. But Julia McElhattan Williams, among those reviewers who have tended to disagree with Deane's claim, has made the following response:

> *The Field Day Anthology* represents literary editing on a grand scale, the apotheosis of choice, judgment, and critical perspective. The anthology introduces newcomers to Irish literature (those who can explore the volumes in the library, at least) to a spectrum of authors and works, while confirming for practiced scholars of Irish studies the range of texts classifiable as "Irish." The "story which the anthology has to tell" that Deane refers to proceeds on two levels: first, it is the story of Irish oppression at the hands of British imperialist forces since the Elizabethan Plantation; second, and perhaps less apparently, it is the meta-narrative of anthology-making, and thus illustrates the theoretical problem I alluded to earlier. It is certainly an odd moment in literary history for an

editor to present such a massive collection of texts, odd because what Deane has given us looks remarkably like a canon of Irish writing···though Deane may claim that *The Field Day Anthology* is only an "example of the way in which canons are established and the degree to which they operate as systems of ratification and authority."[35]

Edna Longley also criticises this absence of Irish women's writing in the Anthology as 'unjustified':

Might the anthology's exiguous representation of writing by women be justified on aesthetic grounds? But the General Editor [Seamus Deane] does not believe in aesthetic grounds: "The aesthetic ideology which claims autonomy for a work of art is a political force which pretends not to be so." Logically, then, the printed poems of Field Day directors Heaney, Deane and Paulin might just as well make way for women contributors.[36]

Longley argues that there is no excuse for 'omitting the documents of Irish feminism' in the light of the anthology's inclusion of non-literary texts of political writings by men including those by Michael Collins, Eamon De Valera, Ian Paisley, John Hume and Gerry Adams.[37] The latest two volumes of *The Field Day Anthology* (2002) on Irish women's writing provide sufficient evidence to prove that there are many Irish female writers as 'good' as those (mostly male) who have been collected as representatives in the course of Irish literary history in the first three volumes of the anthology. The key point here is the attitude of those editors and critics who subscribe to the double critical standard of a male literary tradition, resulting in the exclusion from the 'canon' of many established female writers.

It is a fact that female writers do write frequently about love and marriage in their fiction. However, stories about love and marriage by Fanny Burney, Jane Austen or the Brontës are now being reviewed positively as contemporary observations on gender dialogue and social values rather than as sentimental love stories. It is not difficult to note that many women's lives have been, and still are, bound deeply and closely with these types of human relationship. Marriage and the family still have a profound impact on women's lives by endorsing their 'natural' roles as daughters, wives or mothers. This area comprises a complex mosaic of social change and power dynamics in respect of gender issues. In Ireland, where women have so often been undermined in various fields, many Irish female writers explore issues of love and marriage in their writing and, in so doing, they evoke the dialectic relationship between social forces and gender relations from varied perspectives. The 'love and marriage' issues Irish female writers address in their stories differentiate themselves starkly from the Mills and Boon romances which usually mask the reinforcing gender stereotypes of 'women's sexual, racial and class submission' by superficially showing women's success as well as giving a voice to female freedom of expression in the quest for love and passion (or sexuality).[38] By contrast, many contemporary Irish women's short stories discussed in this chapter may be termed as those with a 'feminist awareness' even though the substance of many of these stories is still love and marriage. Certainly, women's writing cannot always be assumed as aligned with feminism. However, many Irish women's short stories not only tend to give voice to muted female experiences but also reveal an awareness of female challenge to, as well as rebellion against, unfairness or bias which appears 'feminist' in terms of questioning these gender presumptions. In this way Irish female writers do not express only this aspect of female experience but also convey messages, implicit or explicit, through their choice of subject matter and the issues in their stories.

Particularly, motifs of pursuit, submission and subversion appear archetypal in Irish women's short stories about love and marriage, which examine the meaning of marriage as well as the problematic fundamentals of the way men and women in this particular culture perceive love. Marriage has been classified in the views of some feminists, such as Jo VanEvery, Adrienne Rich or Trudy Hayes, as an enclosure of socially conforming force and a 'hegemonic form of heterosexuality' in its power and dominance.[39] Therefore, women in these stories are depicted as seeking love whilst these social forces of conformity give them little choice but to comply with marriage norms, willingly or unwillingly. These norms used to be the destiny women had to face and submit to as their sole lifetime career without any other options. Presumably marriage is perceived as involving certain fixed gender roles for both sexes in their capacities as husbands and wives in a nuclear social unit such as a family. In the Victorian and earlier periods, when generally women had to rely on men (fathers or husbands) to win the bread, marriage seemed to be women's primary goal in life and, in many cases, probably the only possibility for material survival as adults. Thus, the fulfilment as well as the meaning of life for a woman depended on the marriage she made. This was especially the situation when many women had to depend financially on their husbands.

Historians generally regard marriage in western societies as a term for a social institution which involves the regulation of heterosexual sexual relations through monogamy or mandatory blessing of reproduction by the Christian church, with the ultimate goal of clarifying and regulating issues of wealth, ownership and inheritance.[40] The historian Edward Westermarck has said that marriage probably developed out of a 'primeval habit' which was then reinforced as a social institution.[41] Westermarck's theory derived from his observations of male/female union based on natural instincts of reproduction and nurturing in the animal kingdom. However, in his book on the history of marriage, Westermarck also seems to suggest that the separate gender roles in human models of male-female union are 'natural.'[42] Westermarck's assumptions are not far removed from a line of biochemical and socio-psychological research which aims to show that attraction between the sexes is primarily chemically determined (through pheromones, etc) and so is based on a subliminal, non-rational response through chemical manifestation within the human brain. From these scientists' view, human behaviours (such as the chemistry of love, mothering or reproduction) are largely predetermined by biological factors. As a result, such scientific research seeks to provide a 'logical' (rational) explanation based on biology to justify so-called 'typical' maleness or male behaviour (such as male sexual aggression) and femaleness, which in turn also lead to different (and 'predetermined') gender roles.[43] This simplistic essentialist view on human interactions, exemplified by Westermarck's explanation of the origin of marriage, needs to be reconsidered and challenged, especially in the light of contemporary feminist and also multi-cultural scholarship, because it seems to reinforce gender stereotypes. Nancy Chodorow, for example, has challenged such scientific assumption:

> Natural facts, for social scientists, are theoretically uninteresting and do not need explanation. The assumption is questionable, however, given the extent to which human behavior is not instinctually determined but culturally mediated. It is an assumption in conflict with most social scientists' insistence on the social malleability of biological factors, and it also conflicts with the general reluctance of social scientists to explain existing social forms simply as relics of previous epochs····.We must question all assumptions which use biological claims to explain social forms, given the recent rise to prominence of socio-biology and the historically extensive uses of explanations allegedly based on biological sex (or race) differences to legitimate oppression and inequality.[44]

While it is clear that biologically determined factors play some role in human reproductive behaviour patterns, the institution of marriage is a complex, socially constructed form of power in human society rather than simply being predetermined by natural laws, as argued by Westermarck. If Westermarck's claims were accepted as 'truth,' it would be difficult for women not to follow preprogrammed, natural roles as wives and mothers in the domestic arena instead of engaging in pursuit of their own development and achievement, as men do in other areas. From such a perspective, improvement of women's position in society seems impossible and 'unnatural.' Nevertheless, although many academics in the twentieth-first century avoid being charged with essentialism by simplistically applying the biological instincts from animals to human beings as so-called unchangeable natural forces, this is not to assert that the physiological and chemical regulatory processes which function in human bodies do not play any roles in human behaviour and psychosis (such as schizophrenia). Perhaps these also need to be understood, not as a basis for judgmental generalisation assuming a universal fixed model of cause-and-effect for all human beings of varied gender, ethnic groups and cultures, but more as a way of appreciating individual complexity.

Around half a century before Westermarck, Mona Caird had already questioned the marriage institution where women were treated as 'purchase' on the marriage market.[45] Luce Irigaray also argues that women were being treated as commodities to be exchanged or traded between tribes or families for the benefit of the clan.[46] Similar to Caird's approach, and also echoing that of Luce Irigaray, Irene Boada-Montagut in her feminist study of marriage and women's literature, *Women Write Back* (2003), views marriage as a patriarchal institution regulating and controlling women in male-dominated tribes.[47] The marriage institution was set up, according to Boada-Montagut, in order to ensure the clear paternal line for the continuum of the family, or to maintain the 'pure' blood.[48] Marriage is to be considered as a form of social force to control the two sexes (especially women), to create a socially acceptable way for men and women to relate to each other and to provide economic advantages which will enhance survival as well as ensure the continuity of human beings. Under such circumstance marriage does not necessarily involve 'love' as a component in a male/female union. The romantic idea of a 'love marriage' instead of an arranged marriage by parents seems to have emerged as a new ideal for marriage in general during the Victorian period. According to some historians, a reality in the way people wished to pursue love marriages in Victorian society also seems to be reflected in the popular theme of the pursuit of marriage for love in the contemporary literature. Marilyn Yalom, for example, argues that 'modern' western marriage or love marriage may have emerged in the period between the American Revolution and 1830.[49] The issue of 'love,' Yalom has stated, as the most celebrated criterion for choosing a spouse also appears in the themes of the contemporary women's literature of that period.[50] Scholars such as Jenni Calder and Shirley Foster seem to echo the idea that the pursuit of a love marriage is reflected in Victorian women's literature.[51] This phenomenon in Victorian women's literature may have indicated that young people wished to rebel against a tyrannical control by hierarchal (parents) and economic (material survival) forces through their pursuit of a romantic 'love marriage.' However, does this ideal of love marriage actually result in the happy-ending of a balanced relationship between the man and the woman? Inevitably, there are paradoxes which underlie the confusion over how this form of 'love' is perceived by both males and females and how it is manifested in gender relations in a patriarchal context.

Therefore, for female characters in many Irish women's short stories, the purpose of getting married may appear a romantic idea on the surface, presumably the pursuit of 'happiness' if in fact they ever visualise what it involves; however, underneath it is still often associated with practical goals. These stories uncover the unromantic aspect of the 'love marriages' that female characters tend to confuse in many Irish women's short stories with their need for love. The notion of 'love' as expressed in the stories is problematic. Generally, 'love' appears as one of the major recurrent issues in contemporary Irish women's short stories. But these stories, which disclose the problematic nature of 'love' between men and women in the existing male-dominated society of Ireland, frequently evoke the question of the basis for love, or this kind of love, between men and women. Feminists such as Adrienne Rich and Ti-Grace Atkinson also regard the problem of love between men and women as a form of patriarchal bondage for women. Atkinson thinks 'love' between men and women is based on 'friction,' a magnetism of opposite poles between the two sexes.[52] One could argue Atkinson's view of 'magnetic attraction' of opposite poles in male-female union is a determinist approach, since she seems to suggest men and women are 'naturally' opposite to each other. But what Atkinson proposed was to question the 'gender norm' from the social conditioning of a male-female relationship in which the woman is generally expected to behave a certain way in order to be 'complementary' (thus, 'attracted') to the man's superiority, based on unequal roles that have been placed on both parties by society.[53] Adrienne Rich even argues that heterosexuality is a socially (male) compulsory form of behaviour enforced on women as 'a means of assuring male right of physical, economical, and emotional access.'[54] Similarly, Trudy Hayes, in her 1990 article on the politics of seduction between sexes, claims that heterosexuality emphasised as 'normal sex' by society is an 'oppressive aspect of our sexual culture' because her 'reliable' source of statistics indicates that around ten to twelve percent of women are, in fact, lesbians.[55] Hayes argues that the hegemony of heterosexuality has been institutionalised (such as in the form of marriage) and widely accepted as the only 'normal' sexuality in society, therefore, many women (and men too) are socially conditioned to suppress other sexualities which might exist within themselves. Given the questions raised by some feminists about the problematic basis of heterosexual love, is it possible to attain love in a male/female relationship, or if so, is 'equal love' ever possible in a relationship or marriage? Certainly, it seems difficult to define the meaning of 'love,' a term which can denote and connote a variety of meanings in varied contexts. In the context of this study, so-called 'love' or 'equal love' refers to a purely emotional mutual response and experience between two persons (a heterosexual couple in this case) beyond the 'containment' of certain (usually unequal) gender roles or stereotypical ideologies and assumptions. This is an interesting question which many contemporary Irish women writers seek to address through their stories about love and marriage.

The Old Role and the 'New Woman'

In 1879, Henrik Ibsen shocked his nation and Europe with his revolutionary image of a 'new woman' in his *A Doll's House* (1879). Near the end of the play, the female character Nora cries out to reject her biologically determined role as a 'doll-wife.' Nora wants to pursue her own development as a 'full' human being even at the cost of her secure life with her husband and her family. Considering the times in which *A Doll's House* was written, Ibsen's 'new' image of womanhood radically subverted the conventionally accepted social role for women in his time and place. Ibsen did not actually invent his 'new woman' character. The 'new women' were already a familiar social phenomenon in Ibsen's time. The term 'new woman' itself was actually first used by Sarah Grand as an expression to describe this type of woman in the USA.[56] The new woman was recognisable by 'her education, her independence, her tendency to flaunt traditional family values and blur the boundaries between conventional male and female behaviour.'[57]

As the 'new woman' phenomenon began to emerge in the nineteenth century, those women who were being associated with the image and the idea of 'new women' were actually attacked severely by their detractors and demonised as viragoes or freaks. Nevertheless, there were also supporters. The new women's challenge to the existing fixed roles of women was seen as an attempt to overthrow the existing social order, and as a threat to sacred institutions such as marriage and motherhood, both of which were highly valued and deeply embedded in traditional beliefs and religions. The concept of the 'new woman' is validated by the fact that, especially in today's western society, many women may pursue their own achievements in the wider world outside the home with the associated recognition of professional competence and thus go beyond their biologically determined roles. In this recognition of the 'new women,' to fulfil a family role becomes a personal choice instead of an imposed, determined duty for women. What average women may achieve today in western society would have been deemed unthinkable for many women perhaps even half a century ago.

However, prevailing conservative notions about gender roles still threaten to try to conform men and women by evoking certain models and patterns as 'norms,' which are actually dictated by these social forces, as opposed to some other liberating perceptions about gender relations.

Contemporary Irish women's stories reflect this dilemma underlying celebration of the 'new woman' and of female individuality insofar as they represent the ambivalence of the struggle between ideals and the reality of external factors and constraints such as gender roles or norms in marriage, or heterosexual relationships. Women in these stories may be portrayed as more free within themselves in terms of choosing their own career or life direction, but sometimes they still face a struggle and find it difficult to compromise with the 'gender norms' in their relationships with men. The forces of social conformity seem to manifest themselves in many ways to regulate and to dictate the interpersonal relationships. Gender norms and roles are consciously drawn attention to in many Irish women's short stories. Irish female writers often tend to mock, attack or ridicule gender stereotypes and male stereotypical attitudes toward women (or the difference between what men assume women think and the 'reality,' as well as men's ignorance of this 'reality') in heterosexual relationships: for example, the way in which they are portrayed in Helen Lucy Burke's 'Grey Cats in the Dark,' Kate Cruise O'Brien's 'Losing,' Clare Boylan's 'Housekeeper's Cut' and 'The Wronged Wife,' Mary Beckett's 'Saints and Scholars, ' Éilís Ní Dhuibhne's 'Bill's New Wife,' Trudy Hayes's 'The Virgin' or Julia O'Faolain's 'Man in the Cellar.' It appears that Irish women's stories on women's love relationships with men are more or less characterised by a motivation to expose, question or subvert certain gender ideologies.

If marriage can be considered an age-old institution constructed under patriarchy, it also seems to reveal a certain form of role-playing for men and women which reinforces and consolidates the foundation of the patriarchal system. The roles involved in a marriage are generally accepted and understood as consisting of appropriate social functions such as husband and wife, father and mother, or breadwinner and homemaker. The gender roles in this system also seem to operate in a binary mode that involves domination of one by the other. No matter the domestic set-up, it always seems to be the man who plays the dominant, decisive role. It may be speculated that such a concept of power/dominance might easily suggest to the dominating sex and society in general a sense of superiority and inferiority following on from and diluted through a traditional justification differentiating men from women. For example, women are regarded as incomplete 'flawed' men, a deformity, in Aristotle's theories, just as Freudian assumptions emphasise the deficiency of women in relation to men.[58] According to Christian belief women are 'fallen' as they are exemplified by Eve, the first woman, in the Bible. This sense of superiority over women appears as an unspoken 'pride' within the male mentality or sense of self. This 'male pride' appears to be a totem that women cannot offend or challenge. This paradoxical perception of so-called 'male pride' is perhaps the disguised male anxiety about 'masculinity' crisis. Once men's 'masculinity' has been threatened or challenged, (therefore, their 'pride' is offended) no matter how useless or weak the men concerned may actually be in the real world, not rarely do they express their resentment by brutal behaviour against women in order to disguise their embarrassment, frustration or powerlessness. In Mary Beckett's 'Saints and Scholars,' it is almost a 'sin' for a wife to criticise or condemn her husband instead of being able to honour him or, in other words, to maintain his 'pride.' It is the wife's duty to accustom herself and adjust to the husband's way. Otherwise, if anything goes wrong in a marriage it will presumably be deemed the wife's fault or failure for not managing the marriage well. The mother-in-law character in 'Saints and Scholars' is similar to one in Julia O'Faolain's 'Man in the Cellar' who goes as far as to declare that 'a woman's first obligation is to her family. No matter what her husband does, she must work to keep it together' (MC 20). Even as late as the 1960s, an eminent psychiatrist could still claim with impunity the following:

> Just as the fate of personality development hangs largely on the effect of mother on child, so, I believe, the fate of a marriage hangs largely on the effect of wife on husband...overwhelmingly the flow of crucial influence is from the woman to the man, requiring adaptation or defense on his part...It is the woman who "makes or breaks" a marriage.[59]

This analysis could be interpreted as a misogynistic notion which treats women as the 'scapegoat' for any problems or failures in a marriage. It seems also that women often internalise such self-blaming: for example, the eponymous female character Mrs. Reinhardt, a stereotypically submissive wife, in Edna O'Brien's story. She is described a woman as the following:

> [Mrs. Reinhardt] used to do a million things for Mr. Reinhardt to please him, and to pander to him. She used to warm his side of the bed while he was still undressing...When she knit his socks in cable stitch she always knit a third sock in case one got torn or ruined.

(FH 413)

Mrs. Reinhardt blames herself for being the one responsible for her husband's infidelity because she did not try harder to rescue their marriage:

> [Mrs. Reinhardt was] crying for not having tried harder on certain occasions, as when Mr. Reinhardt came home expecting excitement or repose and getting instead a typical story about the nonarrival of the gas man. She had let herself be drawn into the weary and hypnotizing whirl of domesticity. With her the magazines had to be neat, the dust had to be dusted, all her perfectionism had got thrown into that instead of something larger, or instead of Mr. Reinhardt.
>
> (FH 409)

Even if domestic violence occurs, women normally consider it shameful, as it seems to suggest they have failed in their marriage. Injured 'pride' can be abused as a pretext to express male misogyny through acts of aggression and violence towards women—either verbally (humiliation), physically (beating) or sexually (rape). Leland Bardwell's 'Out-patients' shows such a wife, who has to find various excuses for her injuries to mask the domestic abuse by her husband. Anne in Fiona Barr's 'Excursion' or Kate in Mary Dorcey's 'A Sense of Humour' have to endure the husband's humiliation in brutal physical as well as sexual violence. Kate almost internalises the brutal way her husband treats her in 'A Sense of Humour':

Like the time she had forgiven him—all those times; made up with him because she could not bear to see only the violence. She had told no one. It was their shame—only theirs. The hurt was buried inside her and only he could comfort it. In the end she did not even try to escape. She knew she deserved it. He would not beat her and abuse her unless she did; unless she was all the things he called her. The pain was final then. She knew that she was stupid, vicious, ugly; everything he named her and when she slept with him again it made her the whore he said she was. But only he could absolve her because only he knew how base she was. That knowledge was what had kept her with him so long.

(NW 38-9)

In Maeve Kelly's 'Orange Horses,' the violent abuse towards Elsie is even justified by her mother-in-law's reasoning that '[a] man won't take that kind of treatment from any woman and I wouldn't expect him to. He has his pride' (OH 29) (italics my own). In such a situation, the victim is indirectly accused of being at fault rather than the abuser, simply because it offends men to lose their 'pride' in public. Frances Molloy's 'Women are the Scourge of the Earth' and another story by Leland Bardwell 'The Dove of Peace' both suggest that the husband's violence and abuse have contributed to the wife's nervous breakdown. Even after the tragedy has happened, the husband still condemns the wife and justifies his own behaviour for doing so because she is not tamed as the narrator claims in 'Women are the Scourge of the Earth':

A woman is supposed to obey her husband, is she not? She's supposed to do what he bids her, is she not? Isn't that what the law says? Isn't it? And isn't it wrote in the bible by the hand of the almighty Himself? Well, that woman never did my bidding in her life. Never once in fifteen years could I get her to do my bidding.

(WS 34-5)

Often in these stories the violence is associated with male 'Dutch courage' gained through alcohol abuse. Even though the man may be a loser in public, in private (at home) he may seek to compensate and bolster his sense of personal 'pride' by seeking recognition and acknowledgement from his wife of his authority and prestige—often by showing aggression or violence. This type of man and husband is invariably shown as brutal, abusive and violent but also as weak and powerless in the face of external reality, not rarely escaping from the latter into alcohol. In such stories the woman's subservience to the man appears to be accepted as a social norm.

While men are generally seen as providers for the family, it is taken for granted that women should support them in the background by managing the home in a comfortable way for them. This norm also associates women with bondage by confining women to the private sphere in which they have to deliver what they are taught are their major duties, for example, household chores like cooking, cleaning or looking after children. Even when women need to work outside the home to support the struggling family economy, they still have to fulfil their household duties as a double role. The man is presumed to be the master of the house and so the woman has to fit in and assume within the marriage enclosure whatever role is imposed on her. Mary Lavin portrays such a submissive wife and masterful husband in 'The Haymaking' where Fanny wants to be a good wife by adapting herself to her brutal husband but, once the honeymoon is over, her husband shows little affection, merely rudeness, regarding her as one of his possessions, something useful and maybe productive. In Lilian Roberts Finlay's 'In the Beginning,' Eily realises at the dusk of her honeymoon that her role as a wife is meant to please, to accommodate her husband and his world instead of creating a new world of their own, as in romances:

> Was marriage for two people or only for a woman? The two people entering into the holy bond of matrimony, did that not set them apart? Both of them or only the woman? Did the man lay himself open to ribaldry, exposing himself for the gratification of fun-makers? Vaguely Eily had thought of marriage as a sacred place, a secret cell into which two people walked hand-in-hand. No one else ever came there, no one knocked on the door. If Tom was totally unaware of this lovely, solemn cell, then she must be in there by herself. She wondered if marriage could be a trap with steel teeth, ready to snap on her.
>
> (BF 14)[60]

Outside the formal enclosure of marriage, a similar pattern of domination and submissiveness is also shown in the male/female relationships in the stories. For example, despite Evelyn Conlon's heroine in the story 'Beatrice' appearing to be an independent career woman, who also can pursue passion in her own way without disguise, her love affair still has to be a game in which 'he has the control, this is how he likes it, he's not the sort to like it otherwise, [she] will have to wait' (TL 146). Likewise, Kate Cruise O'Brien portrays such a relationship in her story 'Losing,' conveying the unbalanced roles which society assigns to men and women in a relationship. Women always appear to have to wait or to sacrifice their own needs in heterosexual relationships with men. The courtship between men and women like this normally involves a process of man's chasing woman instead of the other way around. It appears that the male control, domination and the initiative taken in any further action of courtship characterise the nature of such heterosexual relationships. Women are adorable and desirable when they are passive, that is, submissive and therefore less threatening (or in other words, devouring) to men. In a heterosexual relationship like this, men still dominate women in order to play their own games instead of sharing equally. Éilís Ní Dhuibhne depicts such a courtship in 'Holiday in the Land of Murdered Dreams':

> Conor liked girlish women — slim and modest, noble and strong, long-haired and beautiful, mysterious but subservient to him — like the girls in his favourite novels by Walter Macken....When Conor looked at her, he unlocked a different Detta, a Detta who normally hid inside the skin of the polite, friendly, obliging Detta....He changed all that. She felt herself glowing and dancing, jokes tripped off her tongue, trite details grew into riveting stories. He was in love too....But his personality did not change as hers did. She was recreated by him. He remained what he always had been.
>
> (MF 102-3)

Another example from 'Losing' shows how Anne has to risk breaking up her relationship if she does not obey her partner's demand. But if Anne obeys her partner's will, she is left no choice but to sacrifice a chance to pursue her own welfare by getting a job. The key point is that the woman must obey her lover because his 'pride' must be satisfied at all costs in their relationship as intimate partners. Therefore, even if the male/female relationship does not have any formal legal status such as in a marriage, women are still depicted as existing in bondage within the male power-dominance arena, and thus inevitably have to play certain roles or remain passive, as in 'Beatrice' and 'Losing.'

In Helen Lucy Burke's 'Grey Cats in the Dark,' the 'male pride' is highlighted by abuse of power towards the women, and at the same time, the man still benefits from women—either through sex or money. Philip's attitude towards women is extremely misogynistic, referring to women as vampires who '[suck] men's vital fluids,' while in fact it is he who manipulates the situation in relation to women (SM 119). He exploits and treats women as transferable commodities to satisfy his own lust as well. Obviously, Philip does not see his economic dependence on Clare as parasitic, even though he is spending her money and does virtually nothing but 'mess around.' When men are no longer the only providers or breadwinners or in any position of superiority in terms of survival, but rather the converse, the men still uphold the assumption of superiority over women in the name of their 'pride.' Philip feels offended when Clare is concerned about his work progress, and he sees it as an indicator she does not trust him, as an act of humiliation intended to damage his 'pride.' Philip, as described in 'Grey Cats in the Dark,' thinks women are masochistic and need to be tamed. Thus he sees his act of bullying women as justified because he only does so 'when they [women] deserved it' (SM 118). This way Philip not only depersonalises women but also devalues them as objects.

The problematic crisis of 'masculinity,' disguised as so-called 'male pride,' manifested itself at a time when men were faced with the emerging independence of women, especially since the later period of the twentieth century. Polly Young-Eisendrath has explained this paradoxical attitude in men's relations with women in terms of 'the two polarities of feminine beauty,' the public power and the private pleasure.[61] Young-Eisendrath claims such oppositional duality often takes the form of ambivalence towards female individuality. This is due to the fact that traditionally the wife is considered the man's 'property,' so that the wife's charm, beauty and graceful manners all reflect the husband's accomplishments and refined taste, and in this way honour him by giving him enhanced status in society as a whole and with his male peers. If a man's wife appears too independent and becomes a powerful person in her own right, his dignity or 'pride,' which in fact is his sexual domination, is threatened. A man in such a position might feel 'castrated' by the strong woman and become literarily or even physically impotent.[62] Thus, 'the feminine beauty,' which is her individuality as an independent strong woman, evoking the public power that she represents in her own right rather than through his reflection, somehow makes the male feel her too powerful to embrace in intimacy (his private pleasure) because his 'pride,' his sense of superiority, is threatened. A knight cannot prove his heroism if there is no dragon to kill nor maiden in distress to rescue. In other words, the woman's vulnerability and the man's strength and sense of dignity are interdependent in a certain way. In Trudy Hayes's story 'The Virgin,' for example, the male character 'I' explicitly and obsessively eroticises the objectification of women who are shown weak and ready to be (sexually) conquered by him:

> And yet what beasts men are. I cannot help looking at women as they pass by—gazing at their thighs, their bare arms. I fantasise about women—I cannot help it. I'm sure most men do. Women are so soft, so vulnerable, so delicious.
>
> (VH 100)

This again goes back to the ritual of male-female courtship, the game in which the male chases the female. The male eroticism of the courtship between men and women lies in showing male superiority over female vulnerability. Virginia Woolf has used the image of the mirror to address the issue of female self-recognition as the social construct in which women are forced to see themselves and to be seen as the 'Other,' a reflection of men. Woolf describes women as 'looking-glasses possessing the magic and delicious power of reflecting the figure of man at twice its natural size.'[63] This relates to the perception that women's vulnerability is constructed to prove men's strength and subjectivity, and in fact, superiority. The male erotica in pornographies for the male audience, as argued by Clodagh Corcoran, Ethna Viney and Trudy Hayes, largely manifests in presenting male superiority (domination) and female inferiority (vulnerability and submission) by showing sexual abuse and violence towards women such as women being chained, bound, tortured or even murdered.[64]

Simone de Beauvoir has pointed out that women are designated by society to be men's opposite or negation as the inevitable consequence of the fact that men set themselves up as free beings and subjects of their own desire.[65] Elsie in 'Orange Horses,' for example, is disapproved of and disliked by her husband for having learnt too much, therefore becoming too 'smart' for him to manage. Another wife, Lena, in Mary Beckett's 'Saints and Scholars' has to hide her intelligence and pretend to be stupid in front of her plain husband. Here the wife complains:

> I've read nothing but these magazines you complain of, since Peter was born? Did you never think I was sick looking at faces in them empty of all but their lipstick? Just because I discovered that Malachy tortured himself with scrambling after my reading, I confined myself to these so that he could feel his lofty supremacy. I have gone to all length to encourage his self-respect.
>
> (SC 47)

Edna, in 'Queen,' is a lady of graceful manners but her 'femininity' is threatened by her strong will, leading her to dare to compete with men in a chess game, which is 'believed to be played well only by men or boy prodigies' (OH 189). Although Edna often wins, her skill is hardly recognized due to the fact that she is a woman and because 'women aren't good at dealing with abstract ideas' (OH 191). Edna is also sneered at and blamed as a woman who 'has more money than is good for her, who drove her husband to a lifelong binge' (OH 192). Again, the woman-blaming approach positions Edna merely as a failed wife instead of seeing her as an individual of intellect. Constance, in Kate Cruise O'Brien's 'Breaking,' is deemed 'difficult and ambitious' by her own mother in the story (IO 73). But this 'ambition,' unlike in a man, is seen as negative rather than positive for a woman like Constance, and this view inevitably condemns her as being 'selfish, terribly selfish' for not sacrificing her welfare for other people (IO 73). In Patricia Scanlan's 'Ripples,' Alison appears to be a 'virago,' who is blamed by other people (and also by her own daughter) for her neglect of domestic duties as well as for being 'bossy' and for 'nagging' that drives her husband crazy. Alison is portrayed as 'the virago and bad mother' in contrast with Kathy 'the gentle housewife and good mother' in this story. A woman who is far from a gentle 'feminine' type sometimes attracts negative or destructive associations; for example, the evil female figure in fairy tales (such as *Cinderella* or *Snow White*) is typically portrayed either as a devouring stepmother or a devitalising hag. The condemnation of women if they claim their authority (they might be seen as controlling, dominating or aggressive), and blaming of women if they don't (they might be viewed as manipulative, dependent or immature) creates a double bind of female authority.[66] The double bind is reinforced by the misogynistic belief that women are designated by patriarchal ideology to be wanted, to be desired, rather to exert control in their own right with their own power. Thus, a demanding woman is to be 'dreaded and subdued' instead of being known or loved.[67]

Since we have explored earlier the issues of male bias in gender norms as described in some stories, Éilís Ní Dhuibhne's 'Bill's New Wife' which deals with reversed gender stereotypes, may provide some subversive insights for reflection on the basis of gender differentiation. Even the title of the story is symbolic, suggesting new wife (as in the term 'new woman') as opposed to the traditional old wife, that is, looking at the traditional view of how a woman and wife should behave in relation to existing stereotypical ideas about 'femaleness' and 'maleness' as well as gender roles. Éilís Ní Dhuibhne ridicules gender stereotypes via a parody which dramatises the implications associated with conventionally assumed female inferiority, emotionalism and vulnerability in contrast with male superiority in rationalism; however, there is a role reversal (that is, the husband adopts the traditional female's role and manners, and vice versa) in her story. For example, whilst the husband Bill is busy with household chaos, nagging and complaining about the unfair household duties which 'normal housewives' are assumed to carry out, conversely, Catherine is engaged in her intellectual activity studying ancient Greek, ignoring his complaints and feeling irritated by such trivial disruption (as 'normal husbands' are often shown to react). Another passage shows the juxtaposition of Bill's vanity in self-gratification (the 'ritual' of dressing up or beauty treatment) and Catherine's artistic taste in Dvořák's New World symphony. This passage is extraordinarily amusing because it deliberately contrasts the inner depths of Catherine and Bill—artistic intellectual depth juxtaposed with one's 'skin-deep' vanity. Bill's behaviour might appear quite acceptable for a 'normal' woman but appears odd and surreal for a so-called average (and heterosexual) man. Behaving like a 'woman,' that is, being sissy, is devalued as a taboo for a man. The reverse role-play in this story deliberately subverts the 'Self' identification and the exclusiveness of 'Not-I' in gender because vulnerability and emotionalism are regarded as 'sissy' (femininity), and not approved characteristics belonging to masculinity in general. These attributes of each gender are assumptions that are generally accepted as the stereotypes which define or differentiate a man and a woman, even on the very superficial level of mannerisms. Certainly the gender issue is not as simplistic as whether or not it is more desirable for either sex to be homemakers or politicians, or who should do what in the household. Rather it is a subconscious compelling 'impulse' which has been constructed and conditioned by society with the effect of shaping each gender into a certain model. This in turn generates various gender specific roles, and these roles are also coloured by varied cultural and ethnic factors.

However, a 'full' human being may not be rigidly categorised by a black and white duality as in these stereotypes, which may exaggerate one aspect and claim that it represents the whole picture. Éilís Ní Dhuibhne may not actually have intended to reverse stereotypes as another gender model in this story but rather to ridicule the paradox of the rigidity of gender and roles in an amusing way. Ní Dhuibhne closes her story with this ironic paragraph:

> [He] had grown at last to be like her, and she had grown to be like him....The battle of the sexes, siege of the kitchen sink, was over. The best part of life was beginning. But how late it was, how late! How many years had bee given over to the conflict! And how long would the best part last, how long, how long?
>
> (II 76)

Perhaps men and women are better with each other when they are growing more like each other instead of implementing a clear-cut apartheid in terms of their assumed, respective roles and mutual expectations. When the 'should-be' stereotypical ideas are not imposed upon either side, male and female may be more free to be themselves instead of playing roles and games in a relationship according to externally imposed rigid gender principles. Moreover, Ní Dhuibhne's story seems to evoke some more thoughts about 'gender' beyond its surface level of gender differentiation and roles. Ní Dhuibhne leaves some scope for readers to delve into the depth of what may manifest itself behind these gender issues and behaviour with an ambiguous description that 'he had grown at last to be like her, she had grown to be like him' (II 76). Here Ní Dhuibhne remains obscure, albeit open-ended, in describing how both sexes grow more like each other, by which she may mean either physical appearance or inner depth of mind or indeed something else entirely in this story.

Nevertheless, Ní Dhuibhne's story may seem to echo the vision of the 'androgyny' ideal theorized by scholars such as Jung or Young-Eisendrath, wherein men and women are no longer torn by 'should' or 'should-not' or possessed by negative complexes but rather are confident within themselves and relate to (and also compromise with) each other as well as valuing human life objectively with a broader perspective. The idea of androgyny, the unity instead of segregation of the sexes, was also visualised by Virginia Woolf as the ideal model for men's and women's coexistence. Woolf posed the idea of 'androgyny' as the unity of the mind and developed this ideal in Chapter Six of her book *A Room of One's Own* (1977), in which she gave an example that it is like 'a couple getting into a taxi-cab': the mind comes together again in a natural fusion after being divided.[68] Woolf thought it should be natural for the sexes to co-operate with each other. Ní Dhuibhne's story 'Bill's New Wife' also appears to stress the 'co-operation' between sexes. This story ironically presents a gender role reversal which also seems to suggest that the root of the conflict between sexes goes beyond the 'symptoms' of gender roles and behaviour and lies, perhaps, with the framework in which ideological presumptions mould gender stereotypes and behaviour.

There is a range of various controversial issues regarding the idea of androgyny and differentiation of gender debated in academic disciplines such as feminism and cultural criticism. The problematic issue lies in whether there is something basic in 'maleness' or 'femaleness' or if there is another direction in which to reconsider gender. These issues such as the problem of gender 'contingency' are raised by Judith Butler, who thinks gender may not always be as coherent as it seems, for example, the strategy to imitate or parody the set category in the personae of butch lesbian or drag queen. Perhaps the understanding of the concept of gender (as in male and female) may even be altered or not accepted uncritically as 'natural,' especially after some other new insights have been forthcoming from the debates on gender.

Wanting to be Wanted: Pursuit and Submission

The entrapment of women in the dilemma between freedom and survival, and women's resistance to gender norms in some Irish women's short stories, have now been examined. Conversely, women in some other stories are portrayed as actually longing for and pursuing submission to male principles. The pursuit of love and marriage in these stories is presented as indicating that the female characters concerned do want to be desired, want to be wanted. This aspiration appears to be regarded by these characters as a pursuit of 'happiness,' or a 'salvation' which can rescue women from harsh reality. Women portrayed in this way in the stories sometimes appear confused as to whether they love their partners or just need them as an escape from their own problems, for example, to provide economic support or to relieve loneliness. At issue is the fact that the patriarchal attitudes towards women as dependent possessions of a husband are also reinforced by many women who accept this position as a trade-off for a non-competitive existence in which they need take no responsibility for their survival. Women's being wanted or desired can be a way of gaining control over a male and determining his responses in a very intimate way. Emily in Éilís Ní Dhuibhne's 'Estonia' sees a 'happily-ever-after' marriage as the only blueprint for her future life because she feels that, in such a situation, all her problems in her life would 'fall into insignificance. Being married to Lars would compensate for its shortcomings. It would liberate her' (II 186). Similarly, the female narrator/character in Anne Devlin's 'The Way-Paver' seeks to escape by marrying someone in England so she would be rescued from her the burden of family responsibility as well as the troubled environment of Northern Ireland. Such a pursuit by women in some stories appears to be closely linked with pragmatic needs instead of with love and emotions. Clare Boylan tells a story like this in 'Villa Marta.' The female characters Sally and Rose actually weave into their men-hunting dreams a speculation of better material prosperity, although they do not seem to realize their dream is illusory:

> Sally detailed a red sofa and Japanese paper lanterns. Rose was going to have a television in the bedroom....She gathered in her mind from the assorted periods of films she had seen, a white convertible with a rug and a radio on the back seat, a beach house

with a verandah, an orchestra playing round the pool in the moonlight. All Americans had television in the bedroom.

(CS 242-6)

Lily in Éilís Ní Dhuibhne's 'Lili Marlene' is lucky to have been able to find a nice generous husband so she can indulge herself as a princess, including having an affair with another man. Lily does not think she marries for money and she thinks she loves her husband. But this love she claims sounds more like mere gratitude for her husband's protection than love:

> I have never told him about John, but I think he must know. I think he knows and I think he forgives me. And I love him for that. I love him for being there, for being kind, for giving himself to me. For marrying me and for trying make me a lady of leisure, a princess in a garden.
>
> (II 102)

However, here in Lily's case, material considerations still seem to play a key role, because of which she can afford to indulge herself. Also, Lily appears quite happy to be kept as a doll by her husband. Women like Lily may be lucky enough to be glamorous; others, like Mary in Edna O'Brien's 'Irish Revel,' are not. Mary also fantasises a husband-guardian figure, who appears and rescues her from a lifeless world: 'If only I had a sweetheart, something to hold on to, she thought' (FH 197). In such circumstances, women are bound to jump from one web to another trap.

Women's attempts to escape into marriage with such expectations can hardly become an antidote to their problems in a harsh reality.

Women's 'wanting to be wanted' may be regarded as a 'damaging affliction' in respect of women's development in a society where they are generally expected to please men.[69] It seems to express itself as a compulsion to become desirable as a means for women to find power and control but by proxy instead of by their own achievements. A beautiful woman seems to have power over men because men will fight with each other over her in order to 'possess' her. A pretty woman may even think she is superior to other women because she has the power to evoke this kind of competitive response in men. Using this kind of power, women seem to build their self-esteem mainly on attracting men's attention and acceptance and avoiding the fate of becoming unwanted old maids. To do so, they have to be pretty, attractive women who are desirable and therefore valuable. Perhaps what the teenaged girl character Jane Anne in Sheila Barrett's 'Ellie's Ring' actually wants to do is to demonstrate she is attractive (and therefore superior to other girls) by the act of elopement with her boyfriend, because 'girls who eloped were invariably beautiful' (IO 17). It seems that only vanity excites Jane Anne instead of the reality of the world of commitments and responsibilities which marriage entails, and eventually she admits she is not ready for 'a world of forever' (IO 30). Catherine, in Ita Daly's 'Growth,' can only affirm herself, ironically, after she is harassed by an old man on a night train. Rather than feeling offended, Catherine feels a sense of triumph over the glamorous American girl Janet because it is she who draws the attention of that man. In other words, Catherine feels flattered by male admiration even if it is actually an act of sexual harassment: at least it proves she is attractive enough to stimulate him to act in this way. Similarly, the widow Mary, in Mary Lavin's 'In a Café,' 'hankers after the approval, admiration and support of the man' because she appears to be one who loses individuality and identity in her new capacity as a single person after her husband's death.[70] A woman's physical appearance seems to be essential in order to attract men's attention. The female character in Ita Daly's 'Aimez-vous Colette' tries to catch boys at the dance with make-up and fancy dress, or Mary in Éilís Ní Dhuibhne's 'Nomads Seek the Pavilions of Bliss on the Slopes of Middle Age' feels a 'pang of anxiety' about having meals with her friends because she wants to preserve her figure for her lover (PG 75-92). Perhaps Mary thinks she is doomed to lose her boyfriend at high school because she is neither beautiful nor from a wealthy background. A beautiful woman like Monica seems to gain prestige through many things, including taking away Mary's boyfriend. It seems that a plain-looking woman needs to work harder than a beautiful woman because to be beautiful grants power over men. Women with this kind of perception hope that if they can appear in a certain way (appear attractive by a prescribed standard) they will transform their lives and the way other people see them. Thus, Anita in Éilís Ní Dhuibhne's 'The Wife of Bath' might believe that if she appears younger and nicer she would win back her lover.[71] Here, women's beauty does seemingly appear as power in the matter of attention and privilege from men. However, as discussed earlier, women with this outlook merely attain the power by proxy, not real power; it is the power of the 'muse,' the maiden of male fantasy, gained by becoming men's object of desire (to become possessed by him she actually surrenders her own power). One might put it like this: such a woman seems to exert 'power' over a man up to the point where she is possessed by him, after which it is he who has the power. Women learn to bring things under control by behaving and appearing in a certain way, and to make emotional accommodations based on the needs of other people and on a sense of self-image derived from the reflection of other people. Trudy Hayes argues it is in fact the manifestation of sexual politics, such as the ritual of seduction, existing in male/female courtship and relationship, which results in obsessive fetishsation of female bodies epitomised in 'the Page 3 girl,' the advertisements on diet, cosmetics or beauty treatment or the 'Miss World Competition':

> [The] ritual of seduction [is] as a conquest, and maybe men like to see themselves as the aggressor in order to affirm their sense of masculine superiority....This fetishisation of women's bodies places an abominable pressure on women to live up to an image of idealised beauty which is a pressure men simply do not experience as they see themselves in the role of sexual aggressors or 'seducers'. Women, however, may feel they must conform to a stereotyped female image in order to be attractive to men, which is a very unhappy burden for any women to have to carry around.[72]

Thus, in this way women become the second sex, the lesser sex. The beautiful woman of patriarchy may be seen as a 'symbol of male power' because her legacy is about 'power' between and among men, not about real and actual power of and for women.[73] In her book on women and female sexuality, *Women and Desire*, Polly Young-Eisendrath argues that this dynamic between men and women might be rooted in the 'widespread psychological and social constraints on female power.'[74] Women are allowed and encouraged to appear attractive under the patriarchal 'law' in order to divert them from focusing on areas seen as male domains for the exercise of power and acquisition of status. Trudy Hayes also portrays male anxiety towards female power in 'The Virgin.' The three female characters are no quiet passive virgins at home but are shown as energetic, sensual, assertive, independent and intelligent. However, all three terrify the male character in the story. He sees these female lovers as destructive forces of seduction, luring him to deadly sin, throwing his own existence into crisis and struggle as a result of the love-hate conflicts. His resistance masks his anxiety about an overwhelming female power beyond his capacity to control.

Liberating Marriage: Love, Freedom and Subversion

In Irish stories marriage certainly appears as an intimate relationship between man and woman but it is not always based on love. In many stories women are portrayed as having to marry either for survival or other practical reasons. For example, a single mother is forced to find a husband to legitimise her status with the baby in Mary Beckett's 'Theresa'; or women are caught in the web of forces of social conformity which internalise within them that marriage is the major goal they should pursue in their lives, as in those stories discussed earlier where women 'want to be wanted.' While some women in stories are longing for the love symbolised by marriage, others are rebelling against marriage for the sake of love or selfhood. Such female characters in Irish stories subvert marriage, the socially accepted and legally recognised form of male/female relationship, in the name of freedom. Irish female writers actually present a smashed world of disillusioned 'love conquers all' fantasies in which the women no longer believe in marriage as their major or sole goal in life or as a means to finding love. In these stories women who lose their husbands or marriages are sometimes portrayed as relieved and happy rather than sullen or lonely like some of the miserable widows portrayed in Mary Lavin's stories. A woman like Kay in Mary Rose Callaghan's 'Windfalls' feels relieved to have somebody to take over her wifely duties, which appear heavy and monotonous, after she discovers her husband's affair with a younger woman. Or Lillian in Patricia Scanlan's 'Ripples' describes it as 'bliss' to become a widow, which for her means 'to be free.' Instead of having undergone a sense of loss or loneliness in an empty nest, Mary Beckett's Hilary in 'Heaven' sees her husband as an intruder interrupting her peaceful life alone at home. Women who choose to be away from men or remain single, but not celibate, see marriage as a burden to carry or a waste of their lives. Edna in Maeve Kelly's 'Queen' rejects a younger man's courtship and proposal. Edna considers it lucky to be able to escape marriage because '[it's] not a bed of roses....It's lonely being married, too...That's the worst loneliness of all. Never get married just to avoid being lonely' (OH 193). She suggests that, if it turns out to be a loveless marriage for whatever reason, it might be a hell that would imprison and trap both men and women. Edna O'Brien also describes unhappy women in or out of marriage under the disguise of a picture of superficial peace and harmony in their lives in stories such as 'Number 10,' 'A Woman by the Seaside,' 'Mrs. Reinhardt' or 'Paradise,' where women are sometimes depicted with physical disorders such as sleepwalking or vomiting as symptoms of their inner sense of disintegration and disorientation or where a beautiful woman such as Eily is portrayed as withered and trapped in a loveless marriage as the 'poetic justice' of Eily's transgressing the sex taboo in 'A Scandalous Woman.'

Women in these stories who seek to subvert the institution of marriage are depicted through their difficult roles as women, as people who have to live double lives which compel them to adapt themselves to the expectations of other people such as their husbands, willingly or unwillingly. These stories reveal it is the compulsory unequal gender roles imposed on women, which they strive to challenge and subvert in marriage. Marriage is sometimes portrayed in Irish women's stories as the sarcastic anti-climax of a fairytale in which the prince and the princess do not live happily ever after. The fixed (usually unfair) gender roles inherent in this system tend to suffocate any initial love in the marriage as well as the personal development (of the woman or perhaps both partners). Many of these women struggle or/and yearn to change through various means— through rejecting, escaping or subverting the marriage form. Some of them do transform themselves successfully. They rebel and regain a reborn self in the process of transformation (individuation) and then return to their married lives with a fresh outlook. On the other hand, those women who have not achieved this transcendence as transformation (or cannot face the challenges of this kind of development) alienate themselves instead from marriage. Margaret Dolan's 'A Girl Like You' is a good example of a story demonstrating that money and status cannot guarantee a happy marriage. In the story, the woman, as a wife, serves only as one of the husband's possessions; therefore, she eventually decides to fight against his tyranny in order to become completely herself by rejecting the husband and this marriage. Comparably, the heroine in Ivy Bannister's 'Lift Me Up and Pour Me Out' is eventually fully in charge of herself and awakens from her romantic/unrealistic view of marriage, and faces her problems in reality. She, too, learns the lesson and chooses to leave her husband. As Edna in 'Queen' has suggested, the worst thing about marriage is if you have to be stuck with it. It certainly has been the worse scenario, perhaps especially in Ireland, where women either have had to depend on men for survival or actually have had no possibility of escaping the marriage, until the very recent (1995) legalisation of divorce. Marian Keyes's 'Late Opening at the Last Chance Saloon' reflects contempt for the anti-divorce lobby in Ireland, which leads to both men and women being stuck with an unhappy marriage. Although those female characters who seek to marry in the story still cling to the idea that getting married guarantees a happy ending, nevertheless rationally they understand it might not last forever as in fairy tales. Here, fulfilling the marriage norm seems to relieve social pressure as well as providing an antidote to their unhappiness and the loneliness in their lives. Women like these may soon be disillusioned after they enter into the marriage enclosure just like those who marry for money and status. It certainly is not a simple game. Thus, women's escape from pain or loneliness by getting into marriage eventually becomes itself the source of pain, as expressed by Edna in 'Queen,' who views the unhappy marriage as 'the worst loneliness of all' (OH 193).

Some women depicted in the stories as being in loveless marriages choose to transgress the marriage taboo of monogamy for passion out of wedlock. Certainly, marriage is not the synonym of love. A. A. Kelly views this kind of marriage outcome, often typified by characters in Mary

Lavin's stories, as like birds 'ever on the wing and once caged may not sing.'[75] Irene Boada-Montagut even argues that 'the nature of love is free and cannot be reduced to monogamy, fidelity and all the rules and implications of marriage.'[76] Ivy Bannister's Sonia in 'What Big Teeth,' for instance, or Rose in 'Dublin is full of Married Men' smash the fairy tale dream by demonstrating that the freedom of love and passion (or sex, too) is something beyond and different from the bondage of marriage, and also something to be pursued. So, they seem to raise the issue of an inherent opposition between fidelity, loyalty and chastity in marriage as compared to the freedom of spontaneous passion and sexual love.

Traditionally it is clear that chastity is a quality valued and required more in women than in men. Edna O'Brien's central character in 'The Widow' still has to retain her 'chastity' even though she is technically free to find another partner after her husband's death. And this 'chastity myth' results in rumours and accusations, which are in a way responsible for her emotional instability leading to her fatal accident. Similarly, Dolly in Mary Lavin's 'The Young Girls' is viewed by her peers as a fallen woman simply because they assume she goes down to the river alone with a young man whom she has just met for the first time at a dance. Unlike men, women seem often to be in denial about their own bodies as well as their sexuality and desires, associating both with something filthy or shameful. Some women engage in sex only in order to satisfy their husbands or to fulfil one of their wifely duties for the purposes of reproduction. A woman like Helen in Mary Beckett's 'The Master and the Bomb' shows this typical attitude when she says: 'I satisfy his appetites' (BW 80). Thus, in these stories women's pursuit of freedom through passion and sex may be seen as a form of 'female agency' attempting to deconstruct the patriarchal tyranny which cages women in an ivory tower, or with a chastity belt.[77] However, female power such as liberating female sexuality in these stories is often depicted as being demonised and dreaded as a damaging force, which needs to be subdued. For example, Detta was deemed 'slut' (and therefore, not a suitable wife) by her lover after they have tried this forbidden fruit of sex in Éilís Ní Dhuibhne's 'Holiday in the Land of Murdered Dreams'; the woman who has pursued her own freedom in art and passion was seen as 'a common prostitute and will be treated like one' by her husband, who also locked the woman out of her own house in Maeve Kelly's 'The Vain Woman' (OH 102), while in Edna O'Brien's stories 'A Scandalous Woman' and 'Savages' or Mary Lavin's 'Sarah,' heroines are doomed to pay a price for this overwhelming female sexuality.

In Evelyn Conlon's story 'Taking Scarlet as a Real Colour,' there is a powerful message from the female narrator addressed to another female character 'Susan' (and perhaps to readers as well) uncovering liberating female sexuality:

> We are sometimes fat, thin, heavy-breasted, flat-chested, high-hipped; we are sometimes droopy with lust and drowsy with love; we are fast, we are tight, we are so loose the wind could blow a hole in our fannies. But the shape of us is not important. We love sex, we go wild for it at times, but you'd never guess by what they've said, now would you?...The books made us saints, cheap, plastic saints with lack of love, or they called us scarlet, but they didn't see it as a real colour.
>
> (TL 53-4)

In 'Taking Scarlet as a Real Colour,' the female narrator sarcastically challenges the male misogynistic view about female sexuality, in which she invokes Henry Miller's works: 'it's because you understand so little, you think you could eat it; it's the other way about, Mr Miller' (TL 54).[78] Henry Miller, famous for his 'pornographic style' of sex exploration in his novels, attempted to liberate the human spirit for the sake of freedom through the 'divinity' of sexual acts and free expression. However, feminists criticise Miller's barely disguised misogynistic views on women, whom he devalued and distorted by persistent depersonalisation into descriptions of anatomical genitalia instead of developing individual personality in his novels. Here in 'Taking Scarlet as a Real Colour' Evelyn Conlon has explicitly expressed that female sexuality is something which is often restrained and denied (especially by men) in response to the male gaze (such as the view Henry Miller has represented) on female sexuality.

Another of Conlon's female characters, Beatrice, in the story of the same name, also feels a compulsion to escape her stagnant marriage through the freedom of passion and sexuality. However, Beatrice seems to enter into another pattern and game of power and dominance in a love affair with another man. Or women like Anna in Mary Leland's 'A Way of Life' and Mary in Éilís Ní Dhuibhne's 'Nomads Seek the Pavilions of Bliss on the Slopes of Middle Age' appear to acquire a personal sense of liberation and freedom via expressing passion and sexuality. Although, in Anna's case in 'A Way of Life,' this way of life is mainly based on her insecurity and distrust of men resulting from her wounded self due to her failed previous marriage. These fictional women strive to compensate for their dissatisfaction in a lifeless marriage enclosure by turning to the exploration of passion and sexuality as a token of rejecting this traditional fixed model of marriage.

The feminist author Mary Dorcey breaks out of the heterosexual love format and takes her own view of gender norms into a very different sphere. Several stories, especially the title story, from her collection *A Noise from the Woodshed* (1989) openly celebrate homosexual love between women. According to Mary Dorcey's stories, lesbianism is to be more highly valued than a biased, hierarchical, heterosexual relationship. Perhaps Dorcey views 'equal love' as unattainable for women in heterosexual models due to the inflexible unequal roles for men and women imposed by society but, by contrast, sees a homosexual relationship as more genuine and natural for women because, as also argued by Boada-Montagut, lesbianism is a 'young, recently negotiated' form of intimacy between women, which seems to be free from the rigid presumptions and preconceptions about gender roles.[79] Although the phenomenon of 'homosexuality' has had a long history which has been traced back to ancient Greece, the term 'homosexuality,' widely discussed in sexology and psychology, was in fact invented relatively recently in the late nineteenth century (it first appeared in English in the 1890s), to refer to erotic relations between people of the same biological sex. The ancient Greeks prized male homosexuality over heterosexuality with the latter being for reproduction instead of erotic pleasure. The term 'lesbian' used currently to refer to female homosexuality actually originates from the etymological association with the Isle of Lesbos in Greece which was dominated by women of this kind. Sappho (c. 615 B.C.), a well-known lesbian poet, lived on this island and spent her time studying arts and educating women in art and music as well as writing numerous love lyrics to women (many of whom were her pupils). Therefore, where Irene Boada-Montagut and Mary Dorcey refer to 'lesbianism' as 'newly negotiated,' it should be placed in the context of the emergence of modern gay rights movements of the 1960s as well as of sexual politics where heterosexuality is regarded as a patriarchal dominant form for women in western Christian societies (such as Catholic Ireland), which particularly devalue homosexuality.[80] In order to declare her dogma clearly, Dorcey highlights the women's submission to men in heterosexual relationships in her story 'The Husband':

> Adorning themselves for each other—make-up, perfume, eyebrow plucking, exchanging clothes—all these feminine tricks took on new meaning because neither of them was a man. Helen did not need to flatter, she did not need to patronize or idolize, she did not need to conquer or submit, and her desire would never be exploitative because she was a woman dealing with a woman! Neither of them had institutionalised power behind them.
>
> (NW 76)

Dorcey's view seems to echo Adrienne Rich's, Ti-Grace Atkinson's and Trudy Hayes's approach by seeing heterosexual love as a sort of abusive suppression or oppression by patriarchy. Like Adrienne Rich, Dorcey also visualises a gynocentric world which 'rejects the exploitative hierarchies of a male-dominated society.'[81] Lesbianism to Dorcey, as to Rich, serves as a 'metaphor for feminist solidarity and rebellion' for all those women whose lives 'fall outside the enforced androcentrism of heterosexual societies.'[82]

Different from Dorcey's lesbian subversion in some stories, however, Mary Lavin presents a female character, Angela, who chooses to alienate herself from men and reject sexuality altogether as another means to protest against male aggression in heterosexuality in 'The Nun's Mother.' Angela's flight into celibacy as a nun acts as a way to 'avoid male predation' as in male/female relationships, although she still might not avoid 'the inescapability of patriarchal power, whether in the home or the convent.'[83] In other words, Angela may avoid the physical threat of male sexual aggressiveness by gaining her sexual independence from men as a nun but not 'the mental one of ossification, choosing her own form of sacrifice' in the hands of the male-dominated Christian church.[84]

It seems that the female rage resulting from unequal gender and marriage norms seeks to reject them by alienating women from men or totally abandoning this system. Women at this stage of transition may or may not transcend to a further developmental stage but at least women are no longer oblivious to their internalisation of what has been imposed upon them but emerge to challenge and subvert this patriarchal norm.

The representations of love and marriage in Irish women's short stories appear to reveal the problematic nature of the existing gender roles or norms in the marriage institution which are inherent in a heterosexual relationship, depicting these as a microcosm for unequal, unbalanced gender dynamics. Irish female writers tend to expose problems or conflicts in love and marriage between men and women by expressing women's powerlessness and dilemmas in the face of the existing social norms and they do this primarily by plots based on archetypal motifs in pursuit, submission and subversion. The women in these stories appear to be under the negative impact of the animus identification, experiencing an alien, authoritative and abusive male power; therefore, these women assume in various ways the role of warriors against this patriarchal tyranny. They sacrifice, they question, they fight, they subvert or they become alienated from the tyranny symbolised by marriage or heterosexual relationships. Perhaps women should subvert the existing injustice firstly by liberating themselves from the 'false' female power inherited from the patriarchal tradition, the 'wanting to be wanted,' and through this liberation cease to be objectified.

Some stories, on the one hand, show us women who choose to pursue sexual freedom as an indicator of liberation, possibly because women cannot regain their authenticity and re-establish self-esteem if they still deny their own bodies and urges. For example, women are usually demonised as 'fallen women' or 'sluts' or even 'prostitutes' if they dare to express or explore their own sexual desires like many men do. Men tend to eroticise women as objects, and therefore women can only become passive this way. The message from Angela Bourke's 'Mayonnaise to the Hills' expresses this clearly: 'I think landscape turns anyone on. Or it can—but men think sex belongs to them' and 'the thing is, it's me with the land, not me as the land' (BS 166). Evelyn Conlon also explicitly declares that the overwhelming power of female sexuality should be liberated in her story 'Taking Scarlet as a Real Colour.'

On the other hand, some stories reflect women as bewildered and struggling when re-establishing such a connection with themselves through passionate encounters or casual liaisons. Mary Leland's 'A Way of Life' or Edna O'Brien's 'The Love Object' and 'Baby Blue' show these 'wounded' women, however, as tending to become entangled in an 'obsession' rather than with love.[85] Perhaps they can liberate themselves if they overcome the inertia caused by their trauma or their emotional dependence and possessiveness. These women's inertia may result from their very wounded self that yet empowers them with a sense of self-esteem in their own right without the reflection from men (the similar 'syndrome' in widows described by Mary Lavin, Lucile Redmond, Angela Bourke, Mary Beckett or Marilyn McLaughlin). These women might struggle to fight against their victimisation but some of them, such as the heroines in Edna O'Brien's stories, are doomed while some are not, such as in Éilís Ní Dhuibhne's stories. Although the utopian stage of androgyny, where women and men are equal to and coexist in harmony with one other, does not appear to be portrayed in any substantive way in Irish women's stories, some stories suggest that the creation of a 'new' model for male/female or female/female relationships is at least possible if the biased gender perceptions and roles are subverted. Marilyn McLaughlin's 'Honeysuckle' and Éilís Ní Dhuibhne's 'The Truth About Married Love' represent two of those few stories able to picture a world of harmony and mutual affection, rather than depression or unattainability, in marriage. Éilís Ní Dhuibhne tells a story about a heterosexual couple with genuine affection which thrives regardless of their age and cultural differences. At first Sarah's love for Eric is shown more as compassion and fondness rather than passion. However, Sarah is brave enough to accept Eric against all odds. Passion, although it draws people together in the beginning (as with Sarah's for David, who is almost lost in his passionate kiss), might not last long or survive in the face of reality. Perhaps it is because passion actually involves some impulsive reactions from each other and, sometimes, the resultant idealised image reverts to illusion once entangled in the web of indifferent reality. Clare Boylan describes such an 'impulsive reaction,' just as the cliché 'love is blind,' from both sides of a couple while they are at the blindspot of passion in 'L'Amour' or 'Technical Difficulties and the Plague.' In 'L'Amour,' it is clearly stated that 'she sees in his eyes a mirror of her own perfection. Wait until they each discover that the other is not perfect!' (CS 179) Ní Dhuibhne's 'The Truth About Married Love' seems to show us that a happy marriage may be found in the durability of companionship and the profundity of love, certainly based on equal and mutual support and interdependence in any circumstances. Such mutual affection and interdependence is also portrayed in an old couple in Marilyn McLaughlin's 'Honeysuckle.' Here the balance of love seems to lie in the harmony, unlike in some relationships or marriages where one dominates the other or the expectations of one another are not met. The problem of balance in love may lie in the fact that the man's and the woman's respective expectations are not compatible and cannot be mutually accommodated, or in the fact that they just use each other as a means for achieving their own personal goals. Stories like Éilís Ní Dhuibhne's 'The Woman with the Fish' or Mary Lavin's 'A Woman Friend' and 'A Memory' are about this kind of unbalanced love in which one or both sides focus on their own agenda and for their personal benefit or in which one person depends on the other instead of being willing to share life and experience with that other.

Irish women's stories present us with a changing world where old definitions and roles may proceed to take on new meanings and values in the matter of gender issues. Even the perception about 'gender' in terms of two rigid polarities is depicted as something more fluid, flexible or even amusingly 'performative' in Éilís Ní Dhuibhne's 'Bill's New Wife' (contrasted with Mary O'Donnell's 'Strong Pagans') against the backdrop of various gender issues, rather than as the hegemonic rigid gender roles of heterosexuality which used to dominate the sphere of interpersonal intimacy.[86] This changing world also reflects a continuum of progressive dynamics in sexual politics in which the 'new women' are no longer condemned as viragos or freaks but are accepted or may even be valued in society. Irish women's stories about love and marriage presented in archetypal motifs of pursuit, submission and subversion not only attempt to explore relevant issues or to experiment in a new direction, in which gender perceptions are deeply involved, but also disclose ironically and even ridicule some innate difficulties within the basis for constructing and reconstructing male/female relationships. The problematic appears to lie in the power dynamics of which are the manifestation of the fixed gender norm within marriage and heterosexuality, both of which used to be recognised as the dominant, if not the only, 'legitimate' forms of personal sexual relationship.[87] Therefore, a fresh outlook which embraces a more fluid aspect of 'differences' in gender and sexualities is more likely to be explored further in the twentieth-first century. Perhaps before this prospect can be achieved, we need not only to recognise 'the new woman' or 'the new man' but also 'the new gender.'

'The food was what united them, eating off the same plate, using the same spoon, watching one another's chews, feeling the food as it went down the other's neck. The child was slow to crawl and slower still to walk, but it knew everything, it perceived everything. When it ate blancmange or junket, it was eating part of the lovely substance of its mother.'

from Edna O'Brien, 'A Rose in the Heart of New York,'
A Rose in the Heart (1979)

2. Resistance Between Mothers and Daughters

The concept of 'motherhood' exists across human cultures. 'Motherhood' can be viewed as a biological role, as a socially constructed institution, or as an abstract concept within human culture. Undeniably every human being is born through a mother, whether or not one is conscious of the 'mother' as a physical presence. Not surprisingly, then, the theme of the mother and the daughter is a central concern in Irish women's short stories. Clearly, one's interaction with the mother is the primary connection to this mortal world after one's birth. In particular, the relationship between the mother and the daughter, perhaps due to their shared gender identities, is embedded in a complexity of intimacies and conflicts, and this is especially evident under patriarchal culture. This is an emergent area to be explored in respect of Irish women's short stories, since the relationship between the mother and the daughter provides a lens through which to study women's issues within the fundamental social structure and to contextualise female identities and individuality.

This chapter evaluates relationships between mothers and daughters, and attempts to decode this conflicting mother-daughter knot against a background which defines and confines the social norms and roles for mothers and daughters in contemporary Irish women's short stories. This chapter aims to examine fictional representations of the mother-daughter relationship by exploring the archetypal motifs dealing with aspects of conflict, alienation and rejection signified by rebellious or anorexic daughters and 'devouring' or perplexed mothers in mother/daughter relationships within the context of a 'matriphobic' culture. This chapter considers whether contemporary Irish female writers, emerging with attentiveness to women's issues as well as feminist awareness, have rendered some new space for reconciliation and rediscovery in the mother-daughter relationships in their short stories as a response to the distortion of such ill-nurtured intimacy between women (mothers and daughters) under patriarchy. These recurring motifs in which the daughter's ambivalence of identification with the mother or the mother's complex in respect of the daughter's autonomy often lead to passive resistance or open conflict. These motifs are archetypal, revealing as they do the ideology behind the social form of the family institution. They can also be closely cross-examined against the background of the white, middle-class 'dominant' culture and the emergence of feminism in western European/Anglo-North American societies as well as in the context of a distinctively Irish 'feminine' and mother culture. The Irish mother culture and the female emblem as a national symbol in the course of the political development of Irish nationalism appear to intertwine with established 'western white norms.' The dominant norms reinforce an ideology of idealised female role models supported by Irish society, derived from the devotion to the Virgin Mary in Christianity and a conventional gender perception of domestic women as wives and mothers.

The mother in human existence is more than a biological vehicle for bringing new life to the mortal earth. Across varied cultures and societies the concept of the mother, in both a figurative and a symbolic sense, may also take on varied forms and shapes which are deeply rooted in the bases of those civilisations. For example, in an ancient culture such as that of pre-Christian Ireland, the mother is viewed as a symbol connecting human culture and the mythical forces of nature, due to her power to give life which, in turn, symbolises the 'eternal truth' and cycle of human life—birth, growth and death. Ancient Irish society was matri-centred, where women, through association with their 'sacred' biological characteristic as mothers or potential mothers, were highly valued and even worshipped as is indicated in the early Irish literary text such as *Lebor Gabála Érenn* (Book of Invasions). According to Mary Condren's study of early Irish culture in *The Serpent and the Goddess* (1989), childbirth is a 'sacred occasion' and some of the earliest religious centres were those in which women gave birth.[88] The ability to give birth seems to represent the ultimate power and act of creativity of the Goddess to the world.[89] The ancient Irish manuscript tales recount the symbolic ritual of a sacred marriage between the rightful king and the sovereignty goddess or the mother goddess in Irish mythology. It appears that the harmony between humankind and nature was emphasised and balanced in ancient, matri-centred Irish Celtic culture. The 'matri-centered' culture does not necessarily mean 'matriarchal' in the sense that females dominate males, as is the case with patriarchy, but rather that females are preeminent in a society based on partnership and complementarities between females and males, as Condren explains:

> It is important to point out that, although women were held with great respect, matrifocal societies were not matriarchal, that is, societies where all power rested with the women. A matricentered

society was not simply the reverse of patriarchy where public power does indeed rest with men. In a matricentered society descent was sometimes traced through the female, and sometimes through the male, but under patriarchy most forms of descent through women were abolished.[90]

The symbolic marriage between the king and the goddess embodies the concept of the land and its sovereignty as conceived in the form of a female allegorical figure. This powerful female figure also symbolises the rightful throne of kingship in early Irish Celtic tradition. [91] The prospective Irish king's symbolic union with the goddess ensures his sovereignty and, frequently in those ancient stories, after the ritual of union the goddess changes from her former shape of an old hag into a young maiden, thus symbolising the new kingship as a fresh cycle of birth.[92] The (mother) goddess incarnates fertility and a cycle of life and death as well as union between the tribe and its territory in Irish matri-centred culture.

Carl Jung outlines his own concept of the mother as the archetype which, he claims, exists 'universally' to represent phenomena such as those in Irish mythology:

[The] mother archetype appears under an almost infinite variety of aspects. I mention here only some of the more characteristic. First in importance are the personal mother and grandmother, stepmother and mother-in-law; then any woman with whom a relationship exists—for example, a nurse or governess or perhaps a remote ancestress. Then there are what might be termed mothers in a figurative sense. To this category belongs the goddess, and especially the Mother of God, the Virgin, and Sophia. Mythology offers many variations of the mother archetype, as for instance the mother who reappears as the maiden in the myth of Demeter and Kore; of the mother who is also the beloved, as in the Cybele-Attis myth. Other symbols of the mother in a figurative sense appear in things repressing the goal of our longing for redemption, such as Paradise, the kingdom of God, the Heavenly Jerusalem. Many things arousing devotion or feelings of awe, as for instance the Church, university, city or country, heaven, earth, the woods, the sea or any still waters, matter even, the underworld and the moon, can be mother-symbols. The archetype is often associated with things and places standing for fertility and fruitfulness.[93]

Jung tends to view the 'universality' or 'eternity' of the patterns he discovers in human culture as 'timeless.' Although Jung's concept of the 'mother' archetype, associated strongly with powers of fertility and renewal of the natural cycle, goes beyond the individual and personal mother; nevertheless, the implication of Jung's perception seems to associate women's primeval role with the biologically pre-programmed functions of reproduction, nurturing and caring. Such an assumption, which sees human beings in homogenous terms regardless of the variety of race, culture, class, gender or individuality may also need to be reconsidered so it will not reinforce any bias which discriminates against peoples based on differing gender, class or ethnic groups.

Therefore, in recent years the study of motherhood across the diverse academic disciplines of sociology, anthropology, theology, history, philosophy, psychology, psychoanalysis and literary criticism has tended to examine the experience of motherhood from more than a purely biological or social perspective. These interdisciplinary studies deal with motherhood, which had previously been examined from a general rather than an individual perspective, in the light of various sociological, political or historical insights. [94] Many of these studies agree on motherhood and the mothering role as a female experience but, with the evolution of new concepts and definitions of 'gender' and 'family,' there is significant divergence across the disciplines in defining the scope and associations of the terms 'mother' and 'motherhood': whether mothering should be the sole role for women, or whether mothering should be a choice rather than merely a biological duty; whether the mother is a fluid, relational role rather than a fixed, assigned destiny for women. Also, the position of a same sex couple (whether gay or lesbian) in relation to these issues of mothering, and indeed parenting, needs to be addressed in a variety of contemporary contexts.

Despite the matri-centered culture indicated by the powerful Goddess myth and folklore in ancient Irish society, the continuum does not appear in the corresponding role and status of women in present-day Irish society. Likewise, the power of the mother as an elemental force of nature, which was worshipped with respect and awe in some ancient matri-centred cultures, was later transfigured into an ultimate source of anarchy threatening the patriarchal order. Women who represented this kind of power were demonised as evil figures or witches in patriarchal myths and stories. For example, women in the European folk history were sometimes accused of working evil against men as monstrous figures or witches. Similar evil female or mother (and stepmother) figures also exist largely in fairy tales, folklore, mythologies or psychoanalysis. Erich Neumann, for example, observes the dream symbol of the spider as an evil female (maternal) figure:

> [The] souls of women who, having died in childbirth, become demons combining death and birth also belong to the symbolism of the west. As spiders, hostile particularly to men, they dangle from the heavens; and as the demonic powers of primordial darkness, they escort the sun down from the zenith to its place of death in the west.[95]

This view is amplified by the art historian Ferdinand Anton and psychoanalyst Karl Abraham, who also see the spider as a symbol of a wicked mother whose evil capacity is to kill by blood sucking signifying 'castration' of the male during 'incestuous intercourse [with the son].'[96] Likewise, according to the folklore in some rural areas of Ireland, women who are said to have supernatural powers are believed to become evil mother figures who are notorious child murderesses.[97] This gynophobia (or precisely, 'matriphobia') is also clearly epitomised by the (righteous) male victory over the (evil) female symbolised by the matricide in the Greek dramas of the *Oresteia*, or the murder of Medusa in Greek mythology.[98] Thus, instead of a harmonious relationship between humankind and nature such as was described in ancient Irish manuscript tales, nature associated with women as mothers came to be regarded as 'against' human civilised order and culture, as the 'crazy Other,' in patriarchal societies. The profound source of powers from nature, associated with women due to their ability to create new life, is viewed as a force of anarchy, which might need to be regulated by human beings, namely men, otherwise these dangerous chaotic powers might reach beyond their (male) control. This kind of matriphobia tends to emphasise the danger and terror caused by this overwhelming female power. As a result, this perception attempts to suppress the once powerful awe evoked by the capacity of the mother, and leads instead to a tradition in which the mother's voice is both distorted and silenced. Thus, Luce Irigaray claims that western patriarchal culture is based on the 'murder' of the mother.[99] Similarly, Cathy N. Davidson and E.M. Broner argue that the murder of the mother in patriarchal myths represents the imposition of a patrilineal line of descent such as the matricide in the Greek drama of the *Oresteia*.[100] In ancient Greek mythology Medusa serves as a metaphor for the 'dark side of the mother'; therefore, as Davidson and Broner have pointed out, the decapitation of Medusa also signifies a symbolic patriarchal triumph over this terror of anarchic female powers in male mythology.[101] Likewise, the fall of a goddess in Irish mythology, usually symbolised by a rape or death in childbirth, seems to express the overthrow of the matri-centred culture by patriarchy. Mary Condren explains such a power transition from matri-focal to patriarchal in ancient Irish culture:

> Crushing the Serpent/Goddess, therefore, symbolized the overthrow of those societies, together with their religions, which were matricentered [....] Throughout Irish mythology, relationships to the mother are emphasized. The Tuatha Dé Danaan were 'Children of the Goddess Dana." Even famous heroes were called after their mothers; Buanann was "mother of heroes," while the Goddess Anu was known as "mother of the gods." In some

cases men were called, not alone after their mothers, but after their wives [....] The Goddess Macha was one of the most important goddesses in ancient Ireland. She gave her name to the present day Armagh, Ard Mhacha, and to the ancient forts of Ulster, Emhain Mhacha [....] The story of the overthrow of Macha could be described as the foundation myth of Irish patriarchal culture: the story of the Irish "Fall."[102]

There also appears to be a double bind (an 'either-or,' or 'angel or whore' notion) based on a bi-polarity of positive and negative terms associated with mother representations. On the one hand, the ideal, selfless, all-sacrificing mother is glorified by society (and also reinforced by Christianity) for her functional contribution within the family as well as for her female saintly quality, which is implied as being women's natural destiny. On the other hand, the mother is also suppressed and condemned for her 'too powerful inappropriate impact' on the development of the child because the mother may choke or, in Freudian terms, castrate the child with her 'overstuffing' nurturing. Furthermore, the mother may dominate or inhibit the progress of her child towards autonomy (or even harm the child) in favour of her own satisfaction or sense of power—the so-called devouring 'phallic mother' often articulated by psychoanalytic studies and literature.

The mother culture seems to be a long lost tradition, in which the search for the mother and a mother-daughter bond have been lost within a culture which devalues and silences women and mothers. Adrienne Rich in *Of Woman Born* (1976) has remarked that 'the loss of the daughter to the mother, the mother to the daughter, is the essential female tragedy.'[103]

Natalie M. Rosinsky argues that alienation between the mother and the daughter is a patriarchal norm, a way for a woman to develop 'female behaviour and self-identity.'[104] Rosinsky goes on to explain that being a 'good' mother requires 'indoctrinating' one's daughter with false ideals which conform to such patriarchal 'feminine' stereotypes as irrationality and submissiveness. [105] Rosinsky seems to suggest that women as mothers in patriarchal culture have a viable role only when responsible for shaping and conforming under the guise of educating children (especially younger women) into socially acceptable models under the Father's Law. Some Irish women's stories such as Frances Molloy's 'The Devil's Gift,' Fiona Barr's 'Sisters,' Barbara Haycock Walsh's 'Alice' or Julia O'Faolain's 'Melancholy Baby,' attempt to depict such mothers or mother figures (such as nuns in a convent school) who try to shape younger women according to patriarchal norms. Similarly, Mary Daly also notes that 'mothers in our culture are cajoled into killing off the self-actualisation of their daughters, and daughters learn to hate them for it, instead of seeing the real enemy.'[106] The 'real enemy' here, Daly suggests, is the false, distorted ideology and culture in respect of women and this role as mothers under the patriarchy. The older women, the mothers or mother figures, although deprived of their own authority by patriarchy, often become the messengers as well as the deliverers of the rules of 'the Father' to their daughters or younger women through their internalisation of the patriarchal system. For example, many schools, especially the convents, in Ireland were managed and controlled by nuns, the symbolic mother figures, who were charged with the responsibility of educating small children. The convents were also engaged with the roles in education associated with mothering such as the training of girls in their duties, nursing, and charity. These nuns who were successful in the convent culture might be promoted from 'Sister' to 'Mother' and so given greater authority and responsibility. However, even the ultimate head of such an order, the Mother Superior, was still subject to the authority of the priest (the Father) in the church.[107]

In recent decades, significant awareness especially in feminist scholarship has been devoted to issues and research relating to the understanding of motherhood and how mothers function in reality as well as the relationship between this reality and their representations through language and cultural production. Many academics have focused interest and attention on the material genealogy or matrilineage, and also on the 'natural or spiritual' relationship between mothers and daughters. [108] Most notably, literary texts by female writers dealing with motherhood and the mother-daughter relationship are also being studied widely in order to restore a lost voice between women. Medusa, therefore, is now rediscovered as a 'metaphor for powers previously hidden and denigrated' that women need to reclaim and reassure for themselves.[109] Likewise, representations of renegotiation or reconciliation in some contemporary Irish women's short stories which go beyond the 'mother-bashing' assumption can also be regarded as both a response to the conventionally accepted mother culture in Ireland and a reflection seeking to re-visualise a space between women under a patriarchal culture for such a lost tradition inherited from the matrilineage.

The hidden or repressed anxiety and ambivalence between women of different generations uncovered in alienated or even embattled mother/daughter relationships is largely portrayed in archetypal motifs showing the anorexic daughter who rejects the mother's food, the patriarchal domineering 'phallic mother' with a 'wounded self' as well as the mutual struggle and dilemma between separation and identification of both the mother and the daughter in Irish women's short stories. Stories like Edna O'Brien's 'A Rose in the Heart of New York,' 'Cords' and 'The Bachelor,' or Mary Beckett's 'Under Control' and Mary Lavin's 'A Family Likeness' sometimes depict the devoted mother (perhaps also dependent or demanding in a different manner from the daughter's view) with the resistant daughter who seeks to run away from this 'devouring' mother and do it differently. Others such as 'A Walk on the Cliff' by Mary Lavin, Helen Lucy Burke's 'A Season for Mothers,' Clare Boylan's 'The Miracle of Life,' Anne Devlin's 'The Way-Paver,' Ivy Bannister's 'Happy Delivery' and 'Lift Me Up and Pour Me Out,' Mary Beckett's 'Failing Years' or Mary Leland's 'Commencements' reveal the daughter's feeling of alienation as well as the mother's resentment at the daughter's attempts to separate or to deny the 'natural bond' with the mother which indicates the daughter's refusal to repeat 'the mother's story,' in other words, to end up like the mother. Certainly, there are also the daughters who yearn to be reaffirmed and approved by their mothers but, at the same time, even these daughters sometimes feel disappointed they are rejected by their mothers for various reasons, for example, those in Ivy Bannister's 'My Mother's Daughter' or Maeve Kelly's 'Ruth.' The stories not only depict the troubled viewpoint of the daughters; the mothers are also portrayed as depressed, perplexed or helpless in their uneasy relationships and conflicts with their daughters as in Mary Beckett's 'Under Control' or Mary Lavin's 'Villa Violetta.'

The Irish Mother-Daughter Resistance Plot

The short story format is claimed by Park and Heaton to be the 'perfect' genre for captivating the complexity of this relationship between women (the mother and the daughter) due to its 'immediacy and condensed imagery.'[110] Such depictions of the ambivalent relationship between the mother and the daughter in Irish women's short stories may also be regarded as a voice revealing that Irish women have for too long been displaced as the 'Other' in a context that seems both to idealise (or fantasise) and condemn women and mothers. The alienated, sometimes conflicting, interaction between the mother and the daughter appears to be the relationship characterised as distorted, ill-nurtured or even as 'anorexic.' Some psychologists, such as Luise Eichenbaum, Susie Orbach and Luce Irigaray, have linked the 'symbolic symptom' of anorexia to the mother-daughter relationship as women's reaction to patriarchal structures. The clinical anorexic, as studied by Eichenbaum and Orbach, is seeking to gain control over her body as well as mind by creating a new person inside herself and this is prompted by such a person's desire to reject something (whether physical or psychological), which causes disgust about herself. [111] For example, the female character is characterised by this kind of 'disgust' in Marilyn McLaughlin's story 'Aspects: The West-Acolyte' in which the girl tries to stop the process of growing up by actually refusing to eat. The girl is disgusted by the biological 'metamorphosis' within the female body such as her growing breasts or the cycle of menstrual periods, which she loathes as the 'awful smearing shameful juiciness, this dreadful spreading uncontainable stain' (DW 23). In this story, McLaughlin describes a young woman's rejection or denial of her own biological sex which denotes her gender identity, manifested through a clinical anorexic act in the sense to which Eichenbaum and Orbach have referred. The symbolic 'anorexic' anxiety of the daughter in terms of the mother-daughter relationship shows the daughter's ultimate rejection of identification with the mother, struggling to be something other than the mother. Eichenbaum and Orbach argue this anorexic wish is like expressing the following message:

> Here I am. I'm changing....You can't control me. Yes, I can control you, I will transform you. I will not have breasts, I will not have hips, and I will not have periods. I will not be a woman. I will not be like you, mother. I will not reproduce your life and I will not take in your food. I will not take you inside of me, I will make myself into something else, something other than you.[112]

Luce Irigaray, alternatively, claims that the daughter's resistance or rejection is actually a struggle for autonomy because the daughter is 'over-stuffed' by the mother's ill-nurturing and sees herself becoming another repressed, silenced voice like the mother. Irigaray's image of the daughter's being 'anorexic' is more symbolic than a reference to an actual act of starving oneself in the sense of clinical pathology. It is quite common to associate food and eating with the mother, perhaps partly due to a child's primal experience of need fulfilment in food since birth, part of infantile pleasure. Luce Irigaray's description of a refusal to take in the mother's food (milk) implies a symbol of the daughter's resistance and a 'wish' for separation from the mother. Irigaray's description is like this— instead of the child taking the mother's milk, the child (presumably a girl) swallows 'ice,' and this liquid becomes 'poison' which 'paralyses' the child because it 'overstuffs' her—as if the mother wants to feed 'the mother herself' into the child's mouth.[113] From Irigaray's expression in 'And The One Doesn't Stir Without The Other,' it could be speculated that this daughter's 'anorexia,' symbolising the rejection of this mother, is related to, or caused by, the patriarchal tyranny which enforces the conformity of the daughter/woman through the medium of the patriarchally loyal, dutiful mother who has herself represented the same token of subservience. Edna Longley, similarly, in responding to Paul Muldoon's poem 'Aisling,' also utilises the term 'anorexia' and associates it with repression, rejection and denial.[114] Here again, what Muldoon and Longley have represented does not refer to clinical but conceptual anorexia as a symbol in their discussions of Irish culture and politics. Longley argues that 'anorexia' could signify Irish women themselves, who are 'starved, and repressed by patriarchies' through the exploitive way of using female bodies for the purpose of Irish politics.[115] Maud Ellman also suggests the association of hunger and food with patriarchy can be observed as a kind of a response from women towards patriarchy when she argues: 'if eating is the route to knowledge, as the story of Genesis implies, is it possible that anorexia bespeaks a flight from knowledge masquerading as a flight from food?' [116] The daughter protests against the re-modelling by the mother in a symbolic 'hunger strike' rejecting the food from the primal source, the mother. Figuratively, the mother's compelling act of feeding (shaping) the daughter may be also associated with bulimia, compulsive eating which is related to anorexia, since this ritual of feeding, not of the mother herself but of the reproduction of the mother—the daughter—in a way unveils the mother's depressed feelings of self-disgust. This confirms a sense of 'unentitlement and deprivation' under patriarchy because it seems that the mother can only exist as a 'good' mother by behaving like this (producing the appropriate model as female) in patriarchal societies.[117] Bulimia and anorexia are related to each other and share certain specific manifestations; both express a desire to gain a sort of self-esteem by taking control of the body. The compulsive eaters are somehow seeking a comfort and satisfaction they crave from the lack of confidence in their lives by escaping to food consumption. The term 'bulimia' is here used symbolically as is anorexia by Ellman, Longley and Irigaray. The way the mother stuffs and overstuffs her daughter with a paradigm of being a woman (powerlessness) as the mother herself in this framework, manifests itself as if, as Irigaray has argued, the mother wants to feed herself into the daughter's mouth in order to enforce the reproduction from patriarchy into this copy of the mother herself, that is, the daughter.

The association of food, woman/mother and anxiety on the one hand, and with patriarchy on the other, is clearly represented in Edna O'Brien's story 'A Rose in the Heart of New York' which repeatedly links images of food with both female flesh and the relationship between the mother and the daughter. The woman's aversion toward patriarchy as a result of her experience as a vulnerable mother in birth labour (or a woman with no alternative choice) and later the mother's relationship with her daughter are expressed through 'revulsion towards food' in this story.[118] The image of the unsuccessfully cooked goose, of which the flesh is torn as if wounded, is juxtaposed with the wounded mother whose torn flesh is 'gaping and coated with blood' (FH 378). The mother recalls her harsh life experienced through being a female: there is her 'cruel life,' her 'merciless fate' and the 'heartless man,' by whom she '[has] been prized apart, again and again, with not a word to her, not a little endearment, only rammed through and told to open up....She [sees] that she [is] made to serve in an altogether other way' (FH 376). Perhaps when her husband interrupts her labour by showing her the unappetizing goose, the mother feels disgusted by what she feels is the similarity between the goose and herself: her flesh, as a woman in such a 'culminating point in a history of sexual degradation,' the outcome of her labour which underpins her sense of being a mother and her experience of injury from her birth labour analogous to the torn goose meat.[119]

The sharing of food as well as the preference for the same food between the mother and the daughter in 'A Rose in the Heart of New York' represents the emotional bond between them:

> The food was what united them, eating off the same plate, using the same spoon, watching one another's chews, feeling the food as it went down the other's neck. The child was slow to crawl and slower still to walk, but it knew everything, it perceived everything. When it ate blancmange or junket, it was eating part of the lovely substance of its mother.
>
> (FH 380)

The powerful oral image in which the mother attempts to ease the child's pain furthermore strengthens the closeness between the mother and the daughter:

[T]he mother took the poor fingers into her own mouth and sucked them, to lessen the pain, and licked them to abolish the blood and kept saying soft things until the child was stilled again.

(FH 380)

However, later in the story, conversely, the daughter's distaste for her mother's food at home (it is left untouched) and her resentment towards those food parcels sent by the mother afterwards while the daughter is living away from home indicate the breaking of this bond between the mother and the daughter. The overwhelming image associating the mother with food appears omnipresent throughout the story. It is the food they (the mother and the daughter) share, the food they both like, the food which disgusts the daughter, by no means the lovely substance anymore, which seems to overstuff and suffocate the daughter: 'She wished then that her mother's life had been happier and had not exacted so much from her, and she felt she was being milked emotionally' (FH 399).

This type of suffocating 'carnivorous' mother, in Graham's terms, appears again in another O'Brien story about the mother-daughter relationship. In 'Cords,' the daughter ends up blaming her mother for being the source or catalyst of the recollection of past trauma from her childhood, which, the daughter claims, presently overshadows her current adult life, especially in her relationships with men. The alcohol abuse and domestic violence of which 'every detail of her childhood [keeps] dogging [the daughter]' displays how this daughter is packed with insecurity related to her trauma which is recalled by the visit of her mother, who is also associated with this traumatic past (LO 126). The daughter's fear of the colour red, like that of blood, for example, symbolises this trauma from the domestic abuse which she believes is the source of her insecurity and failure in her relationships with men:

> Looking down into rainbows to escape the colour that was in her mind, or on her tongue. She'd licked four fingers once that were slit by an unexpected razor blade which was wedged upright in a shelf where she'd reached to find a sweet, or to finger the secret dust up there. The same colour had been on her mother's violated toe underneath the big, bulky bandage. In chapel too, the sanctuary light was a bowl of blood with a flame laid into it...She told herself that her four fingers had healed, that her mother's big toe was now like any other person's big toe, that her father drank tea and held his temper, and that one day she would meet a man whom she loved and did not frighten away.
>
> (LO 126-7)

Coincidently, both O'Brien's mothers in these two stories have had a harsh life with an abusive or alcoholic husband and both daughters are not successful in terms of their own personal relationships with men or in marriage. Again, in 'Cords,' the daughter's resentful response—rejection of the past associated with the mother—is also suggested through the daughter's revulsion towards the food associated with the mother: 'these were the things her mother favoured, these foods that she herself found distasteful' (LO 117).

In 'Peacocks' Éilís Ní Dhuibhne depicts another uneasy mother-daughter relationship, in which the daughter's (Aisling) hostility towards her mother (Anita) is also reflected by her refusal to eat, especially the food recommended and offered by the mother. Anita's self-conscious maternal guilt turns into her own self-blame and regret when she fails to 'transfer the capacity for wonder at new things which she possesses in enormous abundance at her age' (MF 149). In other words, Anita fails to shape Aisling into the vivid, assertive person whom she thinks she has become. Ironically, Aisling, who deliberately rejects her mother as a role model, actually appears to repeat Anita's past—she is on the verge of anorexia to be slim or, by her ambiguous, flirting manner, threatens to interfere in other people's love affairs (as Anita intruded into Sharon's relationship when she was around Aisling's age). History seems to repeat itself in this relationship between Anita and her daughter, which Anita experiences as a déjà vu:

> In the driver's mirror, she [Anita] sees herself, with her platinum hair, her treble chin, her ridiculous ear-rings. 'I've turned into Sharon,' she says, aloud, in English. 'What' asks the chauffeur. 'Nothing,' she says. 'Nada.' Within minutes she is back in the hotel. She opens the door of the room without knocking. What she finds is not the worst thing. Not Marcus and Aisling in bed together. But it is alarming enough. Marcus is sitting on the sofa, in front of the television set. The curtains have been pulled. Aisling is lying down, her head in his lap. He is stroking her hair. It's hard to see more in the dim room. They turn when Anita comes in, but Ailsing remains where she is and Marcus makes no attempt to push her away.
>
> (MF 162)

The mother's anxiety in respect of the daughter expresses the mother's conflicting feelings in terms of her own freedom and her responsibility for the daughter Aisling. Yet underneath is in fact the threat represented by Aisling's youth and slimness, which stand for female attraction, in particular when compared to Anita herself, who realises 'she is too fat to be graceful, which is what she [Anita] originally specialised in, and is aiming instead at a chunky sexiness' (MF 148). In this story the tension between women merges with an undercurrent of competition for the men's attention, as symbolised by peacocks, such as that between the chambermaid Sharon and Anita, or between Anita and Aisling. This alienation between women which underlies the 'conflicted nature of female subjectivity' may also suggest the 'dangerous [or distorted] instability of female identity in a male–dominated society.'[120] Women see each other as rivals to fight for a place to locate themselves in such a society which especially values women in terms of fulfilment in love and attention from men.

In Mary Leland's 'Commencements,' the daughter's resistance to the mother is conveyed by a description of the daughter's (a narrator in the story) dislike of honey and also having a kind of amnesia by which the daughter has wiped out the memory of the mother:

> If I had been that child I would have had more of my mother. The crepe paper dresses, the parties with singing and dancing in our small suburban garden with its apple-trees, its lavender and Japanese anemones. I would have made different choices. I would have married differently.
>
> (IO 203)

This daughter has also become a mother herself. However, this daughter/mother denies a memory of her own mother, who is recalled by an old acquaintance from the neighbourhood: 'It had not been me. She remembered them from a time before my life began. There had been no me to remember' (IO 205). Again, the narrator's dislike of honey, associated with the memory of the mother, perhaps also reveals her resentment or ambivalence for having to live under the shadow of a past image remembered by other people which is closely associated with her own mother: 'It hurts me now that I have never liked honey. It is too sweet. Too sticky, its traces lasting long beyond its taste' (IO 206). Honey, the sticky, sweet fluid, perhaps reminds her of the mother's milk. It implies a trauma that this daughter seeks to resist: '[m]y impressed bruise has lingered on landscapes long deserted by what I must still call, can only call, my self' (IO 206). Symbolically, and similar to Irigaray's perception, it seems to suggest this daughter's attempt to get away from the shadow of the mother in her past, the mother who was also overwhelmed by the patriarchal repression of women.

Food also symbolises the interaction between the mother and the daughter in Mary Lavin's story 'A Walk on the Cliff,' which shows the daughter's attempt to please the mother as well as the mother's misreading of her daughter in various ways. In the story, the daughter tries to please the mother through the medium of food: for example, scallops specially cooked for the mother's dinner or a lobster as a farewell gift. However, as the daughter says toward the end of the story, it turned out that 'all [the daughter's] surprises went wrong'—the dinner of scallops was almost burnt, there was a disastrous walk on the cliff, and also a calamity happened to the lobster (FLI 41). From the start, the mother is shown as 'uneasy' with her daughter's attempts to show intimacy with her by kissing. The mother feels 'disconcerted' and 'self-conscious' at the daughter's act of kissing her although, in a previous stage of their relationship, the mother used to appreciate this closeness, which represented a 'unique quality of wit and sensitivity she had never found in anyone else [than in her daughter]' (FLI 21). However, the mother and the daughter misunderstand one another from the moment the daughter arrives. This situation escalates through some tense conversations during the walk on the cliff and eventually climaxes in the mother's resistance to whatever her daughter's farewell gift might be (she assumes it must be something she does not like).

Mary Lavin, as in the story 'A Walk on the Cliff,' tends to write stories portraying the mother-daughter conflict, usually involving rejection or alienation from the mother's point of view instead of from the daughter's perspective. By contrast, Edna O'Brien's stories tend to depict this ambivalence between the mother and the daughter from the daughter's point of view. Nonetheless, Lavin's and O'Brien's mothers tend to cling too much to their daughters out of insecurity or a need to compensate, but with the result that their daughters reject the overshadowing burden imposed by mothers of this type. However, Mary Lavin's mothers are usually portrayed as strong-willed and in some ways domineering. Lavin's stories about mothers and daughters, such as 'A Family Likeness' or 'A Walk on the Cliff' (or other stories about the mother and the son such as 'The Patriot Son,' 'A Likely Story,' or 'The Widow's Son'), tend to depict a mother figure who is shown to be more 'actively devouring' than O'Brien's typical mother figure, who is often depicted as a passive vulnerable victim of an abusive or weak husband.

Thus, it is not rare to see Lavin's mother character who, herself, also resists her daughter in respect of the differences between herself and her daughter. For example, in 'A Family Likeness,' Ada frequently attempts to interfere with her daughter Laura's mothering of Daphne and to impose her own judgments and standards on Laura. Laura simply protests against her mother's dominance by declaring: 'Whose baby is she anyway?' (FLI 7) Laura's message to her mother Ada may take on double implications here, in which Laura intends to declare her authority as the mother to Daphne as well as Laura's realisation that the way she attempts to control her daughter Daphne is just as bossy as her mother Ada's attempts to interfere with herself. After all, Laura used to be Ada's baby—the family likeness is suggested here.

Generally speaking, one aspect of the mother-daughter conflict plot discloses the daughter's resentment towards the mother through rejecting foods from or associated with the mother as a typical gesture of protest against the fate of a female which the mother herself has represented in some Irish women's short stories.

The Phallic Mother: The Overwhelming Impact of the Mother

Gerry Smyth notes the tendency towards literary representation of the family image in Irish writing. This image, in which the child cries for autonomy from the fate imposed by the destiny of birth but is eventually forced to recognize the inescapable impact of the ghost from the past, seems to be an 'enduring and resonant' obsession in Irish culture.[121] The 'generation problem' in Irish fiction, as Smyth argues, tends to advocate a 'familial discourse,' which may have exerted an enormously long-lasting influence on the production of cultural representations of Ireland. Therefore, the clash between parents and children (although here Smyth mainly mentions the father and the son) is a 'recurring trope of Irish cultural discourse under the colonial dispensation,' representing a refusal both of received narratives and of the 'seemingly natural mechanism whereby the past dominates the present.'[122] This cry from the soul, rejecting assimilation into the 'past,' also appears to be characteristic of the literary representations of the mother-daughter relationship in contemporary Irish women's short stories, albeit played out in a different dimension from that between the father and the son as presented by Smyth. M. Hirsch argues that anger in this relationship between mothers and daughters appears to be 'the most common aspect of mother-daughter interaction.'[123]

The tendency for the mother to try to interfere with the daughter's way of doing things may be rooted in the process of transition from one generation to the other as experienced generally in patriarchal culture.[124] Mothers may be conditioned to shape their daughters into certain socially accepted roles but these mothers themselves were also daughters, if not repeated victims, who also had to learn what women are in the world through the lens of their own mothers. Eichenbaum and Orbach attempt to defend mothers as individuals condemned to control or dominate daughters' lives. In their analysis of the psychology of the mother-daughter cycle, Eichenbaum and Orbach argue that the mother who is regarded as controlling, domineering or self-indulgent (in other words, not wholly devoted but may save something for herself), was actually an ill-nurtured daughter herself under such a patriarchal system. This symbolic wounded 'daughter,' the 'little-girl-within' in Eichenbaum's and Orbach's term, who also needs to be nurtured and cared for, remains embedded inside the female but has to be repressed both in terms of her true feelings about herself and her attachment to her own mother during her development towards maturity as an adult female. This repression within women (who, later, also become mothers) may seek its release through the socially more acceptable (or encouraged) way of being female; in other words, through selfless acts, taking care of or nursing other people or putting other people's needs before her own. Therefore, according to Eichenbaum and Orbach, this hidden 'little-girl' inside the woman may be revealed when the woman has become a mother and experienced the process of bearing her own baby girl. While the mother is communicating with her baby girl, in a way she is responding to her own self, the 'little-girl within.' The daughter might even be regarded as a kind of mirror image of herself by the mother. In a sense this woman/mother is 'reproducing herself' this way. [125] Therefore, the boundary between the identities of the mother and the daughter may tend to be blurred and fused, perhaps due to the combination of their shared gender and the mother's inevitable projection onto the baby girl of some of the feelings or expectations the mother actually has about herself.[126] Unlike a boy, in this way it may be more difficult for the daughter to differentiate herself from the mother due to their shared gender, which might suggest their 'would-be' shared destiny. Eichenbaum and Orbach analyse the problem of the mother's ambivalence towards separation from her daughter:

Inevitably, the daughter's attempts at separation are somewhat ambiguous and dovetail with mother's ambivalence. The message from mother during the period of infantile dependency has been, 'Take care of yourself, don't depend on others, don't want too much,' but these injunctions, which in effect seem to push the daughter away, have been combined with the unstated, unconscious message: 'Stay close, don't stray, don't go too far, it's dangerous.' As a result, the process toward separation has to contend with a tug to stay close to mother and share the boundaries she inhabits....A daughter's moves toward independence are bound to diminish a mother's sense of being needed. Brought up to see her central role as that of mother, she may feel empty, depressed, confused about who she is; she may lose her sense of purpose. If she has not been able to separate psychologically from the mother, she may in turn cling to her daughter.[127]

This woman, being shaped in such a culture, may feel it difficult to adjust to the time when she as a mother has to face up to her daughter's independence or realise and accept the difference in values or the path the daughter follows in pursuing a life dissimilar to that of the mother's own. As Eichenbaum and Orbach have observed, the once fusional boundary between the mother and the daughter, the mirror image of the mother or rather the little-girl inside, which drives the mother to seek to shape the daughter in the model that the mother actually expected herself to become, gradually diminishes. In other words, the mother's indispensable role, her personal sense of being needed, no longer matters in her daughter's life when the daughter has grown up. Frequently, the mother may find it difficult to accept the 'unexpected outcome' that her daughter eventually becomes a rather different individual to herself. Hence, it is significant to explore not just the invariable pattern of a resistant daughter against a tyrannical mother, a mother who controls too much, but also that of a resistant mother against a 'rebellious' daughter, in other words, the daughter who intends to behave in many ways differently from the mother, in Irish women's short stories dealing with the mother-daughter relationship.

Some of Mary Lavin's mothers appear to be resistant mothers who tend to impose their way onto their daughters such as those in 'A Family Likeness' and 'A Walk on the Cliff,' and, moreover, there are examples showing that the mother and the daughter somehow misread one another in various ways. Ivy Bannister, in 'My Mother's Daughter,' depicts such a 'resistant mother' who reflects this confrontation by showing her envy that her daughter's life is happier than hers. In this story, the mother finds it difficult to accept the reality that, in old age, she is no longer physically attractive to other people in the way she once was, and the fact that she lives away from her daughter (in her view she is abandoned by her daughter to the nursing home). The mother's feeling for her daughter, who is in her prime and has both an enjoyable career and family life, appear complicated and ambivalent. Instead of feeling happy to see her daughter's life as a successful career woman as well as a working mother, this mother simply resists her daughter's efforts to try to build a better relationship with her by her own cynicism and bitter remarks towards her daughter. The mother's criticism of, sometimes even attacks on, her daughter reflects the mother's resentment towards her daughter and perhaps also reveals a response to her own 'little girl inside' who is ill-nurtured, in want of love and attention, and has turned sour: 'I never had what I wanted, not when I wanted it' (MO 34). At the same time, the mother also seems to acknowledge a sense of loss of her own self-value, when faced with the reality that her daughter obviously does not need her guidance anymore, nor has the daughter repeated the mother's 'destiny.' Rather, this daughter, part of a younger generation living in changed times, has turned out even better than her mother in terms of career, marriage and family life.

A jealous mother like the one described by Ivy Bannister may be difficult to please. However, the mother figure in Helen Lucy Burke's 'A Season for Mothers' is even more aggressive. This mother not only disagrees with her daughter's different way of living her life—her daughter's 'almost sinfully luxurious style of living' and the way the daughter herself remains a 'dried-up old maid'—but also attempts to intrude into the private territory of her daughter's life (SM 24). As a result, the daughter feels 'a simultaneous access of cold to her heart. She knew what her mother was planning. And all her life her mother had won' (SM 34). Although the daughter actually feels uncomfortable about her mother's visit and her mother's inevitable interference and judgment, unlike some other rebellious daughter characters such as Claire in Edna O'Brien's 'Cords,' she does not fight against her mother in the same resentful way as those other daughter characters in Edna O'Brien, Mary Lavin's or Ivy Bannister's stories.

Conversely, Mary Beckett's controlling mother in 'Under Control' provokes the daughter's contempt for the mother resulting in the daughter's self-hatred, which eventually leads to her destructive response when attempting to shake off the mother's control of her life. This mother figure, Kathleen, claims that '[she doesn't] want to boss people about or control their lives, but [she has] never found anybody else prepared to make the decisions' (FL 97). However, her daughter Stella seems to perceive her mother from a totally different perspective because she always struggled to achieve whatever the mother had planned for her. Ultimately, this daughter rebels against her mother's plans for her life by taking the radical step of becoming a single mother. This drastic act is destructive for the mother, who is from a background in which 'illegitimate' pregnancy is deemed a huge shame to women. Stella's fatherless baby appears to signify her own shame and self-loathing as well as her revenge for the mother's dominance over her own life. This kind of conflict in the mother-daughter relationship plays out in an extraordinarily tragic way in Mary Beckett's 'Under Control,' but in fact the depiction of alienation between mothers and daughters is not uncommon in Irish women's short stories.

Nevertheless, Mary Beckett characterises another mother figure who also shows her resistance against her daughter but for different reasons in 'Failing Years.' This mother, Nora, reveals her resistance in her disapproval of her daughter Una's marriage as 'unsuitable' in her view:

> Why should she [Una] have married before she was twenty a man so old for her? When he [Una's husband] died eventually, Nora wondered what sympathy she should feel for her daughter. "It was not," she said to Alec, "as if it was a real marriage, like ours."
>
> (BW 100)

In fact, this mother seems to find it hard to negotiate herself within her own married life but she still manages to conform to her role as a dutiful wife and mother:

> Nora didn't feel it was as good as the fires of her childhood where the glow behind the bars was a dangerous delight, but she joined in Alec's praises with gratitude.
>
> (BW 102)

Nora's insecurity makes her depend on her husband for protection and reassurance. Like some mother figures in Mary Lavin's stories such as 'A Walk on the Cliff' or 'In a Café,' Mary Beckett's Nora in 'Failing Years' later becomes a widowed mother. She was so attached to the lifestyle that she shared with her husband that she finds it hard to restart a new life after his death, which no longer centres on him and his needs. Nora was so deeply attached to and dependent upon her husband that she believes she does not have a life of her own:

> She had often said to him that it would be nice if his car would go out of control and smash into a wall and kill the both of them and not leave one lonely. Now he was gone and she was left waiting. Of course he had gone off and left her waiting many a time on his trips abroad, but then she knew he's be back with a present for her and a suitcase full of dirty clothes. She'd often thought, as the smell of exotic cigarettes and strange rooms rose out of the washing-machine, that that was her share of the foreign travel. She

had never been out of Ireland....But with him gone there was no
one to praise her, no one to laugh at her, no one to touch her

(BW 101-2)

Nora's unsettled feeling, originating from her sense of insecurity, also
alienate her from her own offspring. It seems the daughter, Una, becomes
an intruder in this exclusive world belonging to Nora and her husband:
'Una, I can manage without you. I am not a fool. And it is my house' (BW
100). The mother tends to misread how the daughter behaves or reacts,
and sees her as an irritable intrusion; for example, the daughter's moving
back to the house in order to look after the aging mother results in the
mother's anxiety, sleeplessness and even contempt. The mother resents
the way the daughter treats her as a weak person in need of help, and the
mother is especially irritated when the daughter behaves as if she (the
daughter) has become the 'focus' of the mother's house: 'When the
neighbours called to welcome Una back it was Una who had their
sympathy' (BW 103). Nora fails to recognise that the gap, which always
seems to block her from her daughter (and also her sons and grandchildren
as well), is related to a fundamental sense of her insecurity, particularly
in the absence of her husband. For example, there is her embarrassment
in dealing with her awkwardness with verbal expression: 'She couldn't
think of the words she wanted at all and her tongue felt heavy in her mouth'
(BW 103). Without the protection from her husband, the mother in
'Failing Years' retreats into her own cocoon in which she can hide away
from her daughter and other people:

She would never let them know where she's gone, she repeated to herself. It was something of her own to hold on to. Then she realised that if she were very careful and kept Una at bay, Belfast would still be there for her. She would try again some time in the spring, when the weather was warmer or the Troubles were over.

(BW 111)

This mother resists her daughter, not due to her wish to dominate or meld with her daughter to prevent their separation, but because of the mother's fundamental inability to retain closeness with people. This kind of anxiety and insecurity leading to alienation within relationships among people and families can perhaps be associated with an instability in the society, most notably in Northern Ireland, as depicted by some Northern Irish female writers. For example, there is the exile of the daughter from the mother in Anne Devlin's 'The Way-Paver' or the crisis of trust between people in 'The Wall-Reader.' This kind of anxiety, foreshadowed by the unstable political and societal conditions in Northern Ireland, does not seem to emerge the same way in stories by female writers from the Republic of Ireland. Some Northern Irish female writers depict alienation in human relationships in stories such as Anne Devlin's 'The Way-Paver,' and 'Five Notes After a Visit,' Fiona Barr's 'The Wall-Reader,' or Blánaid McKinney's 'Big Mouth.' It may be not directly addressed in Beckett's story that the mother's anxiety and difficulty are related to the shadow of the 'troubles' in Northern Ireland. Nonetheless, depression and alienation among people in a politically unstable society, expressed through interactions with each other, appear to be distinctive in works by Northern Irish female writers.

The stories on mother/daughter relationships mentioned and examined above uncover the powerful impact of the mother upon the daughter, which appears to be the fate that the daughter attempts to escape, albeit often in vain. This 'devouring' phallic mother is often condemned to 'suffocate' the daughter by overstuffing (imposing herself upon) the daughter, but in fact this 'overpowering' mother might also have been a victimised daughter/ woman herself under patriarchy.

Do it Differently: Daughter Rebels Against the Patriarchal Mother

It appears that mothers are often condemned for blocking their daughters' paths to autonomy by seeking to control or to shape their daughters in a certain way, as we are shown in many Irish women's short stories dealing with the mother-daughter relationship. It has been argued that the Greek classical myth of Demeter and Persephone is also a story about a daughter's struggle to run away from the possessive 'terrible mother.' [128] Luce Irigaray argues that the patriarchy functions by separating women from each other, and this negativity has imprisoned mothers and daughters as 'captives of [their] confinement.'[129] Irigaray also poses a question: '[b]ut how, as daughters, can we have a personal relationship with or construct a personal identity in relation to someone who is no more than a function?'[130] Certainly, the mother will introduce her daughter to what is, from her perspective, the proper way of behaving and feeling as a girl and what is appropriate to prepare the daughter for her future life and roles as an adult female. In this situation, the daughter may see herself as unwanted and unloved, the 'embodiment of [the mother's] own failure and depression,' and in such a situation the daughter can have little sense of her own value and must battle against her mother to try and find her own self.[131]   Some passages in Maeve Kelly's 'Orange Horses,' such as the following one, convey such a daughter's anger in the face of her mother, who is herself powerless under patriarchal tyranny:

> That's why her brothers were so proud and cocky. They could race the wind, and she couldn't. Her father did it once. Her mother never did it. Her mother got beaten and had babies and complained. Her mother was useless....'It's easy. I'll practise. If they see I'm good, they'll let me do it. I'm not like you, Mama. I'm like my Dada and no one will bate me into the ground. You shouldn't let Dada hit you.'
>
> (OH 32, 40)

This anger underlying the mother-daughter relationship is, according to M. Hirsch, the result of an ambivalence stemming from '[fears] of maternal power and anger at maternal powerlessness' under patriarchy.[132] Ann Owens Weekes elaborates Hirsch's notion further by linking the 'invalid' role model of older women, mothers, for younger women, daughters, to the frustration underlying anger, which surfaces in turn in the form of an uneasy relationship between the mother and the daughter:

> Mothers' collusion in their own powerlessness and in communicating this to their daughters may be unconscious, but the children, for whom the mother is 'the primary uncontrollable source of the world's goods,' are reduced to rage and

disappointment when the 'powerful maternal presence' they have relied upon subsequently becomes 'the powerless woman in front of the father, the teacher, the doctor, the judge, the landlord—the world.'[133]

Weekes's remarks uncover some problems in certain aspects of this relationship, which need to be explored further in order to grasp the complexity and ambivalence of mother-daughter relationship representation in Irish women's short stories. This resentment as well as alienation may be linked to the daughter's ambivalent struggle between the need for closeness and her desire for separation and autonomy from the mother. On the one hand, the inter-connectedness between mother/daughter is seen as a 'problem,' both parties being trapped in a web of ambivalence which impedes the development of a constructive identification between women from different generations. On the other hand, social norms seem to emphasise the desirability of separation between the mother and the daughter, due to the high value contemporary society places on autonomy and individuality.

Different from Eichenbaum and Orbach, who have attempted to analyse the mother/daughter relationship from the mother's point of view, Adrienne Rich has noted the complexity of the inter-dependence and identification between mothers and daughters from the daughter's point of view. Rich thinks it is partly because '[mother] stands for the victim in ourselves, the unfree woman, the martyr. Our personalities seem dangerously to blur and overlap with our mothers'.'[134] Actually, as Vivien E. Nice argues, it appears that the issues of identification with and separation from the mother are being presented within a patriarchal framework which treats the mother as a kind of scapegoat who should be held responsible for the daughter's dependence or lack of confidence. Nice attacks the assumed desirability of a separation between mothers and daughters as a kind of distortion by patriarchal culture of which the purpose is to confirm a basis for society which is 'developmentally healthy based on the positive regard of individualism and heterosexism' and leads automatically to the closeness between women (such as between mothers and daughters) being interpreted as 'unhealthy and denigrated.'[135]

The merging identification between the mother and the daughter may become problematic and ambivalent in respect of the later stages of separation between the mother and the daughter as well as the daughter's attitude towards her mother. In her book theorising motherhood, *The Reproduction of Mothering* (1978), Nancy Chodorow explains such a condition as a framework of ambivalence and 'interdependence' between the mother and the daughter.[136] Chodorow thinks that social expectation actually discourages development of an over-indulgent attachment to the mother with, as a possible ultimate consequence, the daughter's criticism or rejection of the mother. The daughter's ambivalence in respect of both identification with and separation from her mother is a dilemma causing anxiety as well as resentment, both of which may underlie the daughter's troubled relationship with her mother.

The depiction of the daughter's ambivalence towards the mother is well presented in Edna O'Brien's 'A Rose in the Heart of New York,' in which love evolves into hatred and suffocation. In the beginning the mother and the daughter are so fused into oneness that 'her mother's body was a recess that she would wander inside forever and ever, a sepulcher growing deeper and deeper' (FH 380). However, the daughter also feels an anxiety about this deepest love from the mother, which acts as a 'gigantic sponge, a habitation in which she longed to sink and disappear forever and ever. Yet she was afraid to sink, caught in that hideous trap between fear of sinking and fear of swimming' (FH 388). The turning point for the daughter's perception of her mother seems to commence when the daughter is forced to separate from the mother, perhaps for the first time in her life, by being sent to a boarding school. A similar depiction of the daughter's changed attitude towards her mother occurs in another story by O'Brien, 'The Bachelor.' Nancy Chodorow argues that the daughter's rejection of such fusion with her mother shows both an attempt by the daughter to escape into another form of 'intense identification-idealization-object loves' and at the same time reveals her 'feelings of dependence on the primary identification with this mother.'[137] Both girls in 'A Rose in the Heart of New York' and 'The Bachelor' seem to be able to find a replacement for Chodorow's 'intense identification-idealization-object loves'—the nun as an idol in 'A Rose in the Heart of New York' and the dream of going to university in the big city in 'The Bachelor'—after they return home from the boarding school. These daughters' previous closeness with the mother metamorphoses into reluctance, avoidance of intimacy with the mother, or rejection of the mother—in 'A Rose in the Heart of New York,' '[n]ow she [the daughter] did the avoiding, the shunning. All the little treats and the carrageen soufflé that the mother had prepared were not gloated over' (FH 390). In 'The Bachelor,' the daughter also alienates from her mother:

I aspired toward Dublin and resented having to stay at home and listen to depressing conversations. I was sarcastic to my mother, shunned my father, and spent most of the time upstairs fitting on clothes, my own clothes and my mother's clothes.

(FH 68)

In 'A Rose in the Heart of New York,' after the break from her mother, the daughter escapes into an unsuitable marriage which eventually fails. In the aftermath of her collapsed marriage, the daughter seems to fall into an abyss of darkness; she is still struggling to flee from the shadow of her mother. This is expressed in the form of a dream in which she attempts to kill the mother, an act showing the daughter wishes she could have stopped her mother giving birth to her:

She thought of choking or drowning. Certainly the method had to do with suffocation, and she foresaw herself holding big suffocating pillows or a bolster, in the secrecy of the Blue Room, where it had all begun....Her mother was on her deathbed, having just given birth to her—the little tonsured head jutted above the sheet—and had a neck rash, and was busy trying to catch a little insect, trying to cup it in the palms of her hands, and was saying that in the end "all there is, is yourself and this little insect that you're trying to kill."

(FH 394)

Although the daughter hates the mother for her 'choking' love and yearns for separation from her completely, the daughter actually feels ambivalent about the breakaway. Partly this is because she fears her denial of being a younger version of her mother would be in vain due to the fact that, genetically, part of the mother is also part of her. This undeniable fact is also acknowledged by the daughter in 'The Bachelor,' who later realises that 'some of her [mother's] fatality had already grafted itself onto [her] and determined [her] disposition' (FH 57). Nevertheless, in 'A Rose in the Heart of New York' the daughter's primary 'emotional dependence' on her mother is apparent when she returns to her family house after the mother's death. The daughter seeks for something that could put together the jigsaw of the hardship in her mother's past, especially her mother's private life, which has always been a mystery to the daughter. At the same time, what the daughter actually hopes to discover is a trace of something left by the mother which will reassure the daughter of her mother's tenderness and closeness towards her. However, the daughter is disappointed in this search and feels abandoned by the mother through the mother's death. This daughter's powerful feelings of love-hate/oneness-separation/dependence-autonomy in 'A Rose in the Heart of New York' exemplifies a typical ambivalence such as that expounded by Chodorow in her analysis of the factors which define the daughter's relationship with the mother.

However, Clare Boylan, in 'The Miracle of Life,' describes this ambivalence, ironically, through a reversal of the typical model of the conforming mother versus the rebellious daughter. Conversely, the mother in this story is portrayed as an unconventional woman of independent spirit. Ironically, this 'subversive' mother is rejected by the daughter because the mother is 'heretical,' that is, the mother does not conform to a socially acceptable role of how a mother should behave; rather, the mother is an outspoken, independent woman. Thus, the daughter instead turns to the female neighbour as her role model as an adult female. Obviously, the daughter's admiration for this neighbour as a substitute mother figure seems to be related to vanity (perhaps the daughter's concern for the impact on her own status of her mother's distinctive behaviour) as well as to her idealised image of a perfect mother who, for her, should project the image of a beautiful, happy housewife— like the glamorous Betty Malibu, who lives in a nice house with high-tech equipment (such as a fridge) and has a car for herself. In a sense, this daughter still identifies with a superficial, unrealistic image shaped by patriarchal stereotypes, and this contrasts with the self-image of a unique, independent individual whom the daughter claims she wants to be. The daughter's ambivalence in respect of her identification with an idealised mother image on the one hand, and with her mother's subversive ideas on the other hand, seems to be symbolised in the story by the daughter's contradictory feelings evoked by the prudishness of the nun, Sister Sophie, and the open female sexuality of a friend's sister, Reenee, whose illness and death appear to the daughter to be a punishment for a 'fallen' woman who has experienced the sinful 'French kissing,' 'lurching' or 'shifting.' Perhaps the daughter's ambivalence towards her heretical mother also illustrates a battle of resistance between the independent female self and the patriarchal forces of social conformity.

In many Irish women's stories about mothers and daughters, the daughter's tendency to do it differently, if not better, or the daughter's alienation from the mother, is also the consequence of the fact that the daughter wishes to see herself as a unique individual separate from her mother. For example, in Ivy Bannister's 'Lift Me Up and Pour Me Out,' the daughter confronts the mother by wanting to become a female different from the mother, whom the daughter detests as a 'sexless freak' (MO 111). The mother forces the daughter to play piano (as the mother has always done) but the daughter rebels and resists becoming like her mother who '[sits] at the ivories, day in, day out, hammering out the one loony tune until it gives everyone the creeps' (MO 112). Another of Bannister's stories, 'Happy Delivery,' shows how a daughter rejects the idea of becoming a mother: she 'ha[s] but one ambition: not to end up like [her] mother' (MO 64). Certainly, the struggle for separation and autonomy (following Irigaray's schema) may lead to alienation, or even to the extreme rejection of identification (merging) with the mother. Alienation in a mother-daughter relationship is often shown as ambivalent anger or conflict (as argued by Chodorow) in some Irish women's stories such as those by Edna O'Brien, Mary Lavin or Mary Beckett.

The Dual Mother: The Ambivalence of Representations in Irish Mother Culture

As noted earlier in this chapter, the phenomenon of the tyrannical mother who controls or shapes her daughter surfaces in the mother-daughter relationships presented in some Irish women's stories. Another dimension of this exploration of such relationships is displayed through depictions involving a tendency to idealise the mother according to the parameters of the dominant patriarchal culture. The so-called 'ideal mother' may exist only in fantasy and any parameters used to judge such an image are also problematic insofar as they tend to be filtered through the lens of male perspectives and priorities. The ideology in this arena as manifested in the Irish context tends to reinforce the making of the stereotypical image or the standard as a model for women and mothers. The perception of 'mother idealisation' in Irish culture, as argued by C. L. Innes, is linked to a fusion of diverse strands from Irish (pagan) culture merged with religious impact, such as the Irish 'feminine idiosyncrasy' manipulating allegorical female figures as the emblem of the Irish nation for varied political agendas in history as well as the veneration of the Madonna in Christianity.[138] This 'feminine idiosyncrasy' in Irish culture and history embodies a tendency to portray Ireland either as maiden or as mother. This is exemplified by the eighteenth-century political aisling genre (meaning 'dream' or 'vision) which influenced James Clarence Mangan's poem 'Dark Rosaleen' a century later, by 'Hibernia,' which figures Ireland as a vulnerable female seeking protection by the English colonisers, by its Irish counterpart, 'Erin,' by Irish nationalists in the nineteenth century, and by the symbolic Queen figure 'Cathleen Ni Houlihan' in W. B. Yeats's nationalistic drama or the poor old woman (the Shan Van Vocht) of Irish legend and ballad. These emblematic female figures as maiden or mother appear to be a complex interweaving of earlier traces of Irish matrifocal culture adulterated with patriarchal values from Irish pagan and Christian ideologies and subsequently pressed into the service of a male-dominated Irish politics, both English colonialism and Irish nationalism.[139] Politics in various forms appears to be expressed through the transfiguration of female bodies in Ireland. Irish women, argued by Edna Longley and Sara Edge, are displaced and exploited once more by this use of female bodies for the purpose of Irish (male) politics.[140] Sara Edge argues that it seems the only role for Irish women in the position of 'double otherness,' which locates them as subservient to both patriarchal male power and to dominant British national identity, is being mothers.[141] This kind of political discourse also tended to reinforce existing gender stereotyping, emphasising the vulnerability of women and consolidating gender roles for women as passive wives and mothers. As Gerry Smyth has pointed out, Irish nationalism 'imposed within Ireland the economy of unequal gender relations that colonialism had constructed between Ireland and England.'[142] It appears that the literary representation of the mother-daughter relationship in contemporary Irish women's short stories also reflects this collective distorted 'tradition' of the powerlessness of mothers, in which women are objectified under male-dominated societies.

Irish mother culture in various aspects is closely connected to the complexity of the ancient Irish matrifocal culture as well as to more progressive female emblems in subsequent Irish society and politics. In the early period of Celtic Ireland, the female metaphor represented by the Mother Goddess symbolises prosperity of the nation and the rightful kingship. This female emblem, represented by ferocious female warriors or goddesses such as Queen Maeve or Macha, signifies a powerful female culture in Celtic Ireland. However, these once powerful female symbols which already existed in Irish culture and society later merged with the dominant social ideology from the eighteenth through early twentieth centuries in Irish society. Richard Kearney speculates that Ireland, mythologised as a 'repressed' motherland, is related to the history of 'dispossession' after the English policy of plantation in the seventeenth century and the Cromwellian occupations.[143] Significantly, the Gaelic aisling genre which emerged after the seventeenth century 'envisages Ireland in a dream vision as a beautiful woman pleading for rescue from the invaders.'[144] The image of those female symbols in the nineteenth and early twentieth centuries tends to be tainted with patriarchal gender ideology, also embodying a stereotypical vulnerable female figure seeking male protection or liberation. Therefore, Irish 'feminine' culture under patriarchy during these periods is dominated either by maiden figures such as Hibernia, Erin, 'Dark Rosaleen,' 'Cathleen Ni Houlihan' and Deirdre in the Irish Literary Revival, or by mother figures such as a betrayed suffering Irish mother dramatised by the literary Revivalists, the Shan Van Vocht and the Virgin Mary of Christianity. These female figures are characterised especially by their vulnerability or their subordinate status to patriarchy. The double vision of Ireland as both a young maiden and an older woman (a mother figure) is associated both with 'being betrayed,' and also with 'dispossession.'[145] Irish culture associates itself with the 'feminine' nature of the maiden and with the mother, and both images act as metaphors for the nation; likewise, both can be traced through a process of evolution from the powerful to the powerless. Gerry Smyth argues that female iconography had played an eminent role in Irish Gaelic culture, and that later this was manipulated into a 'colonialist tradition in which the country was represented as a woman—either an old woman or a beautiful young queen, exhorting the menfolk to oppose the invader.'[146] Obviously this phenomenon, which Gerry Smyth has discussed in post-colonial discourse, can be traced back through a complicated reworking process which 're-invents' female emblems in Irish culture, history and politics by fusing several strands of Irish culture, Christianity and patriarchy.

English representations in the nineteenth century largely portrayed Ireland as the helpless maiden figure 'Hibernia.' 'Hibernia' is an ancient name for Ireland first applied by the Romans, as were the names Britannia

(Britain) and Gaul (France) during the period of the Roman Empire.[147] But 'Hibernia' was then manipulated by Victorian English political propagandists in order to curb Irish nationalism and the Home Rule movement, which represented Hibernia (Ireland) as a mistreated maiden in need of advice from Britannia (Britain) as well as help and protection from the male colonisers of British rule.[148] Jonathan Swift's *The Story of the Injured Lady* (1746) or English political cartoons in newspapers which emerged in the nineteenth century adopted this ancient Roman name, Hibernia, and blended it into an ideology of a virginal maiden who needs to be rescued from the 'barbarian' Irish by British 'civilisation.' This Victorian colonialist 'biased' view of the English is epitomised in a letter from Charles Kingsley to his wife, in which the Irish people were not even regarded as human beings:

> But I am haunted by the human chimpan-zees I saw along that hundred miles of horrible country. I don't believe they are our fault. I believe there are not only more of them than of old, but that they are happier, better, more comfortably fed and lodged under our rule than they ever were. But to see white chimpanzees is dreadful; if they were black, one would not feel it so much, but their skins, except where tanned by exposure, are as white as ours.[149]

On the other hand, Irish representations also saw a female figure representing a nation in crisis adopted by both Anglo-Irish Protestant and Gaelic Catholic nationalists. Examples of this include James Clarence Mangan's political implication in his reworking of an earlier folk song *Róisín Dubh* (Little Black Rose) in his poem 'Dark Rosaleen,' the Celtic twilight of the Irish Literary Revival epitomised by W. B. Yeats's famous figure in his drama Cathleen Ni Houlihan and the popular motif of Deirdre amongst the Literary Revivalists, or the maiden figure 'Erin' in Irish newspapers and magazines which emerged between 1860 and 1914.[150] The image of Erin appears to be an Irish counterpart of Hibernia. These female figures, including Erin, Cathleen Ni Houlihan, Deirdre and Rosaleen, appear to epitomise the nation as a female (a maiden or a queen) in need of protection and rescue (from her suitors or warriors, certainly male).[151] It is interesting to see how the Irish Literary Revivalists favoured the heroine Deirdre over Queen Maeve from their Celtic heritage for their creative inspiration. Lorna Reynolds thinks it may illustrate the change from one system to the other symbolised by Queen Maeve and by Deirdre. That is, the powerful and sovereign Mother Goddess figure of Queen Maeve is overthrown and replaced by a romantic tragic heroine in a society 'where women lose their rights and become chattels' and who would be wronged by inappropriate suitors in the most fundamental way in the patriarchal context.[152] However, we also need to note that the earlier pre-Christian version of the Deirdre story exists as a fable warning that kings must act fairly and justly, and maintain a harmonious relationship between culture and nature. But the later version of the Deirdre story had been revised by monks who transcribed it to fit into the Christian context as well as to emphasise the parallels with the story of Eve.[153] Deirdre also seems to be linked with some later versions of Erin (similar to Yeats's Cathleen Ni Houlihan), serving as a vulnerable female figure who summons young men to fight and die for her in order to 'liberate her from an oppressive suitor.'[154] The Irish poet Seamus Heaney also inscribes traditional gender divisions when describing the relations of the two nations, figuring a male Britain and female Ireland in his poem 'Act of Union,' in which the political implications of this trope have been drawn more self-consciously in the terms of gender relations or marriage.[155]

The maternal figures appear to be distinctive female emblems representing Ireland embodying the poor old lady and the Virgin Mary, both of whom represented a similar 'maiden in distress.' The mother figures are in need of rescue and liberation, they depend on the agency of others in a context which blends traditional Irish folklore and Christianity. The popular figure of 'the poor old woman' (the Shan Van Vocht) of Irish legend and ballad may derive from or combine aspects of a much earlier Irish tradition dating back to at least the eighth century and associated with the banshee (bean sí) and 'Badhb,' who appears to come from the war goddess, Badb.[156] In Irish mythologies, this figure is a goddess of battles who is regarded as one of the triune of Badb (Badhbh), Macha and Mórrígán (Mór-Ríoghain). Patricia Lysaght connects the two aspects as sovereignty and death in the sagas in the figure of Fedelm by arguing the following:

Since the sovereignty of the land was perceived as a [female] who espoused the rightful king and thus conferred on him entitlement to his land and dominion over it, the connection of the death messenger with families in modern folk tradition can be explained in terms of the survivals of the concept of sacral kingship into modern times.[157]

Perhaps the female sovereignty symbol is also associated with the triune goddesses of the land and fertility, who represents the spirit of Ireland: Banba, Fotla and Éire, the last one of whom also gives her name to Ireland. C. L. Innes suggests that the nationalistic play Cathleen Ni Houlihan, composed by Lady Gregory and W. B. Yeats, may have exploited the effectiveness of the powerful emotive response generated by fusing folk versions of such an old woman with the beautiful maiden except these female figures like 'Cathleen Ni Houlihan' or 'the poor old woman' are removed from the 'powerful' image of what the 'banshee' or 'Mórrígán' represented in early Irish mythology. Therefore, such figures are themselves the result of a convergence of varied sources of cultural traditions from Ireland as well as from Europe:

> The strands include elements of ancient Irish mythology and legend, ballad and other oral folk traditions, including the Gaelic bardic traditions, the influence of the Catholic church and the increasing stress in the nineteenth century on the worship of the Virgin Mary as Mother of God, the 'Celtic Twilight' school popularised in England as well as Ireland by Thomas Moore, and the influence of English and European literary and artistic traditions with their uses of medieval and classical motifs and images.[158]

Another strand of Irish mother culture stems from the religious ideology of Christianity, the worship of the Virgin Mary. According to Innes, by the late nineteenth century, the images of Mother Ireland and the Mother of God who is often associated through iconography to

Mother Church in religious paintings and statues, had become 'potent social, political and moral forces in Catholic Ireland.'[159] The attributes of the Irish pagan figure of Mother Goddess, which like other pagan Celtic figures, later became 'Christianised,' also merged with the image of 'Mother Church.'[160] Innes argues that the similarity between Mother Ireland and Mother Church lies in the fact that both are dependent on their children to make them 'whole and glorious,' and both serve as the 'instruments of their children's redemption' through their similar roles as the maiden figure who needs to be liberated through male protectors.[161] This unquestioned gender stereotype, centred around reproduction and received from colonialism and from the identification with the Virgin Mary of the Catholic Church, led to prudishness and conservatism in terms of sexuality and gender issues in Ireland and, as pointed out by Gerry Smyth, appears to be one of the 'most damaging blindspots' in traditional Irish nationalism.[162] 'Mother Ireland,' incarnated in 'Mother Church,' was officially recognised in the Constitution of Ireland in 1937, thus identifying the bodies of Irish women as vessels for the production of children within marriage.[163] Therefore, the image of the idealised, devoted mother from this distinctive Irish mother culture is reinforced particularly by the impact of the devotion to the Madonna in Ireland. Marina Warner thinks there is a link between patriarchal authority and the worship of the Virgin Mary, the Mother of God, in Ireland. Warner argues that the doctrines of the 'immaculate' and 'pure' conception of the Blessed Virgin Mary stress the asexual, idealised in women, which is also an unrealistic, flatly stereotypical image of women, actually denying all biological functions except 'lactation and weeping,' while at the same time reinforcing and demonstrating motherhood as the ideal, or the only, destiny for Irish women.[164] The glorification of the Virgin Mary supports not only chastity and motherhood as female ideals but also their 'humility, obedience and passive suffering.'[165] This concept of mother, a fusion of diverse strands from Irish culture as well as from religion, appears to reinforce and consolidate the notion of an unrealistic (idealised) image of a female social role which finds expression as an all-sacrificing angel, as a passive vessel for hereditary reproduction and/or as an asexual, life-denying shadow without its own viable identity.[166]

Thus, mothers would be blamed if they failed to fulfil such motherly duties as protecting their children, not to mention the loss of children due to incidents or accidents regardless of the circumstances. This kind of 'mother-bashing' tendency is closely linked to a feeling of disappointment in connection with the idealisation of the mother which, itself, brings with it certain implications of 'mother image' reinforced by the dominant culture; for example, images such as that of a happy, glamorous housewife, of a devoted, all-sacrificing angelic mother evolved from the quiet, long-suffering Madonna in Christianity. V. Nice speculates that the 'idealisation of mothering' actually sets the scene for the 'demonisation' of the mother because it might mean that any mothers who fail to live up to this idealised, in fact, rigid and under normal circumstances unrealistic stereotype, would be labelled as bad mothers. Some lines of psychoanalytical studies, Freud among them, also tend to blame mothers for their failure to meet such standards as 'good mothers.' It is suspected that the devotion of these 'bad' mothers may not be so selfless as it is supposed to be, and therefore, maternal love may suddenly turn dangerous and suffocating in Freudian terms.[167] In a Celtic story, Rhiannon, for example, is one such mother victim of the 'mother-bashing' tradition.

Rhiannon was accused of being an evil mother who devoured her own child and was prosecuted.[168] In the story, Rhiannon was betrayed by her own women because they were worried they might be held responsible for the child's mysterious disappearance. Then the women lined up to accuse Rhiannon of having killed her own child while she was asleep. In fact, they killed a couple of puppies and smeared the blood on Rhiannon's face and clothes as the evidence of Rhiannon's 'evil deed.' Thus Rhiannon was punished. For seven years she had to sit by the horse-block at the gate to the city and tell the whole story of her child's disappearance to everyone who came in and offer to carry them on her back wherever they needed to go. This speculation about mothers who may harm their children still pervades in today's society; consider those mothers who are charged with murdering her children in various cases of cot death allegations, in particular, the notorious collapsed case of Angela Cannings in the UK in 2003.[169] It seems that this culture which over-glorifies the mother on the one hand and condemns her on the other tends to perceive the mother as the one who is directly responsible for the catastrophe of the infant's death. The obsession with idealising (as well as demonising) mothers may be also regarded as a consequence of the anxiety and fear of female power beyond male control. As a result, E. Ann Kaplan argues that some psychological or sociological theories tend to construct bipolar stereotypical representations of 'ideal, perfect' 'good' (all-giving, angelic) and 'bad, evil, devouring' (all-withholding) mothers. This bipolarity, Kaplan believes, could reinforce an ideology which is compliant with political or economical purposes, and attempts to manipulate women in, or out of, certain social areas, such as the workforce.[170]

Women's 'maternal guilt,' resulting from failure to comply with the perfect mother ideal (and also related to their compelling wish to be mothers), may turn into a torture of self-blame or depression such as is experienced by those mothers who lose their children in Mary Beckett's 'Sudden Infant Death,' Mary Lavin's 'The Lost Child' or Éilís Ní Dhuibhne's 'The Garden of Eden,' or the woman who is unable to conceive in Mary O'Donnell's 'Breath of the Living,' or the disorientated woman who craves for being a wife and a mother in Clare Boylan's sarcastic story 'Technical Difficulties and the Plague.' The 'mother-bashing' perception which blames women for being barren appears two-dimensional. Firstly, if the couple is sterile for some reason, the woman instead of the man is often the first one to be blamed, as if the woman is solely responsible for conception. Secondly, a sterile woman, that is, one who is unable to be a mother for whatever reason, is either condemned or 'pitied,' as if a woman is invalid if her reproductive function is faulty. Mary O'Donnell exposes this issue by juxtaposing two narratives in her story 'Breath of the Living.' It displays a contrast between the maternal instinct in one story and another story on a Kenyan woman who was battered and stoned because she is accused of adultery, which act is superstitiously believed to render her sterile.[171] They appear to imply glorified motherhood on the one hand and, on the other hand, a fear that female sterility is somehow against 'nature':

> [The] kind of story at which some people might nod their heads, as if something were confirmed, something shared wordlessly, the intent of which extended even to the human race. She could recall

lazily formulated mumblings about "instinct", "the power of nature" and "the call of blood".

(SP 3)

Therefore, the woman in this story is also blamed (by her own parents) for having disappointed her husband by not producing children for him, and this matter becomes a source of great loss in the meaning of this couple's life. The over-glorification of motherhood as well as the indispensable maternal instinct assumed in every 'normal woman' inevitably makes some women in such circumstances feel guilty about their failure to fulfil such roles as mothers.

The so-called ideal, good mother in the stories is normally characterised by an image of a mother who devotes most of her life to her family. For example, the stark contrast between the portrayal of a devoted, 'good mother' and a selfish 'bad mother' is implied in Patricia Scanlan's 'Ripples': 'She was a real mother. She cooked bread and tarts and everything and she made proper dinners' (IO 272). Here again, food is associated with the mother figure to emphasise that a mother's duty and function are located in the household: 'Biting her nails made [Ciara] think of food. She hoped Kathy [her godmother] would cook chicken and mushroom pie for the dinner' (IO 286). By contrast, the image of a busy or working mother seems to be associated with that of a selfish, bad mother, regardless of whether such a mother might also be vulnerable or desperate because of her own problems in dealing with an idle, self-centred husband (like the husband Barry in 'Ripples') who focuses only on his own personal life instead of sharing the responsibility for the family. Alison in 'Ripples' is portrayed as such a mother, and she is blamed by other people and her own daughter because she fails to fulfil her 'motherly duty.' By contrast, in this story it appears people condemn Barry less in terms of parenting responsibility; he even receives some sympathy because he has a 'terrible' wife. A relatively greater degree of condemnation of mother than father in terms of neglect of children suggests the responsibility for childrearing is still regarded as mainly the woman's responsibility, as expressed in 'Ripples.' In this story, perhaps both parents should take equal responsibility for their own mistake when facing their daughter but the story only seems to show the daughter's as well as other people's criticism of the mother.

Mary Lavin, however, tends to defend mothers in her stories about mother/daughter relationships, in which the maternal guilt or 'good-bad mother' bipolarity appears to be ironic and ambiguous. Lavin depicts a widowed mother's (Vera) difficulty in readjusting to her new life with her children in a foreign country after her husband's death as well as another mother figure who was devastated by her daughter's mental shock due to acrophobia in 'Villa Violetta.' Despite Vera's isolation and helplessness in Italy, she was determined and defensive, especially in face of her daughter's criticism:

> But Gloria caught her by the arm and shook her. 'Linda only means back to the hotel, Mother, not back to Dublin.' She looked troubled, though. 'If only you'd stop thinking of yourself all the time, Mother.' Vera couldn't believe her ears. ' – Thinking of myself? It's of you children I'm thinking — all the time.'
>
> (ME 110)

This view from the mother is contrasted with that from the daughter in another story 'A Family Likeness' in which the mother is blamed by the daughter (Ada, who also becomes a mother herself) for being irresponsible and selfish, because 'she [the mother] didn't even have the supper ready in the evening when [the father] came home tired and hungry from the office' (FLI 16). Ada recalled that she had blamed her mother because her mother was too focused on the relationship with her own mother (Ada's grandmother) and, therefore, neglected her maternal duties (namely attention to Ada). On the other hand, Ada envied the closeness her own mother shared with grandmother. It is the intimacy that Ada was seeking but not receiving from her own mother. In the story Ada herself appears to be a domineering mother, which may reflect her wounded 'little-girl-within' in Eichenbaum's and Orbach's term, and therefore she projects her 'wanting of love' onto her relationship with her own daughter Laura. There are also different points of view from Laura in respect of Ada's relationship with her grandmother, Laura's relationship with Ada, as well as with her own daughter Daphne. Laura 'protests' (although not explicitly) against Ada's dominating her life but in a way Laura herself seems to repeat Ada's pattern of behaviour through the way that Laura also tends to control Daphne. Laura's sympathy with the grandmother, whom Ada does not respect, also appears to reflect Laura's ambivalence about the tension with her mother Ada. Mary Lavin often juxtaposes multiple visions in her stories, in which the depiction of so-called 'good' or 'bad' mothers appears ironic and sometimes ambiguous. Lavin's story 'The Lost Child,' for example, dealing with a mother's pain over the miscarriage of her unborn child, dramatises this 'maternal guilt' and ironically turns to questions and debates associated with Christian

(Catholic) dogmas: 'Whether the idea of Limbo is a dogma or not, why were no women given a say about it?' (ML3, 261) Generally speaking, Mary Lavin's stories tend to present strong-willed women in a way sympathetic to mothers or are written from the mother's point of view.

Apart from the standards which are used to judge the mother, the mother is also depicted as feeling alienated from her daughter due to an aversion to female bodies and sexuality in some Irish women's stories such as Mary Beckett's 'Under Control,' Mary Lavin's 'The Nun's Mother,' Ivy Bannister's 'Lift Me Up and Pour Me Out' or other stories about older women's attempts to suppress younger women in respect of female sexuality like Fiona Barr's 'Sisters.' In Mary Beckett's 'Under Control,' for example, the mother's 'prudishness,' which is associated with the female body, sensuality or sexuality may be linked with her convent experience in which she recalls her shame at having been shouted at by the nuns when 'a bit of leg escaped between [her] black stockings and navy knickers' (FL 99). The mother's prudery in respect of human bodies reflects how the mother avoids touching her children when they grow to her height. Her daughter, Stella, also seems to mirror such an attitude of disgust and shame in her reaction of scrubbing all over her body ('every place he had touched') in an attempt to wipe out the sense of shame she experiences after having sex (FL 96). This corporeal revulsion results in the daughter's self-disgust, which alienates the daughter from the mother, and the daughter's drastic response of resistance against the mother. Similarly, the mother in 'Lift Me Up and Pour Me Out' is portrayed as an asexual, life-denying 'freak' who is 'free of sweat or stain' in a 'flowing white gown' like a nun (MO 111). Mary Lavin's 'The Nun's Mother' also tells a story about a mother's alienation from her daughter, not from the perspective of a mother's disappointment or sense of loss as with Eichenbaum's and Orbach's or Nancy Chodorow's theory of mother/daughter separation, but through exposing some complex and uneasy feelings within the mother who is simply unable to be intimate with her daughter for different reasons. Meg in 'The Nun's Mother' seems to have difficulty in being close to her daughter: 'why was it so hard for women to be honest and above board with each other? [Men] didn't behave like that with men!...But [women] with each other it seemed it was virtually impossible' (ML2, 50). Here again there appears a prevailing attitude of denigration of sex, perhaps associated with her 'nonsensical girlish prudery' resulting in turn from her convent experience, which blocks Meg from being honest and straightforward with her daughter Angela (ML2, 50). Meg is conscious of some 'curious embarrassment' or even 'revulsion' that has alienated her from Angela since the latter reached adolescence (ML2, 51). Meg's concern for Angela reveals her anxiety towards her daughter's growth, the ambivalence of which involves knowledge of the potential joy of sexuality, as well as indicates that 'a woman [like Meg herself] bludgeoned by the dogmatic moral conservatism of post-revolutionary Ireland is incapable of voicing.'[172] The suppression of this corporeal fear is embodied by the physical as well as psychological alienation between the mother and the daughter as depicted in Mary Lavin's 'The Nun's Mother,' Ivy Bannister's 'Lift Me Up and Pour Me Out' and Mary Beckett's 'Under Control.'

Some Irish women's stories focus on a daughter's ambivalence or resistance from the daughter's perspective. However, those stories discussed above about the mother's inability to be physically and psychologically intimate with her daughter are in fact due to the mother's self-imposed denial of the female body and sexuality, which is an anxiety still associated with the 'good/bad' or 'virgin/whore' bigotry in society. Moreover, some stories display mother figures who 'conspire,' either actively or passively, in bullying their daughters or younger women due to their own prudery, as in Fiona Barr's 'Sisters,' 'Alice,' Frances Molloy's 'The Devil's Gift,' Margaret Barrington's 'Village Without Men' or Marilyn McLaughlin's 'Witchwoman.' Prudery which confines or represses women is a notable issue in those stories set in a convent by Fiona Barr, Frances Molloy or Edna O'Brien. Here the mother figures are still frequently judged according to the paradigm of bipolarity—either good-bad or virgin-whore. Likewise, the stories, such as 'Ripples' which condemns a bossy working mother as irresponsible and 'A Family Likeness' in which the mother is blamed by her daughter for not fulfilling motherly and wifely duties, appear to show mothers who are still 'judged' by a standard comprising the idealisation of a devoted mother who is associated with domesticity involving nurturing, caring and also passivity. As a result of their representations of mothers in their stories, Irish female writers reveal an aspect of the mother image through a lens which distorts the definitions of women and their roles in society.

Reconciliation and Rediscovery of a Mother-Daughter Bond

Conflict and resistance between mothers and daughters appear to be a dominant and recurring motif in contemporary Irish women's short stories. Irish female writers explore this conflicting aspect of relationships between mothers and daughters in their short stories through archetypal motifs of anorexic reaction (from daughters), alienation, conflict, resistance, and dilemma between identification and separation. Here, overt alienation often intertwines with complex feelings of ambivalence. The mother's ambivalence towards the daughter's separation as well as the daughter's rebellion against conformity to the model which threatens to repeat the mother's role and destiny can be examined and evaluated against the framework of the patriarchal context. Under patriarchy women as mothers and daughters may be conditioned and shaped to conform to certain desired models. Luce Irigaray argues that this is how patriarchal civilisation functions to separate women from each other, emphasising the patrilineal instead of the matrilineal. This patriarchal framework seems also to owe itself to the creation of stereotypes as well as to the demonisation of the mother. Perhaps this characteristic resistance in mother-daughter relationships in contemporary Irish women's short stories may also be viewed as reflecting a voice of anger which seeks liberation from the confinement of mothers and daughters, both of whom have been imprisoned by the negativity of a 'false' identification between women as suggested by Adrienne Rich and Mary Daly and discussed earlier in this chapter.

Nevertheless, reconciliation between mothers and daughters in some stories by Irish female writers appears to open a space for a positive identification between mothers and daughters, for example, Marilyn McLaughlin's 'Witchwoman,' Anne Devlin's 'The Way-Paver' or Maeve Kelly's 'Ruth.' Marilyn McLaughlin's 'Witchwoman' is an allegory of a daughter's re-claiming of her mother's power as well as of reconciliation between the spiritual mother and the daughter. Women (including mothers) under the patriarchy are signified by the raped mother and the tyrannical mother-in-law in the story. The dispossession of women's power by the patriarchy is often symbolised by male acts of sexual aggression towards women. By contrast the witchwoman, who appears to be intelligent and independent in the story, acts as a surrogate mother figure for the young girl Darling. Freedom, which is also the girl's actual name, is symbolically achieved only after the girl has discovered her authentic identity and has identified with the witchwoman as her spiritual mentor. The lost bond between older and younger women is restored by such a new realisation and identification in McLaughlin's 'Witchwoman.' And this identification with the lost power between women seems to act as a source of redemption for women of different generations, liberating themselves from patriarchal dogma.

There are also times when the mother and the daughter reach a pivotal stage of life such as the daughter's becoming a mother or the death or illness of the mother. When the daughter herself becomes a mother, this involves a new identity in which the daughter comes to share the role as the mother. Perhaps it is difficult to make a drastic change in a relationship between the mother and the daughter if they have previously been in a conflicted relationship, but there may still be 'some new ground for sharing and considering compromises.' This 'new ground' may also serve as foundation for a mutually satisfying continuation of this relationship or, alternatively, become the scene of instability and new conflict. [173] Ivy Bannister's 'Happy Delivery' documents a daughter's transformed outlook towards mothering through her new role as a mother herself. In this new stage of life for a female, as Vivien Nice observes, it may be expected that some renegotiation of the relationship will have to take place from the daughter's point of view. Anne Devlin's 'The Way-Paver' also portrays a younger woman who becomes reconciled and renegotiates her relationship with her mother after having been separated from her in young adulthood, when later she herself also becomes a mother. Maeve Kelly's 'Ruth' explores the potential for mutual understanding between the mother and the daughter through recollections of the past and perhaps also due to the fact that the mother and the daughter become more involved with each other when the daughter herself also reaches a stage (motherhood) in which she can share a sense of identity with her mother. This daughter seeks to reaffirm her own existence by assuring her identification with her mother in a shared mother's role, experience and responsibility: 'You need to be reminded of your own existence. You also were born. Once, a long time ago, you inherited the earth too' (OH 206).

Reconciliation and reconfirmation of a close relationship between the mother and the daughter may also happen when the mother dies or becomes ill. Nancy Chodorow's theory of the blurring ego boundaries between the mother and the daughter is represented once more in Mary Lavin's 'Senility,' when both the mother and the daughter share the experience of physical as well as emotional discomfort. The daughter's rejection of the possibility that the mother may die and the mother's unwillingness to reveal her worries about her own health (a view sensed and shared by her daughter and son-in-law, but kept a private matter only to the mother herself) unveil the exclusive closeness between this mother and her daughter and also their difficulty in distancing themselves from each other in the face of death. It is sometimes difficult for the daughter to avoid looking at her mother with a 'childlike gaze' when the mother is alive because the daughter's reconciliation with the mother, and the daughter's understanding of their connections as well as her acceptance of the differences between the mother and herself, may be something the daughter needs to come to terms with within herself.[174] The actual physical death of the mother appears to be a final separation from the daughter leading to a stage of transition for the daughter in which she has to come to terms with herself and with her relationship with her mother.[175] The daughter in Edna O'Brien's 'A Rose in the Heart of New York' intends to reconcile herself with her mother but in vain because still she fails within herself to accept the eternal separation from the mother. Instead, the daughter feels she is abandoned by the mother, deliberately, again:

> A new wall had arisen, stronger and sturdier than before. Their life together and all those exchanges were like so many spilt feelings, and she looked to see some sign or hear some murmur. Instead, a silence filled the room, and there was a vaster silence beyond, as if the house itself had died or had been carefully put down to sleep.
>
> (FH 404)

Irish women's short stories portray the complicated process through which women come to identify with each other over generations. The daughter's 'anorexic' reaction towards the 'ill-nurtured' mother in a tradition that devalues women and mothers is revealed as a rejection of the patriarchal injustice towards women in a male-dominated society. Moreover, the daughter's dilemma sometimes lies in her close identification with her mother. The daughter subconsciously constructs an 'evil' mother in order to move herself away from the mother but the daughter still carries both the burden of guilt at betraying her mother as well as the fear of what she will become in the future.[176]

During the early wave of the women's liberation movements, feminists like Simone de Beauvoir simply rejected and denounced maternity as 'narcissism, altruism, idle day-dreaming, sincerity, bad faith, devotion and cynicism.'[177] Feminists in the 1970s still tended to deny reproduction and the role of the mother as a way of rejecting patriarchy. For instance, Shulamith Firestone even demanded 'the freeing of women from the tyranny of reproduction' in the 1970s, a time when women struggled and fought for the right to choose abortion and contraception.[178] After the generation of de Beauvoir and Firestone in the 1980s, feminists generally no longer merely reject and exclude the experience of motherhood but instead pay more scholarly attention to the lost relationship between mothers and daughters. It is not, as V. Nice argues, the mother who denies the daughter her value, her rights and control over her life, but rather the denial stems from a system which treats women as subordinates to serve men and presents women as devalued, sexualised and objectified for men's needs.[179] The daughters may learn to value themselves and fight for their rights by looking back through their mothers—not in the patriarchal way of denigrating mothers but by valuing mothers' strengths and understanding mothers' needs. [180] Through stories by writers such as Marilyn McLaughlin and Ivy Bannister, Irish female writers have explored a space which deals with the restoration of the mother-daughter bond. Contemporary Irish women's short stories, through a range of archetypal motifs from ultimate rejection through reconciliation and re-identification with motherhood, reflect this vision. These stories pave the way for consideration and reconsideration of Irish women's responses towards women and female power in male-dominated Irish society. The vista may encourage some potentially positive elements and possibilities in respect of transforming in years to come what has been a suppressed, distorted and ill-nurtured intimacy between mothers and daughters in Irish literature.

'Orla has always liked Kathleen but Kathleen hates Orla. It's clear. And now at last she has a real reason for hating her, and a motivation for hurt. Crime Passionnel.'

from Éilís Ní Dhuibhne's 'At Sally Gap,'
The Pale Gold of Alaska (2000)

3. The Ambiguity and Ambivalence of Sisterhood

In recent scholarship on relationships between women as depicted in women's literature, crucial attention has largely been focused on the vertical relationship between women—that of mothers and daughters. Irish women's short stories which engage with this primal relationship between women as mothers and daughters give voice to a series of gender issues as well as illustrate experiences which women share and can relate to, such as those which have been discussed in the previous chapter. However, another category of relationship between women which cannot be neglected in critical studies of women's literature is the horizontal one—that of biological sisters and metaphorical sisterhood. This chapter focuses on the relationships between sisters and women's sisterly closeness with one another as depicted in contemporary Irish women's short stories. However, ambivalence and ambiguity towards sisterly relationships recur as archetypal motifs in these stories. The core of this chapter uncovers this paradoxical aspect of women's relationships with women and sisterhood in Irish women's stories by contextualising archetypal motifs of ambivalence and ambiguity in a western patriarchal framework. These archetypal motifs unveil divided sisterhood and conflict among siblings as another aspect of female difficulties experienced under patriarchy.

Relationships between sisters have provided the plot in fairy tales and literature by both male and female writers in the past and the present as in the *Cinderella* story (1697), William Shakespeare's *King Lear* (1608), Anton Chekhov's *Three Sisters* (1901), Jane Austen's *Pride and Prejudice* (1813), Louisa M. Alcott's *Little Women* (1868-9), and Alice Walker's *The Color Purple* (1982). [181] In all of the above, relationships between sisters are presented in positive as well as negative terms. In areas other than literature, bonds between women sharing a sense of common experience and sympathy for each other provided the basis for some feminists to create an ideal of 'sisterhood' as a means to pursue their shared idea of women's liberation. Feminists such as Robin Morgan regard sisterhood as a utopian state which can empower women to rediscover and rejuvenate a communal source of female power. [182] Feminists call for a coalition of women bonded by sympathy for each other's oppressed state to work together in order to fight against inequality against women under patriarchy. Sisterhood, originally a family kinship term, has been reconfigured into feminist ideals which seem to mimic the form of sibling bonds between women.

Despite the glorification of this collective female power of sisterhood by modern feminists, the phenomenon of women's gathering together as a community seems always to have evoked ambivalence within society. Nina Auerbach, in *Communities of Women* (1978), has pointed out that such female communities are rarely endowed with 'majestic titles' reflecting the solidarity of men (brotherhood) as warriors and heroes, and glorified by mythology and literature. [183] Rather, Auerbach would argue that this kind of female solidarity is usually regarded as presenting an implicit threat or challenge to the accepted social order:

As a recurrent literary image, a community of women [such as the Graeæ sisters or the Amazons in the Greek mythology] is a rebuke to the conventional ideal of a solitary woman living for and through men, attaining citizenship in the community of adulthood through masculine approval alone. The communities of women which have haunted our literary imagination from the beginning are emblems of female self-sufficiency which create their own corporate reality, evoking both wishes and fears.[184]

Auerbach goes further to argue that 'sisterhood' 'tended to veer between extremes of horror and hope' in the Victorian period because '[not surprisingly] these polarized assumptions combined with the sanctity of the home to make of women's sphere the solitary confinement it so often became.'[185] Peculiarly, the revulsion of Victorian conservatives towards the idea of women's communities is reflected also in the outlook of Mary Wollstonecraft, the pioneer feminist in the same period, who objected to the idea that girls were being brought into close contact with each other, on the grounds that such closeness evoked female 'grossness' due to 'knots of young women.'[186] This ambivalence is displayed also at the opposite pole of Victorian conventionalism by Sarah Stickney Ellis, who advocated a cult of domesticity and argued in textbooks on female behaviour such as *The Women of England* (1843) for a traditional role for women as mothers, wives and daughters, subservient to their fathers and husbands, in the private sphere. Ms. Ellis seemed nevertheless to welcome the idea of solidarity between women as an ideal context within which women might develop themselves in a moral and altruistic sense for mutual benefit:

Let us imagine a little community of young women, among whom, to do an act of distinterested kindness should be an object of the highest ambition, and where to do any act of pure selfishness, tending, however remotely, to the injury of another, should be regarded as the deepest disgrace; where they should be accustomed to consider their time not as their own, but lent them solely for the purpose of benefiting their fellow-creatures; and where those who were known to exercise the greatest charity and forbearance, should be looked upon as the most exalted individuals in the whole community.[187]

In *The Women of England*, Ms. Ellis's insistence on the moral superiority of women as well as their great influence within the private sphere upon the external prosperity and overall integrity of the nation was based on a conventional Christian 'white middle-class' interpretation of the world.[188] Women's communities in the charitable or religious spheres of activity have played recognised roles in society. In such communities, nuns are referred to in kinship-derived terms such as 'mothers' or 'sisters' in the church and many of them take on responsibility for educating young women, preparing them for their integration into society. In a society such as Ireland, which remains a Catholic stronghold, it may be a common experience for many young women to have spent their years of schooling within the environment of a convent school, such as those depicted in many of Edna O'Brien's stories. However, various stories such as those by Mary Lavin, Edna O'Brien, Fiona Barr, Mary Beckett or Frances Molloy appear to present the 'sisterhood' of such women's communities as a symbol of suppression/oppression rather than as the manifestation of the kind of 'disinterested kindness' imagined by Ms. Ellis. The solidarity of women in communities like this appears to be portrayed by such writers as, in effect and impact, patriarchal oppression in a different guise. In modern and contemporary literature, as in the literature of the Victorian period, an essentially negative image attaches to demonstrations of female solidarity within communities of women.

Nevertheless, the terms 'sisters' and 'sisterhood' are implemented by writers and literary critics to express diverse levels and forms of relationships among women. Before this argument considers what sisterhood means in the context of contemporary Irish women's stories, it is essential to examine the connotations attributed to 'sister' and 'sisterhood,' and to try to define the scope of these terms. The distinction between both terms appears to be a fluid one, as both derive from a definition of blood sisters which is then extended into a metaphorical concept about female bonds as sisterhood. Linguistically the term 'sister' may simply denote a biological reality within the family unit, as well as implying someone to whom there are ties of emotional affiliation by choice, whether blood related or not. This generally blurry use of the terms 'sister' and 'sisterhood,' as Amy K. Levin has pointed out, results in confusion of two types of bonds between women, which are not necessarily similar.[189] The words 'sister' and 'sisterhood' become metaphors, Levin argues, signifying something different when they refer to abstract concepts of emotional bonding between women or to membership of a 'sisterhood' from when they are used to describe the interaction between biological female family members. This extension in the meaning of 'sister' and 'sisterhood' beyond the biological bonds between siblings serves as a so-called 'second order of reference' derived from the primary semantic definition of biological siblings, and used to explain a phenomenon which appears similar to that which is assumed to exist between biological sisters.[190] However, this displacement of the primary semantic signs, in respect of the terms '(blood) sister' and 'sisterhood,' has come to depict both what is present (bonds similar to those between sisters), and also what is absent (a biological kinship) in the process of 'metaphorisation' by academics and writers, who use the terms to describe closeness between women. In the light of Jacques Derrida's concepts, Levin sees metaphorisation as a process to allow various senses of meaning in words to slip from different levels, which permits a word to have different senses in its 'bottomless overdeterminability' (in Derrida's terms).[191] Some feminists consider 'sisterhood' to be a powerful bonding factor and also a utopian state, part of a process towards female development of individuality, while other feminists regard the concept as highly problematic. The 'sisterhood' bond claimed by some feminists as an ideal model of women's relationships is questioned by other feminists like Audre Lorde, Oyeronke Oyewumi and some belonging to African and minority ethnic groups. They perceive it as a notion informed by racist and classist assumptions about white (bourgeois) womanhood as a universal global norm because this particular idea of sisterhood is largely a legacy of a white Anglo/North American/Western European nuclear family and not necessarily transferable to the experiences of other peoples, ethnic groups and classes in different cultural contexts.[192]

Having studied a series of literary as well as critical works on sisters in British and American Literature from the nineteenth to the twentieth century, Levin identified what she termed a tendency of 'slippage' in literary criticism and theory in respect of using metaphorical and biological sisterhood as synonyms for one another, especially in the context of overt glorification of the positive aspects of women's relationships as sisters as expressed in some feminist theory and criticism.[193] Whilst such sisterhood is emphasised in feminism as an ideal model for female interrelationships, it obscures a 'reality' which is not necessarily reflected in the relationship between blood sisters and their representations in literature. The frequent friction between blood sisters in literary portraits is at odds with the idealised sisterhood which is the core dogma of certain feminist theories. On the one hand, the troubled side of sisterhood appears to be ignored or suppressed to some considerable degree in such feminist theories and criticism. On the other hand, literature appears to focus on the negative aspects of sisterhood. This is a paradox which requires further investigation. Levin's explanation is that the terms 'sister' and 'sisterhood' cannot fully encompass the possibilities for meaning enclosed in them. While the term 'sister' can describe biological as well as emotional kinship, this biological relationship may contain none of the affinities which lead to emotional bonding, a situation summarised in the following remark by Christine Downing:

> Although feminism made us all newly aware of the importance of sisterhood, there was early on a tendency to conceive the sister bond only metaphorically and thus in high idealized terms. Almost inevitably we then found ourselves subject to intense feelings of disillusionment when our "sister" failed us.[194]

Therefore, the highly idealised (and glorified) sisterly relationships of literary theory and feminist criticism tend to obscure in a simplistic and self-serving way the complex and multi-layered issues of identity, competition and self-interest which frequently characterise the sisterly relationship within women's literature. However repressed on various levels, patterns of sisterly relationships involving rivalry and polarisation appear archetypal in sister-centred plots. Levin suggests that this may be embedded in 'the process of separation from the mother' and this phenomenon cannot be 'detached from the history of women in Europe and [North] America.'[195]

The divided nature of sisterly relationships which Amy K. Levin has proposed in her book *The Suppressed Sister* (1992) provides an initial reference point for examining the 'sister' theme in contemporary Irish women's stories because the essence of sisterhood, often that of biological sisters, also appears complex and opaque in these Irish women's stories. At the foundation of such relationships in Irish women's stories, there is a level of ambiguity. Maybe this complexity is related to the fact that blood sisters, unlike metaphorical sisters who actively choose this state, can neither be replaced nor chosen but exist due to their passive genetic bond with each other. That is, sisters by blood have to put up with each other no matter whether they can get along or not, and especially during their early experience of family life prior to adulthood. Some stories about sisters deal with issues such as premarital pregnancy, divorce, exile or alienation and are focused on differences of age, class or religion rather than on the inner lives and values of the sisters themselves; for example, in Mary Leland's 'The Little Galloway Girls,' Edna O'Brien's 'The Connor Girls,' Mary Lavin's "Loving Memory,' 'A Visit to the Cemetery,' or Anne Devlin's 'The Way-Paver.' Nevertheless, such issues are also expressed through variation in views or behaviour between these sisters, thus underlining indirectly the differences between them as individuals. Where the aim of the stories is mainly to describe the outlooks of sisters and the interaction between them, ambivalence always rises to the surface. The theme of sisterly relationships in Irish women's stories evokes various dimensions of women's interrelationships as siblings or peers from ambivalent blood sister ties to collective sister bonds in female friendship and even extending to lesbian erotic love.

To sum up, this chapter aims to unveil the paradoxical dimension of sisterly relationships as represented in archetypal motifs of ambiguity and ambivalence in contemporary Irish women's short stories and to do this against the background of the legacy of the male western conventions in respect of the European/North American nuclear family as well as any female revision of these conventions. Therefore, it begins by examining portraits of blood sisters in the works of Irish female writers. Plots involving relationships between women who are biological sisters in these stories convey traces of the troubling ambivalence already noted by the work of Levin. Sister stories like Éilís Ní Dhuibhne's 'At Sally Gap,' two works both entitled 'Sisters' by Claire Keegan and Edna O'Brien, Moy McCrory's 'The O'Touney Sisters and the Day of Reckoning,' Emma Cooke's 'The Foundress,' Jan Kennedy's 'June 23rd,' Mary Lavin's 'Lilacs,' 'Frail Vessel' or 'A Bevy of Aunts,' Clare Boylan's 'Gods and Slaves' all depict blood sisters and their divided worlds, characterised by ambivalence—jealousy, tension or a dilemma between closeness and separation. The expression of the 'sister bond' through a form of metaphorical sisterhood or erotic love is also examined in some Irish women's stories. For some of the women in these stories, affiliation replaces friction between women as a kind of antidote for female powerlessness, women are shown expressing sympathy and empathy, supporting each other and bonding one to another in profound love, friendship and sometimes, ambiguous intimacy of this female friendship. This is the case with Lucile Remond's 'Anna Mae,' Leland Bardwell's 'The Dove of Peace,' Mary Morrissy's 'Rosa' or Mary Dorcey's lesbian stories like 'A Noise from the Woodshed,' 'The Husband,' 'A Country Dance' and

'Introducing Nessa.' It is also present in the call for a collective liberated enlightenment in respect of female sexuality which is expressed in Evelyn Conlon's 'Taking Scarlet as a Real Colour,' Ita Daly's ambiguous story of female friendship 'Such Good Friends' and Edna O'Brien's 'Sister Imelda.' The last two stories in this list seem to involve an ambiguity of female closeness tempered by sensual eroticism between women. Stories about profound metaphorical sisterly bonds are apocalyptic and inspiring and contrast with those hostilities and unfulfilled affinities between blood sisters in other stories. It seems, from various texts which are examined in this chapter, that Irish female writers demonstrate a tendency to review as well as to revise those conventional model(s) of interaction between sisters (and women) by exposing the root of the conflicting aspects through archetypal motifs in stories. The archetypal motifs of ambivalence and ambiguity about sisterly relationships in Irish women's stories reflect a phenomenon associating with women's status and roles, which have been constructed within the straightjacket of a social context which confines both females and males.

Divided Sisters in Irish Women's Short Stories

It is not rare to find stories about sisters who are rivals or in conflict. Auerbach and Levin have argued that this pattern of 'sister plot' has ancient roots, in fiction constructed within a patriarchal framework.[196] The tale of the Graeæ sisters in Greek/Roman mythology, for example, is a story suggesting that solidarity between sisters can be undermined by separating them. In this story, it is 'heroic' to weaken or even demolish sisterhood insofar as the hero, Perseus, successfully achieves his goal by forcing the

Graeæ sisters to aid him against the other triad of sisters, the Gorgons. The sisters of Graeæ are said to have been born old and to have shared one eye and one mouth between them. Neither of them had ever thought of taking the eye and running away with it. But when Perseus intrudes into their territory and steals the eye, suspicion and conflict occur among the sisters. Eventually they surrender to their information about the location of the nymphs of the North who know how to kill the Gorgons. Perseus at last completes his task successfully by killing the monstrous looking snake-haired Gorgons with the aid of the nymphs of the North.[197] This allegory seems to express the message that sisterhood appears 'powerless against the hero's theft of the communal eye.'[198] When the communal eye of (the Graeæ) sisters is lost, sisterhood itself in this case (the Gorgons) is doomed.

It seems that, according to Levin, in fairy tales and mythology, female power expressed through sisterhood is routinely suppressed so that heroism and heterosexuality may flourish. Cinderella and another Greek myth, the story of Psyche and her sisters, are other typical examples of this motif of suppressed sisterhood. Invariably such stories depict sisters who disagree and who are polarised both in appearance and in behaviour. Before a happy ending, typically marriage, can be achieved, sisters must be separated from or abandon one another. In the story of Cinderella, for example, the sisters are polarised by their appearance (beautiful innocent Cinderella as opposed to ugly wicked sisters) and they are further distanced by their stepsister relationship. The story of Psyche, Levin argues, provides a paradigm of the female quest for womanhood within a patriarchal social framework which suppresses the solidarity of women. This story may therefore be regarded as a patriarchal allegory of women's conformity to heterosexuality:

[T]he sisters initially grieve at the loss of their sister, as if they have lost part of themselves (and indeed they have). It is only when they are reunited with Psyche at the latter's request that their envy and hostility become overwhelming. Difference is the source of this envy; if Psyche's life were exactly like theirs, they would see no need for rivalry. Thus, the original female dilemma of sameness and difference generates this plot, and when Psyche's sisters seek to render her unhappy, they are trying to make her resemble them, to demolish dissimilarities. Their behaviour illustrates how an essential desire for closeness, a longing to merge, exists in opposition to the need for separation.199

Psyche's reunion with her husband, according to Levin and based on Erich Neumann's interpretation, is eventually achieved by coming to terms with her own 'femininity' and the priorities of her life, symbolised by the sorting task, with the assistance of natural forces as well as by separation from her sisters through the death of the latter. These sisters are prosecuted for their open expressions of hostility and their 'verbal seduction,' traditionally reserved as a kind of 'male behaviour,' thus implying the breach of a taboo by transgressing gender norms.[200] The 'moral lesson' and the 'warning' expressed in the story of Psyche may lie in the potential danger posed both by the sisters' openly expressed contempt resulting from feelings of jealousy and rivalry and in their capacity for solidarity when they conspire together to give 'damaging' advice to their sister. This threatens the 'happy marriage' of the heroine, a motif which recurs in other fairy tales and mythologies. These recurring motifs of divided sisters and suppressed sisterhood appear archetypal not only in mythologies and fairy tales but also in literature and

Irish women's short stories on which this chapter aims to focus. The double bind of supportive sisterhood lies in the fact that, on the one hand, it seeks to preserve a harmonious relationship among sisters within the family ideal glorified by conventional society and this desire for harmony suppresses any underlying rivalry. On the other hand, this perceived supportiveness creates anxiety about the sisters being 'too close,' thus neglecting or even dismissing what is assumed to be their primary duty and goal to be wives and mothers and threatening in the process the existing patriarchal system which favours heterosexuality. From this perspective the story of Psyche may be regarded as an archetype, typical of and also exemplifying a recurrent pattern of ambivalence towards sisterhood in literature or fairy tales from different times and cultures.

Mary Lavin's 'Frail Vessel' can be viewed as a reworking of the story of Psyche and her sisters. Lavin's story also depicts the struggle between the choice of being sister or lover. In the end, the sister bond wins out and the lovers are separated. In 'Frail Vessel' the division between sisters is even emphasised by depicting the elder sister Bedelia as a strong-willed mother figure in contrast to her frail, thin, naive younger sister Liddy, a child-woman aged only sixteen. Again, Bedelia's practicality and Liddy's sentimentality and youth polarise the sisters in their personalities, behaviour and choices for life. Bedelia disapproves of and dismisses Liddy's behaviour as silly, unrealistic, inexperienced and simple-minded when Liddy is attracted to and intoxicated by what Bedelia regards as the sentimental nonsense of a slippery, sloppy solicitor named Alphonsus O'Brien, and becomes his sweetheart. Bedelia obviously despises such sentimentality as nonsense, as exemplified in her words:

You know—all that rubbish he went on with—about you being the only one in the world for him—and that he was waiting all those years for you. How can you stand that kind of talk? It's so meaningless.

(ML1, 7)

Bedelia's remarks about Liddy's marriage display contempt, such as when she says Liddy is too young for marriage, the husband-to-be is too old for Liddy, and also, that there is no practical financial basis for a promising married life. However, perhaps Bedelia's contempt results not just from the potential loss of her sister but also from her feeling of unease towards the implications of this marriage for the way she defines herself and her role in life. Bedelia's concern for Liddy appears to derive from her self-proclaimed role as guardian for her little sister, partly also from the practical consideration of the loss of her sister's assistance in the household chores. However, underlying all of this is jealousy based on the 'dissimilarities' between her and her sister:

[Bedelia] was suddenly shot through and through with irritation. Why did this business about Liddy have to blow up on the verge of her own wedding? Goodness know, she [Bedelia] hadn't expected much fuss to be made about her own marriage, what with not being out of mourning, and Daniel having always lived in the house anyway; but it did seem a bit unfair to have all this excitement blow up around Liddy. Two rare, very rare, and angry tears squeezed out of Bedelia's pale eyes, and fell down her plain round cheeks. Because, of course, mourning or no mourning, a young girl like Liddy wasn't likely to get married in serge!…But this last thought made her feel more bitter than ever because it seemed to her suddenly that it was a measure of the difference between them as brides. Already she could imagine the fuss there would be over Liddy—the exclamations and the signs of pity and admiration. Such a lovely bride! Whereas when she—oh, but it was so unfair because never at any time did she regard her own marriage as anything but a practical expedient. It was only that she hadn't counted on being up against this comparison. It was that she minded.

(ML1, 4)

Even at the end of the story, when Liddy is supposed to be devastated by the separation from her husband and an uncertain future, her mysterious glee particularly annoys Bedelia because it is something she can neither understand nor share:

Yet Liddy never seemed to have pondered it at all. Her body, beautiful, frail even in its fertility, was still a vessel for some secret happiness Bedelia never knew, and although she hadn't known it, what she wanted, all the time, was to break it. She thrust herself forward, thrust her face, that was swollen with the strain she had undergone into the face, still so serene, in front of her.

(ML1, 19)

Just like Psyche's sisters, Bedelia also seeks to render Liddy unhappy. In doing so, Bedelia is trying to make Liddy resemble herself by demolishing their dissimilarities. Such behaviour among sisters illustrates the ambiguity over 'an essential desire for closeness, a longing to merge, existing in opposition to the need for separation.'[201]

Bedelia's efforts to try to dissuade Liddy from the marriage do not succeed. Nevertheless, she later 'seduces' Liddy successfully into separating from her husband, who is in financial trouble. However, the story ends with an ironic anticlimax. Liddy presents herself as pregnant, which the conniving Bedelia did not expect in her plan to try to reunite with her little sister within the family (an obstacle also for the help which Bedelia, also heavily pregnant, may be expecting once again with the household chores from Liddy). Although the lovers are separated and on the surface sisterhood seems to triumph over love, on another level sisterhood is seen to have been defeated by the legacy of patriarchal power as symbolised by the unborn baby conceived from Liddy's husband, whom Bedelia loathes so much. The implication is that Bedelia is being 'punished' for showing her contempt (in refusing initially to help her sister with the rent bill) as well as for the boldness of her 'verbal seduction' in seeking to separate the lovers (through the terms she imposed for helping her sister and husband out of their financial trouble). Although Bedelia does not pay with her life, unlike Psyche's sisters, she may be eternally punished by having to take on a triple maternal responsibility (her own baby, her sister Liddy and also Liddy's baby) as well as the associated burden of expenditure, the factor which bothers her the most.

The problem of antagonism between sisters sometimes manifests itself in a dilemma between an instinct towards assimilation with one another and a parallel instinct for a distinct personal identity which drives sisters to seek separation from one another. Louise Bernikow has indicated the apparent paradox of separation and sameness within the sister bond:

> Competition seems to be the language we use for the process of separation, seems to be the kind of activity we throw up against the desire to merge....Boys are encouraged to leave mother, punished for not doing so; girls are encouraged to stay with mother, punished for leaving. When these forces [of separation from the mother] turn lateral, the process is played out among sisters.[202]

Hence, the paradoxical nature of the relationship between sisters appears to be characterised by both 'polarization and interdependence.'[203] In the scenario of the Freudian Oedipus complex, girls, unlike boys, are believed to find it harder to develop a sense of separate identity differentiation from the (same-sex) mother. If this Freudian analysis is accepted, sisters, like blossoms growing from one stem, may find it even more difficult to try to establish a sense of individuality between one another because they see each other as on an identical position in the family hierarchy, each sister in a subordinate position to the mother (but nevertheless a rival), and in competition for the attention of the father, or later, other men. Although feminist psychologists have questioned the Freudian view of female development, Freudianism may at least illustrate a valid phenomenon that has been constructed under the influence of patriarchal structures in western culture and society.

Clare Boylan's 'Gods and Slaves' and Moy McCrory's 'The O'Touney Sisters and the Day of Reckoning' appear to illustrate the tensions induced by rivalry which alienates sisters who compete for male attention. In the story 'Gods and Slaves,' the sisters may appear as amiable and harmonious when performing on stage as a marvellous singing group. However, their attempts to compete for the attention of Phelim, a male tutor, interrupt this harmony:

[T]hey had achieved the primary object of mating, which is to make other women jealous…They grew anxious, inert, waiting for him to make the difficult choice between them.'

(CS 329)

These sisters are divided by the impulse to exclude 'other women,' thus they become rivals in this love game. The sisters in Moy McCrory's 'The O'Touney Sisters and the Day of Reckoning' play a similar game although it is never explicitly mentioned in the story. On the surface the antagonism between the two sisters Brid and Mary seems due to be their polarised views on religion (religious Mary versus atheistic Brid). However the main storyline has an undercurrent which suggests that it is the marriage of the narrator's parents, Mary and the farmhand, which actually distances Brid from Mary. The plot deals with Mary's interpretation of her and Brid's rescue by the farmhand as a miracle, and with the surprising hospitality extended by their stingy Aunt Liddy. These, in a sense, suppress the underlying alienation in the relationship between Brid and Mary. But this alienation is somehow reflected by the way in which Brid has gradually changed, growing out of the young laughing girl she used to be, and turning later into a spinster of 'tiredness' and 'bitterness.' The narrator seems to have sensed this distance between them when she says: '[b]ut to me they were always distant with each other, the remnants of sisterhood only present in their furious arguments' (VH 37). This statement reveals that a factor which cannot be directly addressed has perhaps become central in their relationship with each other. Bernikow argues that this kind of 'compelling' competition for male attention or for authority between women (a similar principle to that which we see in

Cinderella and King Lear) is the way 'masculine power' manifests itself to isolate women as 'the woman alone—motherless, sisterless, friendless—can fix her eyes solely on father, brother, lover, and therefore peace will reign in the universe.'[204]

The polarisation is sometimes manifested in an oppositional duality of 'good' and 'bad,' comparing one child to the other(s) in order to establish their separate identities. Elizabeth Fishel thinks that 'good' and 'bad' do not necessarily refer to absolutes but vary depending upon the definitions in different families.[205] A 'good' child may generally be decoded as a child who is adult-orientated, sharing adult values and fulfilling parental expectations whilst a 'bad' one may mean the rebellious, angry child resistant to parental control and who turns to peers for sense of identity.[206] These labels are like different informal roles which are assigned to each daughter and act as a model that Robert W. White speculates may be a catalyst for an ongoing situation of underlying tension within the sister relationship:

> [A good child and a bad child] come into existence because they serve some purpose in the family social system, helping at least to describe the members, define their relations, and make things somewhat more predictable. They continue as long as they serve this purpose and perhaps, out of inertia, for some time beyond; but if the pattern becomes too frustrating for one member, or if it ceases to perform its function for the group, informal role assignments may change or fade out.[207]

This process of polarisation may make each daughter in the family an incomplete person, denying them the chance to develop fully their potential as individuals. Since they are tied together within the family unit, so they seek fulfilment through one another instead of through their own agencies.[208] Echoing Downing's view, Toni McNaron claims that polarisation acts as an 'unspoken, unconscious, pact that neither sister need develop all her potential.'[209] This has the consequence that women remain within a smaller social framework, attached to and submissive to the family because each woman 'depend[s] upon the other to continue to act in certain ways.'[210] The need for self-definition among sisters which results from the identical position of girls (sisters) in the family hierarchy leads them to insist on their differences and in a way reveals why sisters always seem to define themselves in opposition to each other. It appears that the 'mutual self-definition seems typically to proceed by way of polarization that half-consciously exaggerates the perceived differences and attributes of the sisters.'[211]

This emphasis on the polarisation of sisters either in appearance or personality is evident in the depiction of sisters in various stories by Irish female writers such as in Claire Keegan's 'Sisters,' Mary Lavin's 'Lilacs' and 'A Bevy of Aunts' or Jan Kennedy's 'June 23rd.' In Mary Lavin's 'A Bevy of Aunts,' for example, one sister differs from the other in the way she dresses, behaves or the life she lives, each having her 'endearing individual mannerism' (FLI 113). Sometimes sisters are defined not on the basis of their individuality but in a comparative sense by the reflection of one another. Moreover, sisters may even seem to have an identity only in terms of their relationship with each other. However, and ironically, the sister with the apparent 'good' character is not necessarily the winner in any rivalry between the sisters, and the 'bad' one may be the one who leads the more exciting and affluent lifestyle. In 'Lilacs,' there is a strong-willed sister, Kate, who fights against the patriarchal authority (their father) in the family. By contrast, her younger sister is frail, passive and only endures and obeys the father's will. However, being a 'good,' in other words, submissive, daughter is not rewarded in this story. In the end, the rebellious sister (the 'bad' one) has achieved a better future (including winning a marriage for herself) whilst the obedient one is left with nothing but shattered dreams and loss.

In stories like Kennedy's 'June 23rd' and Keegan's 'Sisters,' for example, the devoted daughter at home becomes the dull and sullen one. In 'June 23rd' the dull spinster sister, Martha, appears (she is also a devoted caring daughter) in contrast to the lively, creative, happily-married Edwina. In 'Sisters,' Betty is the dedicated, plain-looking but strong willed (or clever in Louisa's view) spinster sister while her sister Louisa is the passive, beautiful and self-centered (also happily-married) one. The polarisation which characterises these sisters is somehow reinforced by parental intervention such as when Betty's and Louisa's mother describes them as 'chalk and cheese' in 'Sisters' (AN 146). Louisa is described as a pretty girl, popular among men, with beautiful golden hair and a sweet smile with plentiful white teeth. In contrast, Betty is dull, has brown hair, a 'hard and masculine' palm and 'look[s] terrible when [she] smile[s]' (AN 151). These oppositional characteristics not only distance Betty and Louisa in appearance but also determine the choices they supposedly make in their lives, whether willingly or not, such as their marital status. In both 'Sisters' and 'June 23rd,' all the glamour seems to belong to the pretty sister. The pretty one receives admiration and affection from parents and other people, and she leads a lifestyle which is envied by the other sister, the plain, hardworking, home-centred one. Underneath the apparent amiability between the sisters lies alienation. At one point, Martha attempts to 'justify' to herself her selfish sister, who has not taken the responsibility of looking after their elderly parents at home while she (Martha) has been forced to do this herself: 'How could I expect an energetic 20-year-old with such talent to give it all up and come home to look after mother and father?' (FL 179) Nonetheless, underneath Martha feels ambivalent about this. At another point Martha is also bitter about the fact that she is the one without a life of her own:

> But then it's easier to have plenty to say if you're only here for two weeks. Easy to have plenty of stories when you have an office full of people to talk to every day, a husband who adores you and a social life that never seems to slow down. 'Damn,' Martha said to herself, 'that's twice in one day. I really must not go over all that again.
>
> (FL 179)

Martha and Betty perceive that what they have sacrificed for their family at the expense of their own welfare, such as marriage and social life, is actually something of which their sisters, Edwina and Louisa, have dispossessed them. These suppressed feelings turn into a repressed anger and pain which results in their rejection of their sisters at the end of both stories—Martha is no longer prepared to give in to her selfish sister by ruining her own holiday and Betty will not agree to take her sister back into her home as indicated by Betty's act of cutting off Louisa's beautiful hair of which she is so proud. What Betty seeks to demolish may be not just Louisa's pride but also the pretended harmony in her relationship with Louisa, which has become a source of contempt for her. Eventually, the conflict between the sisters surfaces in both stories. No matter which sister attempts to resolve the conflict in order to maintain a surface amiability in the family which conforms to socially accepted norms, the polarised division of roles between them becomes a major source of friction.

Notwithstanding the above, there is a myth of devotion between sisters which evokes a repressed desire for closeness. Powerless themselves in the face of the power the authority of the family or society wields this desire is frequently manifested through one sister's attempt to control her sibling. It seems that one of the factors underlying such contradictory behaviour between sisters is the unfulfilled longing for intimacy. However, this is also related to the divided framework within which sisters interact with each other.[212] In Mary Lavin's 'Frail Vessel,' Bedelia reflects such a longing for intimacy with Liddy by presenting herself as a mother figure to her sister. Bedelia is deeply disappointed by Liddy's behaviour, turning against her due to the row about Liddy's intention to marry a stranger of whom Bedelia disapproves:

> "Liddy," she said sharply, "I hope"—she paused—"you know how I have always felt towards you, like a mother"—she caught herself up—"well anyway, like a guardian," she corrected, "but perhaps lately with my own taking up so much of my time I may not have given you as much supervision as I used—as much as you should have had perhaps—I can only hope that you haven't abused your freedom in any way?"
>
> (ML1, 7)

Bedelia is angry because Liddy is so 'ungrateful': 'Bedelia felt just like as if a mean trick had been played on her! After all I've done for her! She thought. After being a mother to her!' (ML1, 5) The way Bedelia still regards Liddy as a child reflects Bedelia's resistance to acceptance of the fact that Liddy is, after all, an individual with her own ideas which cannot be controlled by Bedelia. Liddy's desire for independence may be what hurts Bedelia most— or rather, the consequence of this desire for independence, which is the potential loss of intimacy with Liddy. Hence Bedelia sees Liddy's desire to separate from her, from this family, as an act of betrayal. This relationship is rendered unstable and troubled by the contradictory perspectives which each has on the meaning of sisterhood and what sisterhood means in their interaction with each other. In 'Frail Vessel' one sister's possessiveness towards the other sister turns into hostility and opposition when the latter tries to break away from the former. Sisters' ambiguous feelings of intimacy towards one another can sometimes lead both to attempts by the one to dominate the other as well as to hostility by this individual if the attempt at domination fails.

This desire for domination disguised as sisterly closeness is expressed as ambivalence about this closeness in Mary Morrissy's stories 'Rosa' and 'Agony Aunt.' In 'Rosa,' for example, the narrator is presented as a caring elder sister, devoted to her sister Rosa, for whom she is even willing to commit a murder in order to resolve her sister's problem. On the one hand, the narrator describes how she and Rosa are emotionally interdependent with each other: 'it seems that without her I would barely exist, that I would be a mere spectre, passing in and out unseen through the sullen doorways of her life' (LE 27). On the other hand, the narrator feels uneasy that Rosa still reserves some space which she does not share: 'Was it then I passed over into Rosa's world? No, even then, there were corners of it into which she retreated that I could only guess at' (LE 31). The narrator's longing to 'merge with' her sister uncovers her ambivalence towards the intimacy of her sister's involvement with her lover as well as the bliss of sexual love. The narrator behaves as if she wishes to protect her sister but in fact what she seeks to demolish is the intrusion into their relationship by her sister's lover. The narrator reveals that she imagines 'a coldness in their [Rosa's and her lover's] pleasure' and expects 'he would abandon her, and [the narrator] simply waited' (LE 29). Then the narrator and Rosa would still cling to each other and face their lives together with their closeness secured between them.

Likewise, the narrator in another story by Mary Morrissy, 'Agony Aunt,' expresses a similar desire for intimacy with her sister, coupled with ambivalence. The manner in which the narrator juxtaposes both positive and critical remarks about her sister (whose name is not mentioned but with an alias, 'Mavis,' in the story) invokes a feeling of ambiguity in this story in respect of their sense of sisterhood. On the one hand the narrator appears to be delighted at the prospect of Mavis becoming a mother: 'I think she'd [Mavis] make a wonderful mother…[s]he has a practical, capable air which inspires confidence. She is a big-boned and ample—for God's sake, she's looked like a mother for years' (LE 192-3). On the other hand, the narrator recalls Mavis's dislike of children and questions her motivation for having children, implying with distaste that Mavis is simply attempting to prove her capability for childbearing instead of expressing a genuine maternal instinct. Although the narrator claims 'Mavis and [she] have always been close,' actually the narrator's reminiscences tell a very different story (LE 197). They convey an anxiety expressed through fragments in her memory, which recall how she (the narrator) was excluded by Mavis's 'close-down look' at the girly party, her 'strange, savage' smile, the traumatic experience of Mavis seeing how the narrator was conceived through the ferocious 'rape' of their mother, and Mavis' hostility towards the narrator as an unborn baby—"Mavis looked as if she might kill me that day.' She [mother] paused. 'But I think it was you she was after…" (LE 202). Such memories resurface as an expression of the narrator's anxiety about the true nature of the relationship with her sister and also through the pretext of her agonising about Mavis's suitability as a mother in this story.

Éilís Ní Dhuibhne's 'At Sally Gap' evokes another form of anxiety and ambiguity for want of intimacy in sisterhood. Orla and Kathleen in 'At Sally Gap' can only retain a sisterly relationship by physically separating from each other. The only trace of emotion they share is expressed through the tension and sense of malice between them: 'The grim smile, the tight-lipped jokes, all make sense' (PG 145). When their 'common ground' is uprooted by the death of their mother, their relationship is bound to collapse. Orla herself feels a sense of ambiguity about her relationship with her sister although, ironically, Orla claims she 'always likes' her sister. Nonetheless, this claim by Orla of a sisterly bond swiftly resurfaces as a murderous anxiety and suspicion that Kathleen 'always' dislikes and intends to hurt her. Eventually this ticking time bomb explodes:

Orla notices a lump in the big pocket of her kaftan. It could be a bottle. A book. A knife. A gun. Kathleen is mad enough to kill her. Suddenly Orla realizes that her sister has always hated her. She has hated her….The reluctant visits, the dearth of invitations. They have never gone shopping together. They have never had a tête-à-tête, a girly drink. Always meeting at funerals, at their mother's house, at Christmas in the bosom of their families. Orla has always liked Kathleen but Kathleen hates Orla. It's clear. And now at last she has a real reason for hating her, and a motivation for hurt.

(PG 145)

Orla's illusion that she can keep this sisterly relationship with Kathleen is eventually dispelled by Orla's provocative act of betrayal in having a love affair with Kathleen's husband, to which Kathleen does not turn a blind eye this time. Perhaps deep down Orla dislikes Kathleen as much as Kathleen hates her. The sisterhood between Orla and Kathleen is then demolished and they are separated eternally by the Irish Sea.

Bonds Between Women in Relationships

While competition and friction are not rare in depictions of blood sisters in some Irish women's short stories, by contrast, some other stories visualise a bond between female peers analogous to sisterhood. Such closeness between women is not an uncommon topic in women's literature, whether this theme is treated in an ironical manner or depicts a regenerating strength which helps the women to survive in a male-dominated world. Annis Pratt observes the general depiction of women's closeness with each other in some women's fiction as 'passing phenomena on the road to marriage' which is sometimes shown with irony the clash with patriarchal values or battles about 'dominance and submission, self-punishments and despair' among the female characters and others by American and British female writers of the 1970s.[213] However, Pratt also observes anxieties over such battles as well as some new space for regeneration in the female characters' intimate relationships in women's fiction of a later generation.[214] A similar tendency of depicting female intimacy and lesbianism is also noticed in Irish women's short stories. There is a stark contrast between oblique expressions and hints of ambiguous 'female friendship' in Ita Daly's 'Such Good Friends' and Edna

O'Brien's 'Sister Imelda' in the 1970s and 80s, and those direct descriptions of lesbianism openly celebrated in Mary Dorcey's 'A Noise from the Woodshed' and 'A Country Dance' in late 1990s. Stories like 'Sister Imelda' and 'Such Good Friends' express an ambiguity and an anxiety about women's intimacy with each other triggered by a potential conflict with existing patriarchal values. Mary Dorcey's politically feminist stories about lesbianism also reveal the dilemma faced by women in such a social framework. Nevertheless, apart from lesbianism, the 'metaphorical' sisterhood between women in Irish women's short stories appears to visualise a new opening of the female 'communal eye' of women's solidarity. This idea or ideal of sisterhood serves as a model for women to aspire towards while also reflecting the difficulties of dealing with the inevitable clash with existing social norms.

A hint of lesbianism in women's close relationships is expressed in Edna O'Brien's 'Sister Imelda' and in Ita Daly's 'Such Good Friends,' but this affection between women is implied rather than overt and is suppressed either by an act of sublimation or by eventual rejection with revulsion. The narrator in Edna O'Brien's 'Sister Imelda' develops an intimacy with a nun at a convent. Passion and potential sensuality are sublimated into a spiritual attachment of sisterhood between the narrator and Sister Imelda. In the context of the convent, where celibacy and chastity are highly valued and maintained by the women (whether nun or schoolgirl), such ambiguous closeness would inevitably be condemned, although a consummated heterosexual relationship would be condemned more than a 'mental lesbian liaison.'[215] The narrator's obsession with this love for Sister Imelda suggests 'a possibility of union,' more likely a transcendent and spiritual than a physical one, which lures the narrator to emulate the nun in the process of seeking this union.[216] For example, the narrator starts to imitate Imelda's handwriting and expresses the wish to become a nun—although '[the narrator and Sister Imelda] might never be free to express [their] feeling, [they] would be under the same roof, in the same cloister, in mental and spiritual conjunction all [their] lives' (FH 136-7). Imelda's humanity is revealed through the sensuality displayed during a fling with a boy on the night prior to her taking her religious vows in the church, as well as through her inappropriate friendliness with the narrator, the ambiguity of which somehow assumes both a spiritual and a physical (or sensual) dimension.[217] Sister Imelda takes pleasure in feeding the narrator jam tarts, an act through which the bond between them is transfigured into a 'maternal sacrifice' which disguises this forbidden intimacy between women:

> "Eat them you goose," she said, and she watched me eat as if she herself derived some peculiar pleasure from it, whereas I was embarrassed about the pastry crumbling and the bits of blackberry jam staining my lips. She was amused. It was one of the most awkward yet thrilling moments I had lived, and inherent in the pleasure was the terrible sense of danger. Had we been caught, she, no doubt, would have had to make a massive sacrifice.
>
> (FH 130)

Although in the end the narrator gives up the idea of becoming a nun, her fear of seeing Sister Imelda involves a sense of shame connected to the way in which she has been taught in the convent to loathe her sexual body, in other words, the virgin identity Sister Imelda stands for and which the narrator now avoids: 'I began to wipe off the lipstick' (FH 143).[218] In fact, what troubles the narrator the most may be a profound grief at a lost, unrequited love for Sister Imelda—'I knew that there is something sad and faintly distasteful about love's ending, particularly love that has never been fully realized' (FH 143).

The unacknowledged love between women is conveyed indirectly and dramatised as rejection in Ita Daly's 'Such Good Friends.' In this story intimacy is disguised from the outset as a friendship of peers but is also interwoven with an ambiguous sensuality between the women concerned. Although the narrator, Helen, is described as a 'typical' woman who also fits in with the heterosexual norm by enjoying satisfaction from male attention and marriage, she actually reveals that she cannot attain mental closeness with men: 'I knew that I was bored a lot of the time and often lonely. I felt that something was missing from my life' (LR 124). This seems to suggest that Helen tends to regard the physical contact in relationships with men as of secondary importance when compared to profound impact of emotional closeness with women. In Helen's view, men, such as her husband, are people whom she likes and to whom she is grateful but such feelings are still far removed from the 'love' which she is able to discover in the relationship with another woman, Edith. Helen's unexpressed mental closeness with Edith appears as an ambiguous love involving selfless dedication as well as possessiveness. Helen indicates that she just has nothing in common to share with men in the way she does with Edith:

> It was not only that we shared values and views and interests, but there was a recognition, on both our parts I thought, of an inner identification, a oneness. I knew that I would never have to pretend to Edith, that she would always understand what I was trying to say. I

knew that a bond and a sympathy had been established between us
and that I could look forward with joy to the times that we would talk
and laugh and cry together....Edith became my source of pleasure.

(LR 118-9)

This sense of oneness which Helen claims to experience with Edith seems
analogous to the sort of inseparable passion often found in heterosexual love.
This also generates an inclination to jealousy and possessiveness which leads
Helen to try to interfere with Edith's private affairs, to try to dominate Edith
as well as to seek to end her love affair with Declan. Helen behaves like a
passionate lover towards Edith and attempts to make Edith her own: 'I saw
all the possibilities of her beauty, felt like a creator when I thought of dressing
her' (LR 123). The story does not directly express the perspective of Edith in
this relationship but this is conveyed later in the story through Edith's
hostility to and rejection of Helen with revulsion when Helen tries to comfort
Edith by kissing her: 'Leave me alone. Go away you — you monster' (LR
127). This response indicates a clear detestation as well as denoting a
'gynophobic' anxiety on the part of Edith. Edith's fear of such an obscure
relationship between women seems to coincide with some psychological
assumptions which regard lesbianism as abnormal, unhealthy or childish.

Theoreticians of lesbianism tend to see lesbianism as a 'childish'
phenomenon originating from an intense yearning for emotion, the
consequence of childhood deficiency of want of affection, which Phyllis
Chesler summarises as 'regressive, and infantile: even if it isn't, it leads to
undeniable suffering, and is therefore maladaptive, regressive, etc.' [219]
Psychologists like Freud think lesbianism is a pathological problem, a
perversion, in which females are considered as wounded daughters deprived

of the father's love or in which the female expresses unfulfilled and suppressed childhood inclination towards incest with her brother. A woman who is a lesbian may be explained as a person who is unable to achieve a fulfilled woman's life and roles or adopts lesbianism as a substitute after failing to achieve a successful relationship with a man. However, feminists like Luce Irigaray and Judith Butler consider these theories of lesbianism projected in psychoanalysis as 'symptomatic' of patriarchal biases. Irigaray and Butler think it is because psychoanalysis tends to subscribe to a 'compulsory' heterosexuality as a norm imposed by patriarchy, and therefore '[prohibits] the representation of all sexualities, sexual practices and sexual relations conceivable within its system.'[220]

The depiction of homosexuality in Irish literature has caused scandal. For example, Kate O'Brien's *Mary Lavelle* (1936) and *The Land of Spices* (1941) were banned as 'obscene' by the Irish Censorship board and her lesbian figures often had to exile to other countries in her works. In general, depictions of lesbian figures and relationships (or about sex) tended to be oblique and restrained in Irish fiction until the early 1980s.[221] Then within a decade, the fact that Mary Dorcey's *A Noise from the Woodshed* (1989) won the Rooney Prize has opened a new page for lesbianism in Irish fiction. Lesbian writers, as argued by Emma Donoghue, are no longer marginalised as a 'limiting label' in Irish literature.[222] The groundbreaking title story of *A Noise from the Woodshed*, openly pronounces, celebrates and presents lesbianism in an optimistic and positive atmosphere. After the advent of sexual liberation in the 1960s and 1970s, Mary Dorcey created a landmark in Irish literature by presenting happy Irish lesbians and lesbian sexuality without concealment in an Irish social context.

The period of the late 1980s was an era of significant law reforms in the history of Irish gay and lesbian rights movements. In 1988, after a decade of struggle, the Irish Senator David Norris eventually won his case with support from the European Court of Human Rights that the anti-gay laws in Ireland were unconstitutional. Although lesbianism was not literally mentioned in the criminal legislation, this does not mean lesbians have suffered less discrimination than gay men in Ireland.[223] In 1989, *The Prohibition of Incitement of Hatred Act* was passed in order to abolish the criminalisation of the act of homosexuality in Ireland, and also to protect those people whose sexual orientation is different from the heterosexual norm from being harassed and discriminated in employment. Some law reforms such as *The Criminal Law (Sexual Offences) Act* (1993), *The Unfair Dismissals (Amendment) Act* (1993) and *The Employment Equality Bill* (1997) were passed to protect groups of persons in any sexual orientation from discrimination and offences in Ireland.[224]

As an active feminist, Dorcey claims she chose to be a lesbian woman through her desire for self-determination in a feminist cultural context.[225] The powerful title story in *A Noise from the Woodshed* is narrated in a mode of experimental interlude mingled with fragmentary episodes of eroticism and 'chaos' that blur the boundaries of time and space. Emma Donoghue argues that the symbolic odyssey of lesbianism in this story is echoed by a noise of lesbian lovemaking from the woodshed just as the voices of Irish lesbians have eventually been recognised and 'come out' into the open air in Irish fiction.[226] Dorcey admitted that she intended to express the 'gleeful energy which is seldom talked about and certainly doesn't find its way into literature,' and to 'capture the quality of fertile chaos and the common experience of women who have to balance the practical, the emotional, the political and the sensual all in one day' in this story.[227] The story is a highly experimental utopian exercise seeking to establish a space for female intimacy as well as eroticism outside the patriarchal model for sexuality. Dorcey's 'A Noise from the Woodshed' describes a process of association of female sensuality with sexuality, and coordination with harmony and chaos within the context of an intimate relationship between women rather than telling a story in any conventional way.

This bond between females in a lesbian paradise depicted in Dorcey's 'A Noise from the Woodshed' embraces the ideas as well as the ideals of collective female power largely advocated strongly by some feminists. Dorcey sees the potential of consolidated female power being realised either through sisterhood and female solidarity or through lesbianism because she regards heterosexuality as patriarchal dominance and tyranny against women. This is expressed in her allegorical story 'The Orphan,' in which the female character is exploited sexually by 'father' and 'the men' while she struggles between self-loathing and a distorted view of her self.[228] By contrast, Dorcey portrays lesbian relationships with a more equal power balance between both partners in some of the other stories such as 'A Noise from the Woodshed,' 'A Country Dance,' 'Introducing Nessa' or 'The Husband' in A Noise from the Woodshed. Dorcey's lesbian haven, one in which the women enjoy equality of relationships in her series of lesbian stories, indicates her objective to serve through her writing the political agenda of feminists like herself, even though the 'fundamental' power dynamics of lesbian relationships may still remain controversial issues. The views of feminists tend to vary in respect of whether heterosexuality is compatible with feminism. For example, Jane Freeman points out that in some definitions lesbianism may not always involve sexual relationships with females but just the withdrawal from sexual relationships with males. As an example, cites the Leeds Revolutionary Feminist Group whose statement of the 'political lesbians' means a 'woman-identified woman who does not fuck men.'[229] Freeman argues lesbianism defined in this way does not signify compulsory sexual activity with females. Certainly, in 'A Country Dance' and 'Introducing Nessa,' Dorcey also recognises some difficulties that lesbian women may encounter in reality in which lesbians are frequently faced with, even threatened by, male aggression (especially sexually) as well as by biases and prejudice which seek to demolish this 'abnormality' between women. In 'The Husband,' Martina's decision to leave her husband for her lesbian lover Helen is considered by her husband as a morbid joke beyond his comprehension:

> How could any normal man have seen it as any more than a joke?…He had had to keep himself from laughing. He was taken by surprise, undoubtedly through he should not have been with the way they had been going on—never out of each other's company…She was too fundamentally healthy, and too fond of the admiration of men. Besides, knowing how passionate she was, he could not believe she would settle for the caresses of a woman.
>
> (NW 70)

Stories like Lucile Redmond's 'Anna Mae' and Leland Bardwell's 'The Dove of Peace' describe female powerlessness struggling to survive male dominance or oppression, domestic violence and sexual abuse. However, unlike the narrator in Mary Dorcey's story 'The Orphan,' who is portrayed as eventually regaining her lost self, and thus symbolising a triumph of female power, both female characters—Anna Mae in 'Anna Mae' and Columbine in 'The Dove of Peace'—are not lucky enough to survive their tragic destinies and both die in childbirth. In any society in which medical technology is either primitive or scarce, the mortality of women is often endangered by childbirth. In Celtic mythology, death of women in childbirth also appears as a metaphor symbolising the defeat of female power as well as its suppression by patriarchal tyranny.[230] Female solidarity threatened by male tyranny in 'Anna Mae' and 'The Dove of Peace' shows sisters are united in sharing painful experiences. This 'shared pain' experience between women not only has been recognised by some feminists (however, debated or opposed by others) but also by a conventionalist like Sarah Stickney Ellis who considered it as a bond between women:

> [Unlike men], women do know what their sex is formed to suffer; and for this very reason, the most endearing, the most pure and disinterested of any description of affection which this world affords…[This bond] arises chiefly out of their mutual knowledge of each other's capacity of receiving pain.[231]

This 'traditional' picture of downtrodden women under patriarchy has been gradually altered in Irish literary imagination since women's liberation re-emerged in the 1970s.[232] Contemporary Irish female writers are able to present some stronger female characters as warriors and survivors, or provide a happy ending that is not necessarily related to women's being 'rescued' by men, as in Mary Lavin's 'Lilacs,' Mary Dorcey's 'The Orphan' or Éilís Ní Dhuibhne's 'Gweedore Girl,' 'Wuff Wuff Wuff for de Valera,' and 'Holiday in the Land of Murdered Dreams.'

There appear to be several varied modes of sisterhood in Irish women's short stories including blood sisters, metaphorical sisters and lesbian lovers, all serving as vehicles to express women's intimate relationships with one another. The relationship between biological sisters or female peers, unlike that between mothers and daughters, seems to provide a less hierarchal, more equality based model for women's relationships. Christine Downing argues the 'parent-child' model for female relationships tends to be 'oppressive and misleading' because it still implies a power structure based on authority and hierarchy.[233] According to Michel Foucault, power is associated not with repression or inhibition or straightforward domination but works through institutionalised and accustomed discourses which open up delimited forms of action, knowledge, and being. The exercise of power seems constitutive and inescapable while Foucault argues that 'analysis, elaboration, and bringing into question of power relations…[are] a permanent political task in all social relations.'[234] This model could be transformative or transcendental for individual female development although in Irish women's stories this primal relationship between female peers in the family appears to be problematic, showing through archetypal motifs of ambiguity and ambivalence evoking alienation and conflict as well as closeness and inseparability.

Biological sisters are not necessarily like those people with whom one may establish a bond and befriend through one's freewill. Whether sisters can get along with each other or not, a sister cannot be replaced by choice. Each female child in the family is defined by comparison with the other, because each is interdependent on the other for a sense of identity within the totality of this family. If a family is constructed under this discourse, each individual female will inevitably face a dilemma in respect of identification as well as individuality. Perhaps due to this interconnection, sisterhood between blood sisters sometimes tends to generate difficulties for the development of these females because this development itself denotes separation. Blood sisters are intertwined with one another as 'blossoms from one stem.' Sisters encouraged to be harmonious and supportive, at least on the surface, instead of expressing overt rivalry with one another are ambivalent towards this sisterhood which may sometimes be too intimate to endure (such as when sisters fall in love with the same person). Frequently, there is an underlying conflict between a search for individual development and the pressure to submerge this individual development in the intimacy of sisterhood. On the one hand, sisters seek their own separate uniqueness. On the other hand, sisters may not be delighted to accept dissimilarity, such as happiness in life, when one compares herself to the situation of another. Whenever one party uses force in an attempt to overwhelm the other, the balance and harmony within the relationship between sisters are bound to be spoiled. This dilemma is frequently displayed in Irish women's stories in the form of one sister who tends to dominate her sibling as well as by creating clearly defined roles or emphasising disparity in character and appearance. Nonetheless, in reality this urge to differentiate may, in fact, be a reflection of their inseparable identification and repressed desire for intimacy with each other. Within such a framework each sister seems to shape the other into a common identity so as to achieve a sense of wholeness in the family unit.[235]

It seems that sisterhood is potentially too powerful to control so women are actually discouraged from staying too 'intimate' with each other under patriarchal culture. In Greek mythology, for example, the heroism of Heracles or Theseus is defined in part by their ability to confront and disperse the solidarity of ferocious women, the Amazons, or by the loss of the communal eye of the Graiæs, contributing to the successful killing of the Gorgons by Perseus.[236] Communities of women are sometimes portrayed as murky and vicious, for example, in Irish stories like Margaret Barrington's 'Village Without Men' or Marilyn McLaughlin's 'Witchwoman,' where groups of women represent the collective power of horror and suppression. That groups of women are shown, as a recurrent stereotypical literary image, oppressing each other and fighting against one another, is perhaps the female 'grossness' which Mary Wollstonecraft criticised, the 'cattiness and disloyalty' of the female jungle, which Elizabeth Janeway argues was shaped by rivalry for male approval in the patriarchal framework.[237] If women are conditioned to conform to such an arrangement, then the whole male-female system can function effectively. Since this conception is sustained, then obviously women in conflict with each other will not be able to consolidate collective power against any existing patriarchal framework.

Perhaps the anxiety about and fear of the power of sisterhood or female intimacy also hints at potential danger involving female sexuality. In Victorian England, for example, one of the many hindrances to female education seems to have been the reluctance to bring girls into close contact with each other, as expressed in the following extreme opinion on the subject:

We need not shrink from saying that the congregating of young girls of a certain age, either in boarding schools, true colleges, or any other gregarious establishment...is a downright forcing of minds which ought, for the moment, to be kept as dormant as possible. By minds we do not mean intellects; we mean what everybody who is acquainted with human nature will understand. It is on this account, and on this alone, that female boarding-schools are so unspeakably pernicious.[238]

By expressing 'minds,' here the author actually denotes 'bodies.'[239] The impact of young women on each other must, to such commentators, invariably be considered as a sort of corruption, a transgression of a profound sexual taboo. Even Mary Wollstonecraft revealed her ambivalence towards women closely together as repulsive because they are 'too intimate':

> Women from necessity, because their minds are not cultivated, have recourse very often to what I familiarly term bodily wit; and their intimacies are of the same kind. In short, with respect to both mind and body, they are too intimate....On this account also, I object to many females being shut up together in nurseries, schools, or convents. I cannot recollect without indignation the jokes and hoyden tricks, which knots of young women indulge themselves in, when in my youth accident threw me, an awkward rustic, in their way. They were almost on a par with the double meanings which shake the convivial table when the glass has circulated freely.[240]

Such female intimacy that Wollstonecraft loathed and the writer of the *Imperial Review* was anxious about is, as Auerbach argues, actually an 'embarrassing reminder of the observer's own sexuality, a violation of the right to private distance.'[241] Although the female intimacies celebrated in one of Wollstonecraft's novels, entitled *Mary: A Fiction* (1788), has been assigned to what Adrienne Rich has termed the 'lesbian continuum' by critics, Wollstonecraft herself attacked such 'grossly familiar' relationships spawned in female communities.[242] The anxiety about the possibility of lesbianism (involving lesbian sex) between females seems to alarmingly evoke people's suspicion and fear towards female intimacy. Resistance to 'otherness' in society seems to wrench from women the possibility of consolidating this unrecognised power of communal sisterhood. In spite of the prevailing 'homophobia' about female intimacy among some people, diverse views about homosexuality or female sexuality still gradually emerged and have been voiced in today's western societies through legalisation which recognises this 'sexuality' alternative to heterosexual 'norm.'[243]

The archetypal motifs of ambiguity and ambivalence presented in Irish women's stories about sisterly relationships expose the paradoxes and distortions underlying the sisterly conflict and rivalry, which intend to separate sisters and women from being 'too intimate,' in a patriarchal framework. Nevertheless, the communal eye between sisters (and women in general), as Christine Downing argues, can still be regained and re-opened through our recognition of the inner sister as mutual giver and receiver. In Anne Devlin's story 'The Way-Paver,' despite the indifference and distance between the sisters, they are drawn closer together by their shared experience of motherhood. Reconciliation between alienated sisters may be possible if sisters, like colours in a painting, are seen as shades of difference rather than contrasting shadows of each other.[244] This relationship can be transformative if seen as one which embraces differences and 'otherness' and also one which bases intimacy on mutual giving and receiving.

Epilogue

This book has examined several areas of human relationships related to women's and gender issues through the prism of contemporary Irish women's short stories. Significantly, women's and gender issues which evolve from patriarchal ideology are presented in recognisable repetitive narrative patterns as motifs in Irish women's short stories. These motifs display a recurrent pattern of female aspiration seeking to challenge or ridicule the prevailing patriarchal dictatorship in respect of gender roles and relationships in the arenas of love, marriage, motherhood and sisterhood.

These recurrent motifs are recognised as archetypal in this book because they manifest a 'tendency' of Irish female writers to 'form and re-form images in relation to [women's] certain kinds of repeated experience' as defined by Lauter and Rupprecht.[245] Irish female writers address key issues and unveil gender ideology constructed by patriarchal society through these motifs, which are symptomatic gestures indicating the female power to resist certain social forces under patriarchy. This critical perspective on gender roles and norms in Irish women's short stories is deemed analogous to a kind of 'feminist awareness' by critics such as Janet Madden-Simpson, Ailbhe Smyth and Christine St. Peter. This book has demonstrated that this 'feminist' view in contemporary Irish women's short stories is presented in a systematic narrative form comprised of archetypal motifs in order to unveil the paradoxes behind social norms and gender roles, which distort human relationships under patriarchal ideology.

This book begins with an examination of the relationships between men and women as lovers and married couples; it then analyses women's relationships with each other as mothers and daughters, and as sisters or female peers. Overall this book reviews the process by which Irish women develop themselves through their relationships with other people against a framework of feminist awareness. In these stories, the female characters seek to negotiate their states of being as women within the changing social context of Ireland, from a situation in which Irish women had no choice but to depend on men for physical survival to one in which women fight for their individuality and become choice makers for themselves. The conventional views and values about the nature of women and about gender roles are deliberately rendered problematic through the use of such archetypal motifs in Irish women's short stories, reflecting Irish women's rebellion and their challenge to the ideological manifestations of patriarchy.

Appendix: Alphabetical List of Short Stories

The individual stories mentioned in this book are here listed alphabetically, followed by the names of the authors and the abbreviations of each story collection. Full titles of collections can be found in the Abbreviations section at the beginning of the book. This list is for the reader's convenience and is intended to provide easy access to the primary sources of the stories which have been discussed in the body of the book. For further publication details please refer to the Bibliography.

Story Title	Author	Story Collection Abbreviations
A Beast of a Man	Mary O'Donnell	SP
A Bevy of Aunts	Mary Lavin	FLI
A Country Dance	Mary Dorcey	NW
A Dream Woke Me	Marilyn McLaughlin	DW
A Family Likeness	Mary Lavin	FLI
A Girl Like You	Margaret Dolan	IO
A Life of Her Own	Maeve Kelly	LH, OH
A Likely Story	Mary Lavin	ML2
A Literary Woman	Mary Beckett	LW
A Memory	Mary Lavin	ME
A Noise from the Woodshed	Mary Dorcey	NW
A Rose in the Heart of New York	Edna O'Brien	RH, FH
A Scandalous woman	Edna O'Brien	SW, FH, SC
A Season for Mothers	Helen Lucy Burke	SM
A Sense of Humour	Mary Dorcey	NW
A Single Lady	Mary Lavin	ML1
A Visit to the Cemetery	Mary Lavin	ML1

A Walk on the Cliff	Mary Lavin	FLI
A Way of Life	Mary Leland	LG, CN
A Woman by the Seaside	Edna O'Brien	RH
A Woman Friend	Mary Lavin	ML2
Agony Aunt	Mary Morrissy	LE
Aimez-vous Colette	Ita Daly	LR, SC
Anna Mae	Lucile Redmond	WB
Aspects	Marilyn McLaughlin	DW
At Sally Gap	Éilís Ní Dhuibhne	PG
Baby Blue	Edna O'Brien	RH, FH
Beatrice	Evelyn Conlon	TL
Beauty Treatment	Angela Bourke	BS
Besieged	Marilyn McLaughlin	DW
Biddy's Research	Moya Roddy	VH
Big Mouth	Blánaid McKinney	BM
Bill's New Wife	Éilís Ní Dhuibhne	II
Breaking	Kate Cruise O'Brien	IO
Breath of the Living	Mary O'Donnell	SP
Bridie Birdie	Marilyn McLaughlin	DW, CN
Commencements	Mary Leland	IO
Concerning Virgins	Clare Boylan	CS
Confession	Clare Boylan	CS
Cords	Edna O'Brien	LO
Deep Down	Angela Bourke	VH, CN
Dublin is Full of Married Men	Ivy Bannister	MO
Ellie's Ring	Sheila Barrett	IO
Estonia	Éilís Ní Dhuibhne	II
Excursion	Fiona Barr	SS
Failing Years	Mary Beckett	BW, TV, GM
Fatgirl Terrestrial	Anne Enright	PV
First Bite	Anne Devlin	WP
Five Notes After a Visit	Anne Devlin	WP, FL, CN
Frail Vessel	Mary Lavin	ML1
Fulfilment	Éilís Ní Dhuibhne	MF
Gods and Slaves	Clare Boylan	CS
Grey Cats in the Dark	Helen Lucy Burke	SM

Growth	Ita Daly	LR
Gweedore Girl	Éilís Ní Dhuibhne	II
Ham	Angela Bourke	BS
Happy Delivery	Ivy Bannister	MO
Heaven	Mary Beckett	WT, CN
Holiday in the Land of Murdered Dreams	Éilís Ní Dhuibhne	MF
Honeysuckle	Marilyn McLaughlin	DW
Hot Earth	Éilís Ní Dhuibhne	II
Housekeeper's Cut	Clare Boylan	CS
In a Café	Mary Lavin	ML1
In the Beginning	Lilian Roberts Finlay	BF, CN
In the Middle of the Fields	Mary Lavin	TV, GM
Introducing Nessa	Mary Dorcey	NW
Irish Revel	Edna O'Brien	LO, FH
Journey Home	Maeve Kelly	OH, CN
June 23rd	Jan Kennedy	FL
Knock Three Times	Stella Mahon	FL
L'Amour	Clare Boylan	CS
Late Opening at the Last Chance Saloon	Marian Keyes	IO
Life on Mars	Clare Boylan	CS
Lift Me Up and Pour Me Out	Ivy Bannister	MO
Lilacs	Mary Lavin	SC, ML3, CN
Lili Marlene	Éilís Ní Dhuibhne	II
Looking	Éilís Ní Dhuibhne	BT
Losing	Kate Cruise O'Brien	GH, SC
Love, Hate and Friendship	Éilís Ní Dhuibhne	II
Loving Memory	Mary Lavin	ML2
Man in the Cellar	Julia O'Faolain	MC
Mayonnaise to the Hills	Angela Bourke	BS
Melancholy Baby	Julia O'Faolain	TV, GM
Midland Jihad	Liz McManus	VH
Midwife to the Fairies	Éilís Ní Dhuibhne	BT, TV, GM, MF
Miss Brown, Miss Blonde, and Miss Pleasant	Anna Uí Shighil	FD4

Miss Holland	Mary Lavin	TB
Mrs. Reinhardt	Edna O'Brien	RH, FH
My Mother's Daughter	Ivy Bannister	MO
Nomads Seek the Pavilions of Bliss on the Slopes of Middle Age	Éilís Ní Dhuibhne	PG
Number 10	Edna O'Brien	RH, FH
Oh Susannah	Marilyn McLaughlin	DW
Orange Horses	Maeve Kelly	OH, WT
Out-Patients	Leland Bardwell	DK, CN
Paradise	Edna O'Brien	LO, FH
Peacocks	Éilís Ní Dhuibhne	MF
Queen	Maeve Kelly	OH
Raspberries and the Dream Workshop	Marilyn McLaughlin	DW
Ripples	Patricia Scanlan	IO
Rosa	Mary Morrissy	LE
Ruth	Maeve Kelly	OH
Saints and Scholars	Mary Beckett	SC
Sarah	Mary Lavin	ML2
Savages	Edna O'Brien	RN, FH
Senility	Mary Lavin	SO
Sister Imelda	Edna O'Brien	RN, FH, TV, GM
Sisters	Claire Keegan	AN
Sisters	Edna O'Brien	SW
Strong Pagans	Mary O'Donnell	SP
Such Good Friends	Ita Daly	LR, CN
Sudden Infant Death	Mary Beckett	LW
Swiss Cheese	Éilís Ní Dhuibhne	II
Taking Scarlet as a Real Colour	Evelyn Conlon	TL
Technical Difficulties and the Plague	Clare Boylan	CS
That Bad Woman	Clare Boylan	CS
The Bachelor	Edna O'Brien	RN, FH
The Connor Girls	Edna O'Brien	RN, FH
The Devil's Gift	Frances Molloy	WS
The Dove of Peace	Leland Bardwell	DK, TV, GM
The Empty Ceiling	F. D. Sheridan	SC
The False God	Maeve Kelly	LH, OH

The Foundress	Emma Cooke	TV, GM
The Garden of Eden	Éilís Ní Dhuibhne	EW, VH
The Golden Handshake	Lilian Roberts Finlay	BF
The House	Anne Devlin	WP
The Husband	Mary Dorcey	NW, WT, CN
The Lift Home	Mary Dorcey	VH
The Little Galloway Girls	Mary Leland	LG
The Little Grey Cat	Peig Sayers	FD4
The Little Madonna	Clare Boylan	CS
The Long Ago	Mary Lavin	ML2
The Lost Child	Mary Lavin	ML3
The Love Object	Edna O'Brien	LO, FH
The Man Who Married the Mermaid	Patrick Stokes	FD4
The Master and the Bomb	Mary Beckett	BW
The Mermaid Legend	Éilís Ní Dhuibhne	EW
The Miracle of Life	Clare Boylan	CS
The Nun's Mother	Mary Lavin	ML2
The O'Touney Sisters and the Day of Reckoning	Moy McCrory	VH
The Orphan	Mary Dorcey	IO
The Pale Gold of Alaska	Éilís Ní Dhuibhne	PG
The Palm House	Shirley Bork	FL
The Patriot Son	Mary Lavin	ML1
The Pursuit of Happiness	Mary Beckett	BW
The Search for the Lost Husband	Éilís Ní Dhuibhne	II
The Shaking Tree	Lucile Redmond	WB
The Stolen Child	Clare Boylan	CS, CN
The Story of the Little White Goat	Máire Ruiséal	FD4
The Tale of the Shoe	Emma Donoghue	FD4
The Truth About Married Love	Éilís Ní Dhuibhne	PG
The Vain Woman	Maeve Kelly	LH, OH
The Virgin	Trudy Hayes	VH
The Wall-Reader	Fiona Barr	FL
The Way-Paver	Anne Devlin	WP
The Widow	Edna O'Brien	LS
The Widow's Son	Mary Lavin	ML1

Bibliography

I. Primary Sources

Bannister, Ivy. *Magician and Other Stories*. Dublin: Poolbeg Press, 1996.

Bardwell, Leland. *Different Kinds of Love*. Dublin: Attic Press, 1987.

Barr, Fiona, Barbara Haycock Walsh and Stella Mahon. *Sisters*. Belfast: The Blackstaff Press, 1980.

Beckett, Mary. *A Belfast Woman*. Dublin: Poolbeg Press, 1980.

---. *A Literary Woman*. Dublin: Poolbeg Press, 1990.

Bourke, Angela. *By Salt Water*. Dublin: New Island Press, 1996.

Boylan, Clare. *Collected Short Stories*. (collected *A Nail on the Head*, *Concerning Virgins* and *That Bad Woman*). London: Abacus Press, 2000.

Burke, Helen Lucy. *A Season for Mothers and Other Stories*. Dublin: Poolbeg Press, 1980.

Casey, Daniel and Linda M. Casey, eds. *Stories by Contemporary Irish Women*. New York: Syracuse University Press, 1990.

Conlon, Evelyn. *Telling*. Belfast: The Blackstaff Press, 2000.

Conlon, Evelyn and Hans-Christian Oeser, eds. *Cutting the Night in Two*. Dublin: New Island Press, 2001.

Daly, Ita. *The Lady with the Red Shoes*. Dublin: Poolbeg Press, 1980, 1995.

DeSalvo, Louise, Kathleen Walsh D'Arcy and Katherine Hogan. *Territories of the Voice: Contemporary Stories by Irish Women Writers*. London: Virago, 1989.

---, eds. *A Green and Mortal Sound: Short Fiction by Irish Women Writers.* Boston: Beacon Press, 1999, 2000.

Devlin, Anne. *The Way-Paver.* London: Faber & Faber, 1986.

Donoghue, *Emma.* 'The Tale of the Shoe.' *The Field Day Anthology of Irish Writing.* Eds. Angela Bourke, et al. Vol. IV. Cork: Cork University Press, 2002. 1135-7.

Dorcey, Mary. *A Noise from the Woodshed.* London: Onlywomen Press, 1989.

Enright, Anne. *The Portable Virgin.* London: Vintage, 1992.

Finlay, Lilian Roberts. *A Bona Fide Husband.* Dublin: Poolbeg Press, 1991.

Hooley, Ruth, ed. *The Female Line: Northern Irish Women Writers.* Belfast: Northern Ireland Women's Rights Movement, 1985.

Keegan, Claire. *Antarctica.* London: Faber & Faber, 1999.

Kelly, Maeve. *A Life of Her Own.* Dublin: Poolbeg Press, 1976.

---. *Orange Horses.* Belfast: The Blackstaff Press, 1990.

Lavin, Mary. *The Stories of Mary Lavin.* Vol. 1. London: Constable, 1964.

---. *A Memory and Other Stories.* London: Constable, 1972.

---. *The Stories of Mary Lavin.* Vol. 2. London: Constable, 1974.

---. *The Shrine and Other Stories.* London: Constable, 1977.

---. *Tales from Bective Bridge.* Dublin: Poolbeg Press, 1978.

---. *A Family Likeness.* London: Constable, 1985.

---. *The Stories of Mary Lavin.* Vol. 3. London: Constable, 1985.

Leland, Mary. *The Little Galloway Girls.* London: Hamilton, 1997.

McKinney, Blánaid. *Big Mouth.* London: Phoenix House, 2000.

McLaughlin, Marilyn. *A Dream Woke Me and Other Stories.* Belfast: The Blackstaff Press, 1999.

Molloy, Frances. *Women Are the Scourge of the Earth.* Belfast: White Row Press, 1998.

Morrissy, Mary. *A Lazy Eye*. London: Jonathan Cape, 1993.

Ní Dhuibhne, Éilís. *Blood and Water*. Dublin: Attic Press, 1988.

---. *Eating Women is Not Recommended*. Dublin: Attic Press, 1991.

---. *The Inland Ice*. Belfast: The Blackstaff Press, 1997.

---. *The Pale Gold of Alaska*. London: Review, 2000, 2001.

---. *Midwife to the Fairies*. Cork: Attic Press, 2003.

O'Brien, Edna. *The Love Object*. Harmondsworth, Middlesex: Penguin, 1968.

---. *A Scandalous Woman*. Harmondsworth, Middlesex: Penguin, 1974.

---. *A Rose in the Heart*. Garden City, New York: Doubleday & Company, Inc., 1979.

---. *Returning*. Harmondsworth, Middlesex: Penguin, 1983.

---. *A Fanatic Heart*. New York: Farrar Straus Giroux, 1984.

---. *Lantern Slides*. London: Weidenfeld & Nicolson, 1988.

O'Brien, Kate Cruise and Mary Maher, eds. *If Only*. Dublin: Poolbeg Press, 1997.

O'Brien, Kate Cruise. *A Gift Horse and Other Stories*. Dublin: Poolbeg Press, 1978.

O'Donnell, Mary. *Strong Pagans*. Dublin: Poolbeg Press, 1991.

O'Faolain, Julia. *Man in the Cellar*. London: Faber & Faber, 1974.

Redmond, Lucile. *Who Breaks Up the Old Moons to Make New Stars*. Ennisderry, Co. Wicklow: The Egotist Press, 1978.

Symth, Ailbhe, ed. *Wildish Things: An Anthology of New Irish Women's Writing*. Dublin: Attic Press, 1989.

Walsh, Caroline, ed. *Virgins and Hyacinths*. Dublin: Attic Press, 1993.

II. Secondary Sources

'Mary Lavin Special Issue.' *Irish University Review* Vol. 9 No.2 (Autumn 1979): 233-45.

Ms Muffet and Others. Dublin: Attic Press, 1986.

Rapunzel's Revenge. Dublin: Attic Press, 1985.

The Mabinogion. Trans. Gwyn and Thomas Jones. London: Dent, 1978.

'True College for Women.' *Imperial Review* (1867): 8.

Abraham, Karl, M.D. *Selected Papers of Karl Abraham*. Trans. Douglas Bryan and Alix Strachey. New York: Brunner/Mazel, 1927.

Adam, Barry D. *The Rise of a Gay and Lesbian Movement*. Boston: Twayne Publishers, 1987.

Ang-Lygate, Magdalene, Chris Corrin and Millsom S. Henry, eds. *Desperately Seeking Sisterhood*. Abingdon, Oxon: Taylor & Francis, 1997.

Anton, Ferdinand. *Women in Pre-Columbian Art*. New York: Abner Schram, 1973.

Atkinson, Ti-Grace. *Amazon Odyssey*. New York: Links Books, 1974.

Auerbach, Nina. *Communities of Women: An Idea in Fiction*. Cambridge, Massachusetts: Harvard University Press, 1978.

---. *Women and the Demon: The Life of a Victorian Myth*. London: Harvard University Press, 1982.

Bagehot, Walter. 'The Waverly Novels.' *Literary Studies* Ed. R. H. Hutton. Vol. II (1891): 148.

Barry, Peter. *Beginning Theory: An Introduction to Literary and Cultural Theory*. Manchester: Manchester University Press, 1995, 2002.

Basch, Francoise. *Relative Creatures: Victorian Women in Society and the Novel.* New York: Schocken, 1974.

Beauvoir, Simone de. *The Second Sex.* Trans. H. M. Parshley. Harmondsworth, Middlesex: Penguin, 1949.

Belsey, Catherine and Jane Moore. *The Feminist Reader: Essays in Gender and the Politics of Literary Criticism.* Basingstoke: Macmillan, 1989.

Benhabib, Seyla. '"Feminism and the Question of Postmodernism": Situating the Subject.' *Feminist Literary Theory: A Reader.* Second Edition. Ed. Mary Eagleton. Oxford: Blackwell Publishing, 1996. 373-8.

Bernikow, Louise. *Among Women.* New York: Harper & Row, 1980.

Birch, Dinah. 'Gender and Genre.' *Imagining Women: Cultural Representations and Gender.* Ed. Frances Bonner. Cambridge: Polity Press, 1992. 43-55.

Boada-Montagut, Irene. *Women Write Back: Contemporary Irish and Catalan Short Stories in Colonial Context.* Dublin: Irish Academic Press, 2003.

Boland, Eavan. 'A Kind of Scar: The Woman Poet in a National Tradition.' *A Dozen Lips.* Dublin: Attic Press, 1994. 72-92.

Bolen, Jean Shinoda. *Goddesses in Everywoman: A New Psychology of Women.* San Francisco: Harper & Row, 1984.

Bolger, Dermot. Introduction. *The New Picador Book of Contemporary Irish Fiction.* Ed. Dermot Bolger. London: Picador, 2000. xi-xl.

Bourke, Angela, et al, eds. *The Field Day Anthology of Irish Writing.* Vol. IV-V. Cork: Cork University Press, 2002.

Bradley, Anthony and Maryann Gialanella Valiulis, eds. *Gender and Sexuality in Modern Ireland.* Amherst, Mass.: University Massachusetts Press, 1997.

Brady, Anne. *Women in Ireland.* Westport, Conn.: Greenwood, 1988.

Brooker, Peter. *A Concise Glossary of Cultural Theory.* London: Arnold, 1999.

Brownmiller, Susan. *Against Our Will: Men and Women and Rape.* New York: Simon & Schuster, 1975.

Brunl, Pierre. *A Companion to Literary Myths, Heroes and Archetypes.* London: Routledge, 1995.

Burnap, George W. *Lectures on the Sphere and Duties of Women and Other Subjects.* Baltimore: John Murphy, 1841.

Butler, Judith. Gender Trouble: *Feminism and the Subversion of Identity.* New York: Routledge, 1990.

Byrne, Anne and Madeleine Leonard. *Women and Irish Society: A Sociological Reader.* Belfast: Beyond the Pale Publications, 1997.

Cahalan, James. *Irish Novel.* Boston: Twayne, 1988.

---. Double *Visions: Women and Men in Modern and Contemporary Irish Fiction.* New York: Syracuse University Press, 1999.

Caird, Mona. 'Marriage.' *Westminster Review* (August, 1888).

Caldecott, Moyra. *Women in Celtic Myth: Tales of Extraordinary Women From Ancient Celtic Tradition.* Rochester, Vermont: Destiny Books, 1992.

Calder, Jenni. *Women and Marriage in Victorian Fiction.* London: Thames & Hudson, 1976.

Campbell, Joseph. *The Hero with a Thousand Faces.* London: Abacus Books, 1975.

---. *Transformations of Myth Through Time.* New York: Perennial Library, 1990.

Carr, Jean Ferguson. *Afterword. Images of Women in Literature.* Ed. Mary Anne Ferguson. Boston: Houghton Mifflin, 1991. 569-80.

Casey, Daniel and Linda M. Casey. Introduction. *Stories by Contemporary Irish Women.* Eds. Daniel Casey and Linda M. Casey. New York: Syracuse University Press, 1990. 1-11.

Casey, Juanita. *Hath the Rain a Father?* London: Phoenix House, 1966.

Cavendish, Richard. *King Arthur and the Grail: the Arthurian Legends and Their Meaning.* New York: Taplinger Pub. Co., 1978, 1979.

Chesler, Phyllis. *Women and Madness.* New York: Harcourt Brace Jovanovich, 1972.

Chodorow, Nancy. *The Reproduction of Mothering.* Berkeley: University of California Press, 1978.

Christ, Carol P. 'Margaret Atwood: The Surfacing of Women's Spiritual Quest and Vision.' *Sign* 2 No.2 (Winter 1976): 316-330.

---. *Womanspirit Rising.* San Francisco: Harper & Row, 1979.

Clarkson, L. A. 'Marriage and Fertility in Nineteenth-Century Ireland.' *Marriage and Society: Studies in the Social History of Marriage.* Ed. R. B. Outhwaite. New York: St. Martin's Press, 1981. 237-55.

Cleeve, Brian, and Anne Brady. *Biographical Dictionary of Irish Writers.* Mullingar: Lilliput, 1985.

Condren, Mary. *The Serpent and the Goddess.* New York: Harper & Row, 1989.

Connolly, Linda. 'The Women's Movement in Ireland, 1970-95: A Social Movement's Analysis.' *The Irish Journal of Feminist Studies* 1.1 (March 1996): 43-77.

Connolly, S. J., ed. *The Oxford Companion to Irish History.* Oxford: Oxford University Press, 1998.

Corcoran, Clodagh. 'Pornography: The New Terrorism.' *A Dozen Lips.* Dublin: Attic Press, 1994. 1-21.

Coward, Ros. "'This Novel Changes Lives": Are Women's Novels Feminist Novels? A Response to Rebecca O'Rourke's Article "Summer Reading.' *Feminism: A Reader.* Ed. Maggie Humm. London: Harvester Wheatsheaf, 1992. 377-80.

Cruikshank, Margaret. *The Gay and Lesbian Liberation Movement.* London: Routledge, 1992.

Crow, Duncan. *The Victorian Woman.* New York: Stein and Day, 1972.

Cullingford, Elizabeth Butler. *Ireland's Others: Gender and Ethnicity in Irish literature and Popular Culture.* Cork: Cork University Press, 2001.

Curley, Helen, ed. *Local Ireland Almanac and Yearbook of Facts* 2000. Dublin: Local Ireland, 1999.

Curtis, L. P. *Anglo-Saxons and Celts: A Study of Anti-Irish Prejudice in Victorian England.* Bridgeport, Connecticut: Conference on British Studies, 1968.

Daly, Mary. *Beyond God and Father: Toward a Philosophy of Women's Liberation.* Boston: Beacon Press, 1973.

---. *Gyn/Ecology: The Metaethics of Radical Feminism.* Boston: Beacon Press, 1978.

Davidson, Cathy M. and E. M. Broner. *The Lost Tradition: Mothers and Daughters in Literature.* New York: Ungar, 1980.

Deane, Seamus, Andrew Carpenter and Jonathan Williams, eds. *The Field Day Anthology of Irish Writing.* Vol. I – III. Derry: Field Day Publications, 1991.

Deegan, Dorothy Yost. *The Stereotype of the Single Woman in American Novels.* New York: King's Crown Press, 1951.

Derrida, Jacques. 'White Mythology: Metaphor in the Text of Philosophy.' *Margins of Philosophy*. Trans. Alan Bass. Chicago: University of Chicago Press, 1982.

DeSalvo, Louise, Kathleen Walsh D'Arcy and Katherine Hogan. Introduction. *Territories of the Voice: Contemporary Stories by Irish Women Writers*. Eds. Louise DeSalvo, Kathleen Walsh D'Arcy and Katherine Hogan. London: Virago, 1989. xi-xxi.

---. Introduction. *A Green and Mortal Sound: Short Fiction by Irish Women Writers*. Eds. Louise DeSalvo, Kathleen Walsh D'Arcy and Katherine Hogan. Boston: Beacon Press, 1999, 2001. xi-xxii.

Doan, James E. *Women and Goddesses in Early Celtic History, Myth and Legend*. Boston: Beacon, 1973.

Donoghue, Emma. 'Noises from Woodsheds: Tales of Irish Lesbians, 1886-1989.' *Lesbian and Gay Visions of Ireland: Toward the Twenty-First Century*. Eds. Ide O'Carroll and Eoin Collins. London: Cassell, 1995. 158-170.

---, ed. 'Lesbian Encounters, 1745-1997.' *The Field Day Anthology of Irish Writing*. Eds. Angela Bourke, et al. Vol. IV. Cork: Cork University Press, 2002. 1090-1140.

Donovan, Katie, A. Norman Jeffares and Brendan Kennelly, eds. *Ireland's Women: Writing Past and Present*. Dublin: Gill and Macmillan, 1994.

Dorcey, Mary. 'The Spaces Between the Words.' *Women's Review of Books* 8:3 (December 1990): 21.

Downing, Christine. *Psyche's Sisters: Reclaiming the Meaning of Sisterhood*. New York: Harper & Row, 1988.

Dunleavy, Janet Egleson. 'Contemporary Irish Women Novelists.' *British and Irish Novels Since 1960.* Ed. James Acheson. Basingstoke: Macmillan, 1993.

Edge, Sara. 'Representing Gender and National Identity.' *Rethinking Northern Ireland.* Ed. D. Miller. London: Longman, 1998. 211-27.

Eichenbaum, Luise and Susie Orbach. *Understanding Women.* Harmondsworth, Middlesex: Penguin, 1983.

---. *Between Women.* New York: Viking Penguin Inc., 1987, 1988.

Eisler, Riane. *The Chalice and the Blade: Our History, Our Future.* London: Unwin, 1990.

Ellis, Peter Berresford. *A Dictionary of Irish Mythology.* Oxford: Oxford University Press, 1987.

---. *Celtic Women: Women in Celtic Society and Literature.* London: Constable, 1995.

Ellis, Sarah Stickney. *The Women of England: Their Social Duties and Domestic Habits.* New York: J. & H. G. Langley, 1843.

Ellman, Maud. *The Hunger Artists: Starving, Writing and Imprisonment.* London: Virago, 1993.

Elsbeth, Marguerite and Kenneth Johnson. *The Silver Wheel: Women's Myth and Mysteries in the Celtic Tradition.* St. Paul, Minnesota: Llewellyn Publications, 1997.

Ferguson, Mary Anne. Introduction. *Images of Women in Literature.* Ed. Mary Anne Ferguson. Boston: Houghton Mifflin, 1991. 1-16.

Firestone, Shulamith. *The Dialectic of Sex.* London: Jonathan Cape, 1971.

Fisher, Elizabeth. *Sisters.* New York: Bantam Books, 1979.

Fletcher, R. 'Silences: Irish Women and Abortion.' *Feminist Review* 50 (1995): 44-56.

Fogarty, Anne. 'The Ear of the Other: Dissident Voices in Kate O'Brien's As Music and Splendour and Mary Dorcey's A Noise from the Woodshed.' *Sex, Nation and Dissent in Irish Writing*. Ed. Éibhear Walshe. New York: St. Martin's Press, 1997. 170-201.

---. Preface. *Midwife to the Fairies*. By Éilís Ní Dhuibhne. Dublin: Attic Press, 2003. iv-xv.

Foster, Shirley. *Victorian Women's Fiction: Marriage, Freedom and the Individual*. London: Croom Helm, 1985.

Foucault, Michel. 'The Subject of Power.' *Michel Foucault: Beyond Structuralism and Hermeneutics*. Eds. Hubert L. Dreyfus and Paul Rabinow. Chicago: University of Chicago Press, 1982. 208-226.

Franz, Marie-Louise von. *An Introduction to the Interpretation of Fairy Tales*. Zürich, Switzerland: Spring Publications, 1973.

Freeman, Jane. *Feminism*. Buckingham: Open University Press, 2001.

Frye, Northrop. *The Critical Path: An Essay on the Social Context of Literary Criticism*. Bloomington, Indiana: Indiana University Press, 1971.

Fyfe, Anne-Marie. 'Women and Mother Ireland.' *Image and Power: Women in Fiction in the Twentieth Century*. Eds. Sarah Sceats and Gail Cunningham. London: Longman, 1996. 184-94.

Gallagher, S. F. *Woman in Irish Legend, Life and Literature*. Gerrards Cross: Colin Smythe, 1983.

Gilbert, Sandra M. and Susan Gubar. *The Madwoman in the Attic*. New Haven: Yale University Press, 1979.

---. 'Editors' Introduction, Shakespeare's Sisters: Feminist Essays on Women Poets.' *Feminist Literary Theory: A Reader*. Ed. Mary Eagleton. Oxford: Blackwell Publishing, 1986. 174-80.

Graham, Amanda. 'The Lovely Substance of the Mother: Food, Gender and Nation in the Work of Edna O'Brien.' *Irish Studies Review* No.15 (Summer 1996): 16-20.

Grand, Sarah. 'The New Aspect of the Woman Question.' *Northern American Review* Vol. 58 (1894).

Gray, John. *Men Are from Mars and Women Are from Venus*. New York: Harper-Collins, 1992.

Green, Miranda J., ed. *Dictionary of Celtic Myth and Legend*. London: Thames & Hudson, 1992.

Greg, W. R. 'False Morality of Lady Novelists.' *National Review* Vol.VIII (January 1859): 148.

Gubar, Susan. 'Feminist Misogyny: Mary Wollstonecraft and the Paradox of "It Takes One to Know One."' *Feminist Studies* Vol. 21 No. 3 (Fall 1994): 453-74.

Guerin, Wilfred L, Earle Labor, Lee Horgan, Jeanne C. Reesman, John R. Willingham, eds. *A Handbook of Critical Approaches to Literature*. Third Edition. New York: Oxford University Press, 1992.

Guralnik, D. B., ed. *The Webster's New World Dictionary of the American Language*. Cleveland: William Collins World Publishing Co., 1974.

Hall, Nor. *The Moon and the Virgin, Reflections on the Archetypal Female*. New York: Harper & Row, 1980.

Halpin, Bernadette. *Store of My Heart: Contemporary Irish Short Stories*. London: The Sheba Feminist, 1991.

Hamilton, Edith. *Mythology*. Boston: Little Brown & Company, 1998.

Harding, Mary E. *Women's Mysteries: Ancient and Modern*. New York: Harper & Row, 1971.

Harrison, Jane Ellen. *Prolegomena to the Study of Greek Religion.* New York: Meridian, 1966.

Haskell, M. 'Paying Homage to the Spinster.' *New York Times* Magazine 8 May 1988. 18-20.

Hayes, Trudy. 'The Politics of Seduction.' *A Dozen Lips.* Dublin: Attic Press, 1994. 117-39.

Heaney, Seamus. *Preoccupations: Selected Prose 1968-1978.* London: Faber & Faber, 1980.

Herbert, Máire. 'Celtic Heroine? The Archaeology of the Deirdre Story.' *Gender in Irish Writing.* Eds. Toni O'Brien Johnson and David Cairns. Milton Keynes: Open University Press, 1991. 13-22.

Herman, Nina. *Too Long a Child: The Mother-Daughter Dyad.* London: Free Association Press, 1989.

Hirsch, M. *The Mother/Daughter Plot: Narrative, Psychoanalysis, Feminism.* Bloomington, Indiana: Indiana University Press, 1989.

Hogan, Robert. *Dictionary of Irish Literature.* 2 Vols. Westport, Conn.: Greenwood, 1996.

Hussey, Gemma. *Ireland Today.* London: Townhouse, 1993.

Hutton, R. H. *The Relative Value of Studies and Accomplishments in the Education of Women.* London, 1862.

ICCL. *Equality Now for Lesbians and Gay Men.* Dublin: Irish Council for Civil Liberties, 1990.

Innes, C. L. *Women and Nation in Irish Literature and Society, 1880-1935.* London: Harvester Wheatsheaf, 1993.

Irigaray, Luce. 'And the One Doesn't Stir Without the Other.' *Signs* 7/1 (1982): 60-7.

---. 'Female Hom(m)osexuality.' *Speculum of the Other Woman*. Trans. Gillian Gill. Ithaca, New York: Cornell University Press, 1985.

---. *The Sex Which Is Not One*. Ithaca, New York: Cornell University Press, 1985.

---. 'Women-Mothers, the Silent Substratum of the Social Order.' *The Irigaray Reader*. Ed. Margaret Whitford. Oxford: Blackwell, 1991. 47-52.

Janeway, Elizabeth. *Man's World, Woman's Place: A Study in Social Mythology*. New York: William Morrow & Co., 1975.

Joseph, Gloria I. And Jill Lewis. *Common Differences: Conflicts in Black and White Feminist Perspectives*. Boston, MA: South End Press, 1986.

Jung, C. G. *The Collected Works of C. G. Jung*. Vol. IX. Part 1 and Vol. XVII. London: Routledge & Kegan Paul, 1969.

---. *Four Archetypes: Mother, Rebirth, Spirit, Trickster*. London: Routledge & Kegan Paul, 1972.

Jung, Emma and Marie-Louise von Franz. *The Grail Legend*. Boston: Sigo Press, 1972, 1986.

Kaplan, E. Ann. *Motherhood and Representation*. London: Routledge, 1992.

Kearney, Richard. *Myth and Motherland*. Belfast: Dorman, 1984.

Kelly, A. A. *Mary Lavin: Quiet Rebel*. Dublin: Wolfhound Press, 1980.

Kiberd, Declan. 'Storytelling: The Gaelic Tradition.' *The Irish Short Story*. Eds. Patrick Rafroidi and Terence Brown. London: Smythe, 1979. 42-51.

Kilroy, James F., ed. *The Irish Short Stories: A Critical History*. Boston, Mass: Twayne, 1984.

King, F. 'Spinsterhood is Powerful.' *National Review* 45/14 (19 July 1993): 72.

Kirkpatrick, D. L, ed. *Contemporary Novelists*. New York: St. Martin's Press, 1986.

Lakoff, Robin. *Language and Women's Place*. New York: Harper & Row, 1973, 1975.

Lao Tze (老子). *Tao Te Ching* (道德經). Trans. Stephen Mitchell. New York: Harper & Row, 1988.

Larrington, Carolyne, ed. *The Feminist Companion to Mythology*. London: Pandora, 1992.

Lasser, Carol. '"Let Us Be Sisters Forever": The Sororal Model of Nineteenth-Century Female Friendship.' *Signs* 14 (1988): 158-81.

Lauter, Estella and Carol Rupprecht, eds. *Feminist Archetypal Theory: Interdisciplinary Re-Visions of Jungian Thought*. Knoxville: The University of Tennessee Press, 1985.

Lawrence, Margaret. 'Matriarchs.' *The School of Femininity*. Toronto: Musson Books, 1972.

Leonard, Madeleine. 'Rape: Myths and Reality.' *Women's Studies Reader*. Ed. Ailbhe Smyth. Dublin: Attic Press, 1993. 107-21.

Levin, Amy K. *The Suppressed Sister: A Relationship in Novels by Nineteenth- and Twentieth-Century British Women*. London: Associated University Press, 1992.

Longley, Edna. 'Belfast Diary.' *London Review of Books* 9 January 1992: 21.

---. 'From Cathleen to Anorexia: The Breakdown of Irelands.' *A Dozen Lips*. Dublin: Attic Press, 1994. 162-87.

Lorde, Audre. *Sister Outsider: Essays and Speeches*. New York: Crossing Press, 1984.

Lysaght, Patricia. *The Banshee: The Supernatural Death Messenger*. Dublin: Glendale Press, 1986.

Mac Cana, Proinsias. 'Aspects of the Theme of King and Goddess in Irish Literature.' *Études Celtiques* 7 (1955-56) 76-13; 357-413; 8 (1958-59): 59-65.

---. 'Women in Irish Mythology.' *The Crane Bag* Vol.4 No.1 (1980): 7-11.

Macey, David. *The Penguin Dictionary of Critical Theory*. London: Penguin, 2000.

MacKillop, James, ed. *Dictionary of Celtic Mythology*. Oxford: Oxford University Press, 1998.

MacMahon, Sean. Rev. of 'Concerning Virgins,' by Clare Boylan. *Linen Hall Review* (Summer 1990): 33.

Madden-Simpson, Janet. Introduction. *Women's Part: An Anthology of Short Fiction by and About Irish Women 1890-1960*. Dublin: Arlen House, 1984.

Madsen, Deborah L. *Feminist Theory and Literary Practice*. London: Pluto Press, 2000.

Marcus, David, ed. *State of the Art: Short Stories by New Irish Writers*. London: Sceptre, 1992.

Martin, Augustine. 'A Skeleton Key to the Stories of Mary Lavin.' *Studies* No.52 (Winter 1963): 292-406.

Martin, Máirín. Rev. of 'That Bad Woman,' by Clare Boylan. *Books Ireland* (Nov. 1995): 291.

Matthews, John and Caitlin, eds. *Encyclopedia of British and Irish Mythology*. London: Diamond Books, 1995.

McCafferty, Nell. *A Woman to Blame: The Kerry Babies Case*. Dublin: Attic Press, 1984.

McCurtain, Margaret and Donncha Ó Corráin, eds. *Women in Irish Society: The Historical Dimension*. Dublin: Arlen House, 2000.

McNaron, Toni. 'How Little We Know and How Much We Feel.' *The Sister Bond*. Ed. Toni McNaron. New York: Pergamon, 1985. 1-10.

McRemond, Louis, ed. *Modern Irish Lives: Dictionary of Twentieth-Century Irish Biography*. Dublin: Gill & Macmillan, 1998.

Mead, Margaret. *Male and Female: A Study of the Sexes in a Changing World*. Harmondsworth, Middlesex: Penguin, 1962.

Moi, Toril. 'Feminist, Female, Feminine.' *The Feminist Reader: Essays in Gender and the Politics of Literary Criticism*. Eds, Catherine Belsey and Jane Moore. Basingstoke: Macmillan, 1989. 104-16.

Momaday, N. Scott. *The Way to Rainy Mountain*. Albuquerque: University of New Mexico Press, 1969.

Moody, T. W. and F.X. Martin, eds. *The Course of Irish History*. Cork: Mercier Press, 1994.

Morgan, Robin. *Sisterhood is Powerful*. New York: Random House, 1970.

---. *Sisterhood is Global*. Garden City, New York: Anchor Press/Doubleday, 1984.

Mullett, G. M. *Spider Woman Stories: Legends of the Hopi Indians*. Tucson: University of Arizona Press, 1979.

Murpy, Catherine A. 'The Ironic Vision of Mary Lavin.' *Mosaic* 12.3 (Spring 1979): 69-79.

Murray, James A. H., Henry Bradley, W. A. Craigie and C. T. Onions. *The Oxford English Dictionary*. Vol. I. Oxford: Clarendon Press, 1933, 1961, 1978.

Neumann, Erich. *The Great Mother: An Analysis of the Archetype*. Trans. Ralph Manheim. Princeton: Princeton University Press, 1963.

---. *Amor and Psyche: The Psychic Development of the Feminine. A Commentary on the Tale by Apuleius*. Trans. Ralph Manheim. Bollingen Series, 54. Princeton: Princeton University Press, 1971.

Ní Bhrolcháin Muireann. 'Women in Early Irish Myths and Sagas.' *The Crane Bag* Vol.4 No.1 (1980): 12-9.

Ní Chuilleanáin, Eiléan. *Irish Women: Image and Achievement, Women in Irish Culture from Earliest Times*. Basingstoke: Macmillan Education, 1986.

Nice, Vivien E. *Mothers and Daughters: The Distortion of a Relationship*. London: Macmillan, 1992.

Ní Dhuibhne, Éilís. 'Introduction to International Folktales.' The *Field Day Anthology of Irish Writing. Eds. Angela Bourke, et al. Vol. IV. Cork: Cork University* Press, 2002. 1214-18.

Ó Céirin, Kit and Cyril Ó Céirin, eds. *Women of Ireland: A Biographic Dictionary*. Galway: Tír Eolas, 1996.

Ó hÓgáin, Dáithí. Myth, *Legend and Romance: An Encyclopedia of the Irish Folk Tradition*. London: Ryan, 1990.

O'Brien, Máire Cruise. 'The Female Principle in Gaelic Poetry.' *Women in Irish Legend, Life and Literature*. Ed. S. F. Gallagher. Gerrards Cross: Colin Smythe, 1983. 26-37.

O'Brien, Patricia. *The Woman Alone*. New York: Quadrangle/The New York Times Book Company, 1973.

O'Brien, Peggy. 'The Silly and the Serious: An Assessment of Edna O'Brien.' *Massachusetts Review* 28, 3 (Autumn 1987): 474-88.

O'Brien, Toni and David Cairns, eds. Gender in Irish Writing. Buckingham: Open University Press, 1991.

O'Carroll, Ide and Eoin Collins, eds. *Lesbian and Gay Visions of Ireland: Toward the Twentieth-First Century.* London: Cassell, 1995.

---. 'Interview with Mary Dorcey.' *Lesbian and Gay Visions of Ireland: Toward the Twentieth-First Century.* Eds. Ide O'Carroll and Eoin Collins. London: Cassell, 1995. 25-44.

O'Connor, Anne. 'Images of the Evil Woman in Irish Folklore: A Preliminary Survey.' *Women's Studies International Forum* 11 No.4 (1988): 281-5.

O'Connor, Frank. *The Lonely Voice.* London: Macmillan, 1963.

O'Connor, Pat. *Emerging Voice: Women in Contemporary Irish Society.* Dublin: The Institute of Public Administration, 2001.

O'Hara, Kiera. 'Love Objects: Love and Obsession in the Stories of Edna O'Brien.' *Studies in Short Fiction* 30.3 (Summer 1993): 317-25.

O'Leary, Philip and Rebecca Tracy. 'Two Views.' *Irish Literary Supplement* (Fall 1996): 8.

Oakley, Ann. *Sex, Gender and Society.* London: Temple Smith, 1972.

Onions, C. T., ed. *The Oxford Dictionary of English Etymology.* Oxford: Clarendon Press, 1933, 1966.

Onlywomen, eds. *Love Your Enemy? The Debate Between Heterosexual Feminism and Political Lesbianism.* London: Onlywomen Press, 1981.

Oyewumi, Oyeronke. *The Invention of Women: Making an African Sense of Western Gender Discourses.* Minneapolis: University of Minnesota Press, 1997.

Park, C. and C. Heaton, eds. *Close Company: Stories of Mothers and Daughters.* London: Virago, 1987.

Peach, L. J. *Women in Culture: A Women's Studies Anthology.* Oxford: Blackwell Publishers Ltd, 1998.

Pearsall, Judy, ed. *The New Oxford Dictionary of English*. Oxford: Clarendon Press, 1998.

Phelps, Ethel Johnston. *The Maid of the North and Other Folktale Heroines*. New York: Holt, Rinehart & Winston, 1981.

Pratt, Annis, et al. *Archetypal Patterns in Women Fiction*. Brighton: Harvester, 1982.

Pratt, Annis. 'Spinning Among Fields: Jung, Frye, Levi-Strauss.' *Feminist Archetypal Theory*. Knoxville: The University of Tennessee Press, 1985. 93-136.

Rafroidi, Patrick and Maurice Harmon, eds. *The Irish Novel in Our Time*. Lille: L'universite de Lille, 1975.

Rafroidi, Patrick and Terence Brown. *The Irish Short Story*. Gerrards Cross: Colin Smythe, 1979.

Reingold, Joseph C, M.D. PhD. *The Fear of Being a Woman: A Theory of Maternal Destructiveness*. New York and London: Grune & Stratton, 1964.

Reynolds, Lorna. 'Irish Women in Legend, Literature and Life.' *Women in Irish Legend, Life and Literature*. Ed. S. F. Gallagher. Gerrards Cross: Colin Smythe, 1983. 11-25.

Rich, Adrienne. *Of Woman Born: Motherhood as Experience and Institution*. New York: Norton, 1976.

---. 'Compulsory Heterosexuality and Lesbian Existence.' *Feminisms: A Reader*. Ed. Maggie Humm. London: Harvester Wheatsheaf, 1992. 176-80.

Ricoeur, Paul. 'The Metaphorical Process as Cognition, Imagination, and Feeling.' *On Metaphor*. Ed. Alan Bass. Chicago: University of Chicago Press, 1982. 141-57.

Roiphe, Katie. *The Morning After: Sex, Fear, and, Feminism on Campus.* Boston: Little, Brown & Co., 1993.

Rose, Kieran. *Diverse Communities: the Evolution of Lesbian and Gay Politics in Ireland.* Cork: Cork University Press, 1994.

Rosinsky, Natalie M. 'Mothers and Daughters: Another Minority Group.' *The Lost Tradition: Mothers and Daughters in Literature.* Eds. Cathy N. Davidson and E. M. Broner. New York: Frederick Ungar Publishing Co., 1980. 280-90.

Ruddick, S. 'Maternal Thinking.' *Feminist Studies* 6.2 (Summer 1980): 343-57.

Ruiséal, Máire. 'Scéal an Ghabhairín Bháin' ('The Story of the Little White Goat'). *The Field Day Anthology of Irish Writing.* Eds. Angela Bourke, et al. Vol. IV. Cork: Cork University Press, 2002. 1226-32.

Sands, Donald, ed. *Middle English Verse Romances.* New York: Holt, Rinehart & Winston, 1966.

Sayers, Peig. 'An Caitín Gearr Glas' ('The Little Grey Cat'). *The Field Day Anthology of Irish Writing.* Eds. Angela Bourke, et al. Vol. IV. Cork: Cork University Press, 2002. 1253-61.

Sherif, Carolyn W. 'Needed Concepts in the Study of Gender Identity.' *Psychology of Women Quarterly* Vol. 6 (1982): 375-95.

Showalter, Elaine. *A Literature of Their Own.* London: Virago, 1982.

---. *The New Feminist Criticism.* London: Virago, 1992.

---. *Sister's Choice: Tradition and Change in American Women's Writing.* Oxford: Oxford University Press, 1994.

Smyth, Ailbhe, ed. 'The Contemporary Women's Movement in the Republic of Ireland.' *Women's Studies International Forum* 11.4 (1988): 331-41.

---. Introduction. *Wildish Things: An Anthology of New Irish Women's Writing.* Ed. A. Smyth. Dublin: Attic Press, 1989.

---. *The Abortion Papers.* Dublin: Attic Press, 1992.

---. 'The Women's Movement in the Republic of Ireland 1970-1990.' *Irish Women's Studies Reader.* Ed. Ailbhe Smyth. Dublin: Attic Press, 1993. 245-69.

Smyth, Gerry. *The Novel and the Nation.* London: Pluto, 1997.

Snitow, Ann. 'A Gender Diary.' *Conflicts in Feminism.* Eds. Marianne Hirsch and Evelyn Fox Keller. New York: Routledge, 1990. 505-46.

Somerville-Arjat, Gillean and Rebecca E. Wilson, eds. *Sleeping with Monsters.* Dublin: Wolfhound Press, 1990.

Spence, Lewis. *Ancient Egyptian Myths and Legends.* New York: Dover Publications, 1915, 1990.

St. Peter, Christine. *Changing Ireland: Strategies in Contemporary Women's Fiction.* Basingstoke: Macmillan, 2000.

---. 'Petrifying Time: Incest Narratives from Contemporary Ireland.' *Contemporary Irish Fiction: Themes, Tropes, Theories.* Eds. Liam Harte and Michael Parker. London: Macmillan, 2000. 135-44.

Staley, Thomas F, ed. *Twentieth-Century Women Novelists.* Totowa, New Jersey: Barnes & Noble, 1982.

Stevens, Anthony. *Archetype: A Natural History of the Self.* London: Routledge & Kegan Paul, 1982.

Stevens, Lorna, Stephen Brown and Pauline MacLaran. 'Gender, Nationality and Cultural Representations of Ireland.' *The European Journal of Women's Studies* 7.4 (2000): 405-422.

Stokes, Patrick. 'The Man Who Married the Mermaid.' *The Field Day Anthology of Irish Writing.* Eds. Angela Bourke, et al. Vol. IV. Cork: Cork University Press, 2002. 1280-1.

Strong, Eithne. *Flesh—the Greatest Sin.* Dublin: Attic Press, 1993.

Sullivan, Megan. 'Mary Beckett: An Interview.' Vol. 14 No.2 *Irish Literary Supplement* (Fall 1995): 10-12.

Sweetman, Rosita. *On Our Backs: Sexual Attitudes in a Changing Ireland.* London: Pan, 1979.

Thompson, Richard J. *Everlasting Voices: Aspects of the Modern Irish Short Story.* Troy, New York: Whitston, 1989.

Tóibín, Colm. *Martyrs and Metaphors: Letters from the New Island.* Dublin: The Raven Arts Press, 1987.

Uí Shighil, Anna. 'Ní Mhaol Dhonn, Ní Mhaol Fhionn, Agus Ní Mhaol Charach' (Miss Brown, Miss Blonde, And Miss Pleasant). *The Field Day Anthology of Irish Writing.* Eds. Angela Bourke, et al. Vol. IV. Cork: Cork University Press, 2002. 1247-52.

Valiulis, M. G. and M. O'Dowd, eds. *Women and Irish History.* Dublin: Wolfhound Press, 1997.

VanEvery, Jo. 'Heterosexuality and Domestic Life.' *Theorising Heterosexuality: Telling It Straight.* Ed. Diane Richardson. Philadelphia, P.A.: Open University Press, 1996. 39-54.

Viney, Ethna. 'Ancient Wars: Sex and Sexuality.' *A Dozen Lips.* Dublin: Attic Press, 1994. 45-71.

Ward, Margaret. 'The Missing Sex: Putting Women Into Irish History.' *A Dozen Lips.* Dublin: Attic Press, 1994. 205-224.

Warner, Marina. *Alone of All Her Sex: the Myth and the Cult of the Virgin Mary.* London: Vintage Press, 1983.

---. 'Monstrous Mothers: Women Over the Top,' *Managing Monsters: Six Myths of Our Time*. The 1994 Reith Lectures. London: Vintage Press, 1994. 1-16.

Waters, Frank. *Book of the Hopi*. New York: Viking Press, 1963.

Weekes, Ann Owens. *Irish Women Writers: An Uncharted Tradition*. Kentucky: The University of Kentucky, 1990.

---. *Unveiling Treasures: the Attic Guide to the Published Works of Irish Women Literary Writers*. Dublin: Attic Press, 1993.

---. 'Figuring the Mother in Contemporary Irish Fiction.' *Contemporary Irish Fiction: Themes, Tropes, Theories*. Eds. Liam Harte and Michael Parker. London: Macmillan, 2000. 100-23.

Weekley, Ernest. *An Etymological Dictionary of Modern English*. London: John Murray, 1921.

Wehr, Demaris S. *Jung and Feminism*. London: Routledge, 1988.

Weigle, Marta. *Spiders and Spinsters: Women and Mythology*. Albuquerque: University of New Mexico Press, 1982.

Welch, Robert, ed. *The Oxford Companion to Irish Literature*. Oxford and New York: Clarendon Press, 1996.

Westermarck, Edward. *A Short History of Marriage*. London: Macmillan, 1926.

White, Robert W. *The Enterprise of Living*. Second Edition. New York: Holt, Rinehart & Winston, 1976.

Wilde, Lyn Webster. *Celtic Women in Legend, Myth and History*. London: Cassell PLC, 1997.

Williams, Julia McElhattan. 'This Is (Not) a Canon: Staking out the Tradition in Recent Anthologies of Irish Writing,' 'Irish Women's Voices: Past and

Present.' Eds. Joan Hoff and Maureen Coulter. *Journal of Women's History* Vol.6 No.4 and Vol.7 No.1 (Winter/Spring 1995): 227-235.

Wittig, Monique. 'The Category of Sex.' *Sex In Question: French Materialist Feminism?* Eds. D. Leonard and L. Adkins. London: Taylor & Francis, 1996.

Wollstonecraft, Mary. *A Vindication of the Rights of Woman.* Ed. Charles W. Hagelman, Jr. New York: W. W. Norton & Co., 1967.

---. *A Vindication of the Rights of Woman: An Authoritative Text, Backgrounds, the Wollstonecraft Debate, Criticism.* Ed. Carol H. Poston. New York: Norton Critical Edition, 1972, 1988.

Women in Publishing. 'Reviewing the Reviews: A Woman's Place on the Book Page.' *Feminist Literary Theory: A Reader.* Second Edition. Ed. Mary Eagleton. Oxford: Blackwell Publishing, 1996. 100-3.

Woolf, Virginia. *A Room of One's Own.* London: Granada Publishing, 1977.

---. *Women and Writing.* London: The Women's Press, 1979.

Wright, Elizabeth. *Feminism and Psychoanalysis: A Critical Dictionary.* Oxford: Basil Blackwell, 1992.

Yalom, Marilyn. *A History of the Wife.* London: Pandora, 2001.

Young-Eisendrath, Polly. *Hags and Heroes.* Toronto, Canada: Inner City Books, 1984.

---. *Women and Desire.* London: Judy Piatkus Books, 2000.

Young-Eisendrath, Polly and Terence Dawson, eds. *The Cambridge Companion to Jung.* Cambridge: Cambridge University Press, 1997.

III. Electronic Sources

'Irish Abortion Referendum "Flawed."' BBC News. Online. 1 March 2002.
  Internet. 1 March 2006. Available http://news.bbc.co.uk/1/hi/northern_
  ireland/1846778.stm

'Irish Abortion: Your Reaction to the Referendum Result?' BBC News.
  Online. 11 March 2002. Internet. 1 March 2006. Available http://news.
  bbc.co.uk/1/hi/talking_point/

'Mother Cleared of Killing Sons.' BBC News. Online. 10 December 2003.
  Internet. 30 November 2005. Available http://news.bbc.co.uk/1/hi/
  england/wiltshire/3306271.stm1849624.stm

Aristotle. *On the Generation of Animals.* Book I. Trans. Arthur Platt. The
  University of Adelaide Library E-text Collection, 2004. Online. The
  University of Adelaide. Internet. 24 June 2004. Available http://etext.
  library.adelaide.edu.au/a/a8ga

Ashliman, D. L, trans and ed. 'Cupid and Psyche.' Folklore and Mythology
  Electronic Texts, 23 January 2001. Online. The University of Pittsburgh.
  Internet. 3 August 2019. Available http://www.pitt.edu/~dash/cupid.html

Bunreacht Na hÉireann (Constitution of Ireland). Department of The
  Taoiseach (Roinn an Taoisigh). Online. Internet. 29 July 2020. Available
  http://www.taoiseach.gov.ie/ attached_ files/html%20files/Constitution%
  20of%20 Ire-land%20(Eng).htm

Encyclopaedia Britannica Online. Online. The University of Ulster Library.
  Internet. 31 July 2005. Available http://search.eb.com (Athens Access
  only)

Lau, Beth. 'Wollstonecraft's Daughters: Womanhood in England and France,
  1780-1920,' Wayne State University Press (Summer 1998): n. pag.

Online. Internet. 19 January 2020. Available http://www.findarticles.
com/p/articles/mim222 0/is_ n3_v4 0/ai_ 21182136

Local Ireland. Online. 8 November 2001. Available: www.local.ie/
content/11400.

Oyewumi, Oyeronke. 'Ties That (Un)bind: Feminism, Sisterhood and Other
Foreign Relations.' *Jrnfs: A Journal of Cultural and African Women
Studies* 1.1 (2001): n. pag. Online. Internet. 7 April 2005. Available
http://www.jendajournal.com/vol1.1/oyewumi.html

Rose, Kieran. 'Equality for Lesbians and Gay Men.' *ILGA Europe* (June
1998): n. pag. Online. Internet. 25 March 2002. Available http://www.
steff.suite.dk/report.htm

Ruta, Suzanne. 'The Luck of the Irish.' Rev. of The Inland Ice. By Éilís Ní
Dhuibhne. *New York Times.* 21 December 1997: New York Times
Online. Online. 16 April 2002. Available http://www.nytimes.com

Sheehan, Catherine. Rev. of *A Dream Woke Me and Other Stories.* By Marilyn
McLaughlin.shtml/Literature/books/fiction/

Shumaker, Jeanette Roberts. 'Sacrificial Women in Short Stories by Mary
Lavin and Edna O'Brien.' *Studies in Short Fiction* (Spring 1995): n. pag.
Online. Internet. 1 January 2020. Available http://www.findarticles.com/
p/articles/msi_m245 5/ is_n2_v32/ai_17268505

The Irish Statute Book 1922-2003. The Office of the Attorney General and
Houses of the Oireachtas. *The Stationery Office.* Online. Internet. 9
March 2021. Available http:// www.irishstatutebook.ie/

Endnotes

1　Many Irish female writers work or have worked in journalism such as
Clare Boylan, Mary Leland (the Cork Examiner, the Irish Times),
Margaret Dolan, Janet McNeill (the Belfast Telegraph), Mary Morrissy
(the Irish Times). Maeve Binchy also wrote columns and features for the
Irish Times. Some Irish women work for media broadcasts or drama on
television or radio such as Mary O'Donnell as a broadcaster, Marilyn
McLaughlin as a BBC Radio Foyle researcher, and Anne Enright as a TV
producer with Radio Telefís Éireann. Irish women's stories are also
frequently read and broadcasted on radio such as those by Fiona Barr,
Mary Beckett, Stella Mahon or Anne Devlin. Anne Devlin's story
'Passages' (from The Way-Paver, 1986) was adapted for television as A
Woman Calling on BBC2 Northern Ireland in April 1984.

2　Nevertheless, we should note that some heroines in Mary Lavin's and
Clare Boylan's stories also appear to be strong-willed survivors.

3　O'Connor (1963) 202.

4　C. L. Innes, *Women and Nation in Irish Literature and Society, 1880-
1935* (London: Harvester Wheatsheaf, 1993) 41.

5　For further details about the unequal treatment of Irish women in society
see Chapter 18 in Gemma Hussey, *Ireland Today* (Dublin: Townhouse,
1993) and Pat O'Connor, *Emerging Voices* (Dublin: Institute of Public
Administration, 1998).

6   See *Bunreacht Na hÉireann (Constitution of Ireland)*. Department of The
     Taoiseach (Roinn an Taoisigh). Online. Internet. 29 July 2005. Available
     http://www.taoiseach.gov.ie/attached   files/html%20files/Constitution%
     20of%20Ireland% 20(Eng).htm and Gemma Hussey, *Ireland Today*
     (Dublin: Townhouse, 1993) 419.

7   Stories in anthologies will be cited as the abbreviations of story collection
     titles with pagination in parenthesis in the text of this book. The
     information about stories in individual story collections mentioned in this
     book is provided in the Appendix. See the List of Abbreviations and the
     Appendix for details.

8   Northrop Frye, *The Critical Path: An Essay on the Social Context of
     Literary Criticism* (Bloomington, Indiana: Indiana University Press, 1971)
     24-25.

9   Peter Barry, *Beginning Theory: An Introduction to Literary and Cultural
     Theory* (Manchester: Manchester University Press, 1995, 2002) 124.

10   Judy Pearsall, ed, *The New Oxford Dictionary of English* (Oxford:
     Clarenden Press, 1998).

11   For further information see Carl Jung, *The Collected Works of C. G. Jung*,
     vol. 9.1 (Princeton: Princeton University Press, 1969).

12   C. G. Jung, *Four Archetypes* (London: Routledge & Kegan Paul, 1972) 12.

13   Ibid 14.

14   Whereas there may be some similarities among different cultures, and
     Jung does not mean the actual content of archetypes is fixed, his
     assumption of 'universality' in human culture may incur some problems
     for rethinking as it may apply a generalisation across individuals of
     different races, cultures or gender.

[15] Indeed, Jung tends to be incoherent in making his attributions of anima and animus and sometimes he confuses 'anima' with real women although he also suggests the complimentary qualities of *Yin* and *Yang* as analogous to the harmonious relationship between anima and animus and the concept of 'androgyny,' which has allowed later theorists scope to reconsider gender qualities and the process of constructing gender identity.

[16] Christine Downing, *Psyche's Sisters: ReImagining the Meaning of Sisterhood* (New York: Harper & Row, 1988) 131-2.

[17] Estella Lauter and Carol Schreier Rupprecht, eds, *Feminist Archetypal Theory* (Knoxville: The University of Tennessee Press, 1985) 11.

[18] Ibid 16.

[19] Hussey 423.

[20] For more see Hussey (1993) 422-6 and Ailbhe Smyth, 'The Women's Movement in the Republic of Ireland 1970-1990,' ed, Ailbhe Smyth, *Women's Studies Reader* (Dublin: Attic Press, 1993) 264-6.

[21] Smyth (1993) 266.

[22] Ailbhe Smyth, introduction, *Wildish Things* (Dublin: Attic Press, 1989) 7.

[23] This collection has been reprinted in the USA under a new title as *A Green and Mortal Sound: Short Fiction by Irish Women Writers* (Boston: Beacon Press, 1999, 2000) with a new introduction and bibliographic references.

[24] Unfortunately, this collection is out of print and is unavailable on the market or from the collection of the British Library. The author regretfully could not consult this collection due to the unavailability of the source.

[25] This collection was published in the USA under a different title as *In Sunshine or in Shadow* (New York: Dell Publishing, 1998, 1999).

[26] Dermot Bolger, introduction, *The New Picador Book of Contemporary Irish Fiction* (London: Picador, 2000) xxvii.

27 Mills and Boon is a publisher founded by Gerald Mills and Charles Boon in London in 1908. It is one of several well-known publishers (such as Harlequin Enterprises in the USA and Canada) to publish popular romance novels. They sell in numerous languages worldwide.

28 Elaine Showalter, *A Literature of Their Own* (London: Virago, 1982) 82.

29 Ibid.

30 Ibid 77.

31 R. H. Hutton, *The Relative Value of Studies and Accomplishments in the Education of Women* (London, 1862) 20. Here qtd. in Shirley Foster, *Victorian Women's Fiction: Marriage, Freedom and the Individual* (London: Croom Helm, 1985) 2.

32 Ibid.

33 Walter Bagehot, 'The Waverly Novels' *Literary Studies*, ed. R. H. Hutton, 4th ed., Vol. II. (1891): 148. Here qtd. in Foster 1. See also W. R. Greg, 'False Morality of Lady Novelists' *National Review*, Vol. VIII (January 1859) for further information.

34 Showalter (1982) 73-99.

35 Julia McElhattan Williams, 'This Is (Not) a Canon: Staking out the Tradition in Recent Anthologies of Irish Writing,' 'Irish Women's Voices: Past and Present,' Joan Hoff and Maureen Coulter, eds, *Journal of Women's History* Vol.6 No.4 and Vol.7 No.1 (Winter/Spring 1995): 229.

36 Edna Longley, 'Belfast Diary,' *London Review of Books* 9 January 1992: 21. Here qtd. in Williams 230.

37 Ibid.

38 Ros Coward, '"This Novel Changes Lives": Are Women's Novels Feminist Novels? A Response to Rebecca O'Rourke's Article "Summer

Reading,'" *Feminism: A Reader*, ed, Maggie Humm, (London: Harvester Wheatsheaf, 1992) 378.

39 Jo VanEvery, 'Heterosexuality and Domestic Life,' *Theorising Heterosexuality: Telling It Straight*, ed. Diane Richardson (Philadelphia, PA: Open University Press, 1996) 40. See also Adrienne Rich, 'Compulsory Heterosexuality and Lesbian Existence,' *Feminisms: A Reader,* ed, Maggie Humm (London: Harvester Wheatsheaf, 1992) and Trudy Hayes, 'The Politics of Seduction,' *A Dozen Lips* (Dublin: Attic Press, 1994).

40 Edward Westermarck, *A Short History of Marriage* (London: Macmillan, 1926) 1.

41 Ibid.

42 Ibid 2.

43 For example, John Gray's *Men Are from Mars and Women Are from Venus* (New York: Harper-Collins, 1992) attempts to reinforce certain gender stereotypes in couple counselling in the area of popular psychology.

44 Nancy Chodorow, *The Reproduction of Mothering* (Berkeley: University of California Press, 1978) 14.

45 Mona Caird, 'Marriage,' *Westminster Review* (August, 1888). Here qtd. in Marilyn Yalom, *A History of the Wife* (London: Pandora, 2001) 268.

46 See Luce Irigaray, *The Sex Which Is Not One* (Ithaca, New York: Cornell University, 1985).

47 Boada-Montagut's book provides a concise history of the origin of the marriage institution as well as a discussion of the economic, social, sexual exploitation on women in marriage. See Irene Boada-Montagut, *Women*

Write Back: Contemporary Irish and Catalan Short Stories in Colonial Context (Dublin: Irish Academic Press, 2003) 46-81.

48 Ibid 47.

49 Yalom 175.

50 Ibid.

51 See Jenni Calder, *Women and Marriage in Victorian Fiction* (London: Thames & Hudson, 1976) and Shirley Foster, *Victorian Women's Fiction: Marriage, Freedom and the Individual* (1985).

52 Ti-Grace Atkinson, *Amazon Odyssey* (New York: Links Books, 1974) 43.

53 Ibid.

54 Rich 176.

55 Hayes 125.

56 Sarah Grand, 'The New Aspect of the Woman Question,' *Northern American Review* Vol.58 (1894): xxx.

57 Yalom 268.

58 See Chapter 20 in Aristotle, *On the Generation of Animals*, Book I, trans, Arthur Platt, 2004, The University of Adelaide Library E-text Collection, online, The University of Adelaide, internet, 24 June 2004, available http://etext.library.adelaide.edu.au/a/a8ga

59 Joseph C. Reingold, M.D. PhD., *The Fear of Being a Woman: A Theory of Maternal Destructiveness* (New York and London: Grune & Stratton, 1964) 421-2.

60 The title of this story was mistakenly printed as 'A Bona Fide Husband' in the Irish women's story anthology *Cutting the Night in Two*, eds, Evelyn Conlon and Hans-Christian Oeser (Dublin: New Island, 2001) 63-74.

61 Young-Eisendrath (1984) 100. Young-Eisendrath uses the medieval story of Sir Gawain and Lady Ragnell to illustrate her theory of the two

polarities of 'feminine beauty,' which are symbolised as 'hag' or 'maiden' in the Gawain story. There are various versions of Gawain/Ragnell story, and here Young-Eisendrath uses the version retold in Ethel Johnston Phelps, *The Maid of the North and Other Folktale Heroines* (New York: Holt, Rinehart & Winston, 1981). See also the original medieval version for cross-reference in Donald Sands, ed, *Middle English Verse Romances* (New York: Holt, Rinehart & Winston, 1966).

62   Young-Eisendrath (1984) 101.

63   Virginia Woolf, *A Room of One's Own* (London: Granada Publishing, 1977) 35.

64   See Clodagh Corcoran, 'Pornography: The New Terrorism' (1989), Ethna Viney, 'Ancient Wars: Sex and Sexuality' (1989) and Trudy Hayes, 'The Politics of Seduction' (1990). These three articles are all collected in *A Dozen Lips* (1994).

65   For more see Simone de Beauvoir, *The Second Sex*, trans. H. M. Parshley (Harmondsworth, Middlesex, Penguin, 1949).

66   Young-Eisendrath (2000) 4.

67   Ibid 14.

68   See Chapter 6, *A Room of One's Own* (1977) 91-108.

69   Young-Eisendrath (2000) 2.

70   A. A. Kelly, *Mary Lavin: Quiet Rebel* (Dublin: Wolfhound Press, 1980) 64.

71   This story was first published in *Wildish Things: An Anthology of New Irish Women's Writing*, ed, Ailbhe Smyth (1989), 145-55. Éilís Ní Dhuibhne has edited and rewritten this story, 'The Wife of Bath,' in her published story collections *Eating Women Is Not Recommended* (1991) and *Midwife to the Fairies: New and Selected Stories* (2003), which is completely different from the original version of 1989. Here the citation

is quoted from the original version of 'The Wife of Bath' from *Wildish Things* (1989).

72   Hayes 118, 120.

73   Young-Eisendrath (2000) 55.

74   Ibid 3.

75   Kelly 72.

76   Boada-Montagut 51.

77   Here the term 'agency' refers to 'the role of the human actor as individual or group in directing or effectively intervening in the course of history.' For more information see Peter Brooker, *A Concise Glossary of Cultural Theory* (London: Arnold, 1999) 3-4.

78   There have been some problems and criticism revised by a feminist reading of Henry Miller's tales of sexual exploits in his novels. His famous works include *Tropic of Cancer* (1961), *Tropic of Capricorn* (1961) and *The Rosy Crucifixion: Sexus, Nexus, Plexus* (1965).

79   Boada-Montagut 77.

80   From their origins in Germany in the 1890s, modern gay rights movements in the twentieth century have emerged worldwide since the 1960s. For more see Barry D. Adam, *The Rise of a Gay and Lesbian Movement* (Boston: Twayne Publishers, 1987) and Margaret Cruikshank, *The Gay and Lesbian Liberation Movement* (London: Routledge, 1992).

81   Anne Fogarty, 'The Ear of the Other: Dissident Voices in Kate O'Brien's *As Music and Splendour* and Mary Dorcey's *A Noise from the Woodshed*,' *Sex, Nation and Dissent in Irish Writing*, ed, Éibhear Walshe (New York: St. Martin's Press, 1997) 173.

82   Ibid.

83 Jeanette Roberts Shumaker, 'Sacrificial Women in Short Stories by Mary Lavin and Edna O'Brien,' *Studies in Short Fiction*, (Spring 1995): n. pag, online, internet, 15 September 2004, available http://www.findarticles.com/p/articles/

84 Shumaker, 'Sacrificial Women in Short Stories by Mary Lavin and Edna O'Brien,' internet, 15 September 2004.

85 Kiera O'Hara, 'Love Objects: Love and Obsession in the Stories of Edna O'Brien,' *Studies in Short Fiction* 30 (1993): 318-9.

86 Unlike Éilís Ní Dhuibhne's ambiguous and humorous tone portraying 'gender' in 'Bill's New Wife,' Mary O'Donnell in 'Strong Pagans' depicts the female character's (also the narrator) shock and repulsion when she discovered the secret of her husband's 'perversion' (as a 'cross-dresser' or transvestite) but eventually she accepted him as he is.

87 The legalisation of 'civil partnership' of same-sex couples in 2005 in the UK (like Netherlands, Belgium and Spain) once again seems to indicate that a sexuality alternative to 'heterosexual norm' seems to be more accepted by today's western Christian society.

88 Mary Condren, *The Serpent and the Goddess* (New York: Harper & Row, 1989) 34.

89 Ibid.

90 Ibid 27. For more further discussion of matri-focal culture in pre-patriarchal societies also see Riane Eisler, *The Chalice and the Blade: Our History, Our Future* (London: Unwin, 1990).

91 Proinsias Mac Cana, 'Women in Irish Mythology,' *The Crane Bag* Vol.4 No.1 (1980): 7. For more on Irish women in ancient Irish mythology and the ritual of Irish king's sacred marriage with the Sovereignty Goddess see Proinsias Mac Cana, 'Aspects of the Theme of King and Goddess in

Irish Literature,' Études Celtiques 7 (1955-56) 76-13; 357-413; 8 (1958-59): 59-65. See also Máire Cruise O'Brien, 'The Female Principle in Gaelic Poetry,' *Women in Irish Legend, Life and Literature,* ed, S. F. Gallagher (Gerrards Cross: Colin Smythe, 1983), Mac Cana and Muireann Ní Bhrolcháin, 'Women in Early Irish Myths and Sagas,' *The Crane Bag* Vol.4 No.1 (1980), Peter Berresford Ellis, Celtic Women (London: Constable, 1995) and Lyn Webster Wilde, *Celtic Women in Legend, Myth and History* (London: Cassell, PLC, 1997).

92 Ní Bhrolcháin 12.

93 C. G. Jung, *Collected Works*, 9.1 (Princeton, N.J.: Princeton University Press, 1959) 81.

94 For more information on diverse motherhood discourses see Chapter 2 and 3 in E. Ann Kaplan, *Motherhood and Representation* (London: Routledge, 1992) 17-58.

95 Erich Neumann, *The Great Mother: An Analysis of the Archetype, trans, Ralph Manheim* (Princeton: Princeton University Press, 1963) 184. Here qtd. in Marta Weigle, *Spiders and Spinsters* (Albuquerque: The University of New Mexico Press, 1982, 1994) 22.

96 Karl Abraham, M.D., *Selected Papers of Karl Abraham*, trans, Douglas Bryan and Alix Strachey (New York: Brunner/Mazel, 1927) 326-32. Here qtd. in Weigle 22. See also Ferdinand Anton, *Women in Pre-Columbian Art* (New York: Abner Schram, 1973).

97 Anne O'Connor, 'Images of the Evil Woman in Irish Folklore,' *Women's Studies International Forum*, Vol.11, No.4 (1988): 281-5.

98 Cathy N. Davidson and E.M. Broner, eds, *The Lost Tradition: Mothers and Daughters in Literature* (New York: Frederick Ungar Publishing Co., 1980) 191.

99   Luce Irigaray, 'Women-Mothers, the Silent Substratum of the Social Order,' *The Irigaray Reader*, ed, Margaret Whitford (Oxford: Blackwell, 1991) 47-52.

100 Davidson and Broner, introduction, *The Lost Tradition* (1980) 191.

101 Ibid.

102 Condren 24, 27, 30.

103 Adrienne Rich, Of Woman Born: Motherhood as Experience and Institution (New York: Norton, 1976) 237.

104 Natalie M. Rosinsky, 'Mothers and Daughters: Another Minority Group,' *The Lost Tradition: Mothers and Daughters in Literature*, eds, Cathy N. Davidson and E. M. Broner (New York: Frederick Ungar Publishing Co., 1980) 280.

105 Rosinsky 280.

106 Mary Daly, Beyond God the Father: *Toward a Philosophy of Women's Liberation* (Boston: Beacon Press, 1973) 149.

107 C. L. Innes, *Women and Nation in Irish Literature and Society*, 1880-1935 (London: Harvester Wheatsheaf, 1993) 40.

108 Elizabeth Wright, ed, *Feminism and Psychoanalysis: A Critical Dictionary* (Oxford: Basil Blackwell, 1992) 262. See also Chapter 2 and 3 in Kaplan (1992) pp. 17-58.

109 Davidson and Broner 191.

110 C. Park and C. Heaton, eds, *Close Company: Stories of Mothers and Daughters* (London: Virago, 1987). Here qtd. in Vivien E. Nice, *Mothers and Daughters: The Distortion of a Relationship* (London: Macmillan, 1992) 1.

111 Luise Eichenbaum and Susie Orbach, *Understanding Women* (Harmondsworth, Middlesex: Penguin, 1983) 172.

[112] Eichenbaum and Orbach 173.

[113] Luce Irigaray, 'And the One Doesn't Stir Without the Other,' *Signs*, 7/1 (1981) 60-1.

[114] Edna Longley, 'From Cathleen to Anorexia: The Breakdown of Irelands,' *A Dozen Lips* (Dublin: Attic Press, 1994) 162.

[115] Longley (1994) 162.

[116] Maud Ellman, *The Hunger Artist: Starving, Writing and Imprisonment* (London: Virago, 1993) 29-30.

[117] Eichenbaum and Orbach 171.

[118] Amanda Graham, 'The Lovely Substance of the Mother: Food, Gender and Nation in the Work of Edna O'Brien,' *Irish Studies Review* No.15 (Summer 1996): 16.

[119] Ibid 17.

[120] Ann Fogarty, preface, *Midwife to the Fairies*, by Eilis Ni Dhuibhne (Cork: Attic Press, 2003) xiv.

[121] Gerry Smyth, *The Novel and the Nation* (London: Pluto, 1997) 55.

[122] Smyth 57.

[123] M. Hirsch, *The Mother/Daughter Plot: Narrative, Psychoanalysis, Feminism* (Bloomington, Indiana: Indiana University Press, 1989) 167.

[124] Eichenbaum and Orbach 38.

[125] Eichenbaum and Orbach 40.

[126] Ibid 41.

[127] Ibid 54-5.

[128] See Nina Herman, *Too Long a Child: The Mother-Daughter Dyad* (London: Free Association Press, 1989).

[129] Irigaray (1981) 67.

[130] Irigaray (1991) 50.

[131] Nice 153.

[132] Hirsch 167.

[133] Ann Owens Weekes, 'Figuring the Mother in Contemporary Irish Fiction,' *Contemporary Irish Fiction: Themes, Tropes, Theories*, ed, Liam Harte and Michael Parker (London: Macmillan, 2000) 106. See also S. Ruddick, 'Material Thinking,' *Feminist Studies*, 6:2 (Summer 1980): 343-57.

[134] Rich 236.

[135] Nice 60.

[136] Nancy Chodorow, *The Reproduction of Mothering* (Berkeley: University of California Press, 1978) 133-40.

[137] Chodorow 137.

[138] See Chapter 1 (Mother Country: The Feminine Idiosyncrasy) and Chapter 2 (Mother Culture and Mother Church) in C. L. Innes, *Women and Nation in Irish Literature and Society*, 1880-1935 (1993) 9-42.

[139] Innes 9-25.

[140] See Loneley, 'From Cathleen to Anorexia: The Breakdown of Irelands,' (1994) 162-187 and Sara Edge, 'Representing Gender and National Identity,' *Rethinking Northern Ireland*, ed, D. Miller (London: Longman, 1998) 211-27.

[141] Edge 215-6.

[142] Smyth 56.

[143] Richard Kearney, *Myth and Motherland* (Belfast: Dorman, 1984) 18. Here qtd. in Innes 18-9.

[144] Innes 19.

[145] Ibid 27.

[146] Smyth 55.

147 Greek geographer Ptolemy of Alexandra (c. 100-170 A.D.) drew a detailed map of Ireland mentioning tribal names and places in the second century A.D. For example, the Ulster capital of Emain Mach (Navan fort, near Armagh) was recorded as a city on the map. But it is generally believed by historian and archaeologists that there had been no direct conquest from the Roman Empire to Ireland. For more about ancient Irish history, see T. W. Moody and F.X. Martin, eds, *The Course of Irish History* (Cork: Mercier Press, 1994) 43-60 and S. J. Connolly, ed, *The Oxford Companion to Irish History* (Oxford: Oxford University Press, 1998).

148 It is significant to notice the difference between the representations of the female symbol for Britain (Britannia) and France (Gaul), who were normally shown active and triumphant, and those of Ireland (Hibernia) who are characterised by her passivity and helplessness. Also see Innes 12-3.

149 Quoted by L. P. Curtis in *Anglo-Saxons and Celts: A Study of Anti-Irish Prejudice in Victorian England*, (Bridgeport, Connecticut: Conference on British Studies, 1968) 58. Here qtd. in Innes 14.

150 Innes 15-8.

151 Smyth 55.

152 Lorna Reynolds, 'Irish Women in Legend, Literature and Life,' *Women in Irish Legend, Life and Literature*, ed, S. F. Gallagher (Gerrards Cross: Colin Smythe, 1983) 15.

153 Máire Herbert, 'Celtic Heroine? The Archaeology of the Deirdre Story,' *Gender in Irish Writing*, ed, Toni O'Brien Johnson and David Cairns (Milton Keynes: Open University Press, 1991) 13-22.

154 Innes 34.

[155] Heaney describes how this poem was created and inspired in *Preoccupations: Selected Prose 1968-78* (London: Faber & Faber, 1980). Here qtd. in Innes 10.

[156] For more about the Mythological Cycle see Dr. Dáithí Ó hÓgáin, ed, *Myth, Legend and Romance: An Encyclopedia* (New York: Prentice-Hall Publishing, 1991).

[157] Patricia Lysaght, *The Banshee: The Supernatural Death Messenger* (Dublin: Glendale Press, 1986) 217.

[158] Innes 18.

[159] Innes 40.

[160] Máire Cruise O'Brien, 'The Female Principle in Gaelic Poetry,' (1983) 35-6.

[161] Innes 41.

[162] Smyth 56.

[163] In Article 41, Section 2, subsections 1 and 2 of the Irish Constitution. See *Bunreacht Na hÉireann (Constitution of Ireland)*, Department of The Taoiseach (Roinn an Taoisigh), online, internet, 29 July 2005, available http://www.taoiseach.gov.ie/attached_files/html%20files/Constitution%20of%20Ireland%20(Eng). htm. Also see Gemma Hussey, Ireland Today (Dublin: Townhouse and Country House, 1993) 419.

[164] Marina Warner, *Alone of All Her Sex: The Myth and the Cult of the Virgin Mary* (London: Picador, 1985) 236.

[165] Innes 40.

[166] Ibid.

[167] Kaplan 47.

[168] This story is from the Welsh 'Pwyll, Prince of Dyfed' in The Mabinogion, recorded in the thirteenth century from much older oral versions. Lyn

Webster Wilde retells this story in her book *Celtic Women in Legend, Myth and History* (1997), adopting the translation by Gwyn and Thomas Jones, The *Mabinogion* (London: Dent, 1978).

[169] Angela Cannings was charged with murdering her own children and was sentenced in April 2002. But she eventually appealed successfully and was freed in 2003 due to the inadequate and misleading medical evidence (the so-called 'shaken baby syndrome') put forward by Professor Sir Roy Meadow. For more See 'Mother Cleared of Killing Sons,' BBC News, online, internet, 10 December 2003, available http://news.bbc.co.uk/1/hi/england/wiltshire/3306271.stm

[170] Kaplan 45.

[171] This story on maternal instinct is Liam O'Flaherty's 'The Cow's Death' collected in *Selected Short Stories of Liam O'Flaherty* (London: New English Library, 1970).

[172] Weekes 108.

[173] Nice 179.

[174] Nice 223.

[175] Ibid 221.

[176] Ibid 154-5.

[177] Simone de Beauvoir, *The Second Sex*, trans, H. M. Parshley (Harmondsworth, Middlesex: Penguin, 1949) 528.

[178] Shulamith Firestone, *The Dialetic of Sex* (London: Jonathan Cape, 1971) 221.

[179] Nice 154.

[180] Ibid.

[181] One of the oldest known literary renderings of the Cinderella theme is a Chinese version in the ninth century. The best-known version of Cinderella may be the one which was written by the French author

Charles Perrault in *Contes de ma mere l'oye* (1697; Tales of Mother Goose, 1729) based on a common folk tale earlier recorded by Giambattista Basile as *La Gatta Cennerentola* in 1634. The Grimm brothers also collected the story of Cinderella in their *Childhood and Household Tales* (1812-15). For more information see Encyclopaedia Britannica Online, online, The University of Ulster Library, internet, 31 July 2005, available http://search.eb.com/eb/article-9082662?query=cinderella&ct=eb (Athens access only). There are also elaborate Irish variations of the Cinderella story such as 'Ní Mhaol Dhonn, Ní Mhaol Fhionn, Agus Ní Mhaol Charach' ('Miss Brown, Miss Blonde, And Miss Pleasant') told by Anna Uí Shighil, and 'An Caitín Gearr Glas' ('The Little Grey Cat') told by Peig Sayers. See both stories in Irish and English with headnotes in *The Field Day Anthology of Irish Writing*, eds, Angela Bourke, et al, vol. IV (Cork: Cork University Press, 2002) 1247-61.

[182] See Robin Morgan, *Sisterhood is Powerful* (New York: Random House, 1970) and Robin Morgan, *Sisterhood is Global* (Garden City, New York: Anchor Press/Doubleday, 1984), Magdalene Ang-Lygate, Chris Corrin and Millsom S. Henry, eds, *Desperately Seeking Sisterhood* (Abingdon, Oxon: Taylor & Francis, 1997) or Carol Lasser, '"Let Us Be Sisters Forever": The Sororal Model of Nineteenth-Century Female Friendship,' *Signs* 14 (1988): 158-81.

[183] Nina Auerbach, *Communities of Women: An Idea in Fiction* (Cambridge, Massachusetts: Harvard University Press, 1978) 8.

[184] Auerbach 5.

[185] Ibid 14.

[186] Mary Wollstonecraft, *A Vindication of the Rights of Women* (New York: W. W. Norton & Co., 1967) 194-5. Here qtd. in Auerbach 14-5

[187] Sarah Stickney Ellis, *The Women of England: Their Social Duties and Domestic Habits* (New York: J. & H. G. Langley, 1843) 28. Here qtd. in Auerbach 17.

[188] Beth Lau, 'Wollstonecraft's Daughters: Womanhood in England and France, 1780-1920,' Wayne State University Press (Summer 1998): n. pag, online, internet, 19 January 2006, available http://www.findarticles.com/p/articles/mi_m2220/is_n3_v40/ai_21182136

[189] Amy K. Levin, introduction, *The Suppressed Sister: A Relationship in Novels by Nineteenth- and Twentieth-Century British Women* (London: Associated University Press, 1992) 13-32.

[190] Paul Ricoeur, 'The Metaphorical Process as Cognition, Imagination, and Feeling,' *On Metaphor*, ed, Alan Bass (Chicago: University of Chicago Press, 1982) 211. Here qtd. in Levin 16.

[191] Levin 16. For more on Derrida's notions of metaphors, also see Jacques Derrida, 'White Mythology: Metaphor in the Text of Philosophy,' *Margins of Philosophy*, trans, Alan Bass (Chicago: University of Chicago Press, 1982).

[192] See Audre Lorde, *Sister Outsider: Essays and Speeches* (New York: Crossing Press, 1984), Oyeronke Oyewumi, *The Invention of Women: Making an African Sense of Western Gender Discourses* (Minneapolis: University of Minnesota Press, 1997), Oyeronke Oyewumi, 'Ties That (Un)bind: Feminism, Sisterhood and Other Foreign Relations,' *Jrnfs: A Journal of Culture and African Women Studies* 1.1 (2001): n. pag, online, internet, 7 April 2005, available http://www.jendajournal.com/vol1.1/oyewumi.html or Gloria I. Joseph and Jill Lewis, *Common Differences: Conflicts in Black and White Feminist Perspectives* (Boston, MA: South End Press, 1986).

[193] Levin 16.

[194] Christine Downing, *Psyche's Sisters: Reimagining the Meaning of Sisterhood* (New York: Harper & Row, 1988) 4.

[195] Levin 17.

[196] See Nina Auerbach, *Communities of Women: An Idea in Fiction* (1978) and Amy K. Levin, *The Suppressed Sister: A Relationship in Novels by Nineteenth- and Twentieth British Women* (1992).

[197] For a full, detailed account see Edith Hamilton, *Mythology* (Boston: Little Brown & Company, 1998).

[198] Auerbach 3.

[199] Levin 22-3. Amy K. Levin's illustration is based on Neumann's interpretation of the story of Psyche. See Lucius Apuleius' story of 'Cupid and Psyche' summarised by D. L. Ashliman, Folklore and Mythology Electronic Texts, 23 January 2001, online, The University of Pittsburgh, internet, 3 August 2005, available http://www.pitt.edu/~dash/cupid.html. Also see Erich Neumann, *Amor and Psyche: The Psychic Development of the Feminine. A Commentary on the Tale by Apuleius*, trans, Ralph Manheim, Bollingen Series, Vol. 54 (Princeton: Princeton University Press, 1971).

[200] Levin 23.

[201] Levin 43.

[202] Louise Bernikow, *Among Women* (New York: Harper & Row, 1980) 99.

[203] Levin 37.

[204] Bernikow 77.

[205] Elizabeth Fishel, *Sisters* (New York: Bantam Books, 1979) 121-2.

[206] Fishel 121-2.

[207] Robert W. White, *The Enterprise of Living*, second edition (New York: Holt, Rinehart & Winston, 1976) 96.

[208] Downing 139.

[209] Toni McNaron, 'How Little We Know and How Much We Feel,' *The Sister Bond*, ed, Toni McNaron (New York: Pergamon, 1985) 8.

[210] Ibid 8.

[211] Downing 12.

[212] Downing 166.

[213] Annis Pratt, et al, *Archetypal Patterns in Women's Fiction* (Brighton: Harvester, 1982) 95.

[214] For more details see Chapter 4 in Pratt, et al (1982).

[215] Shumaker, Jeanette Roberts, 'Sacrificial Women in Short Stories by Mary Lavin and Edna O'Brien,' *Studies in Short Fiction* (Spring 1995): n. pag, online, internet, 15 September 2004, available www.findarticles.com/p/articles/msi m2455/is_n2_v32/ai_ 17268505

[216] Kiera O'Hara, 'Love Objects: Love and Obsession in the Stories of Edna O'Brien,' *Studies in Short Fiction*, 30 (1993): 322.

[217] Shumaker, internet, 15 September 2004.

[218] Ibid.

[219] Phyllis Chesler, *Women and Madness* (New York: Harcourt Brace Jovanovich, 1972) 184. Here qtd. in Pratt, et al (1982) 102.

[220] Elizabeth Wright, ed, *Feminism and Psychoanalysis: A Critical Dictionary* (Oxford: Basil Blackwell Ltd, 1992) 218-9. For more information see Judith Butler, *Gender Trouble: Feminism and the Subversion of Identity* (New York: Routledge, 1990) and Luce Irigaray, 'Female Hom(m)osexuality,' *Speculum of the Other Woman*, trans, Gillian Gill (Ithaca, New York: Cornell University Press, 1985) 98-104.

[221] The first account of lesbian sex, pointed out by Emma Donoghue, appeared in Maura Richards's *Interlude* (1982). For more see Emma Donoghue, 'Noises from Woodsheds: Tales of Irish Lesbians, 1886-1989,' *Lesbian and Gay Visions of Ireland: Toward the Twenty-First Century*, eds, Ide O'Carroll and Eoin Collins (London: Cassell, 1995) 158-70. See also Emma Donoghue, ed, 'Lesbian Encounters, 1745-1997,' *The Field Day Anthology of Irish Writing*, eds, Angela Bourke, et al, Vol. IV (Cork: Cork University Press, 2002) 1090-1140.

[222] Donoghue 166.

[223] For more information on gay movements and law reforms see Kieran Rose, 'Equality for Lesbians and Gay Men,' *ILGA Europe* (June 1998): n. pag, online, internet, 25 March 2002, available http://www.steff. suite.dk/report.htm, Kieran Rose, *Diverse Communities: the Evolution of Lesbian and Gay Politics in Ireland* (Cork: Cork University Press, 1994), ICCL, *Equality Now for Lesbians and Gay Men* (Dublin: Irish Council for Civil Liberties, 1990) and O'Carroll and Collins, eds, *Lesbian and Gay Visions of Ireland* (1995).

[224] For more information please refer to *The Irish Statute Book 1922-2003*, The Office of the Attorney General and Houses of the Oireachtas, The Stationery Office, online, internet, 19 January 2006, available http:// www.irishstatutebook.ie/

[225] O'Carroll and Collins, 'Interview with Mary Dorcey,' 30.

[226] Donoghue 167.

[227] O'Carroll and Collins, 'Interview with Mary Dorcey,' 40.

[228] Mary Dorcey, 'The Orphan,' *IF Only* (Dublin: Poolbeg Press, 1997) 105-30.

[229] See Jane Freeman, *Feminism* (Buckingham: Open University Press, 2001) 61. For more also see Onlywomen, eds, *Love Your Enemy? The Debate*

Between Heterosexual Feminism and Political Lesbianism (London: Onlywomen Press, 1981).

[230] For more see Peter Berresford Ellis, *Celtic Women in Celtic Society and Literature* (London: Constable, 1995) and Mary Condren, *The Serpent and the Goddess* (New York: Harper & Row, 1989).

[231] Sarah Stickney Ellis, *The Women of England* (1843) 68-9. Here qtd. in Auerbach 17-8.

[232] Some feminists, such as Katie Roiphe, attack such view of predatory men and victimised women for 'reinforcing Victorian gender stereotypes.' See Katie Roiphe, *The Morning After: Sex, Fear, and, Feminism on Campus* (Boston: Little, Brown & Co., 1993).

[233] Downing 170.

[234] See Peter, Brook, *A Concise Glossary of Cultural Theory* (New York: Oxford University Press, 1999) 177-8 and Michel Foucault, 'The Subject of Power,' Michel Foucault: *Beyond Structuralism and Hermeneutics*, eds, Hubert L. Dreyfus and Paul Rabinow (Chicago: University of Chicago Press, 1982) 223.

[235] Downing 139.

[236] See Nina Auerbach's argument on the recurrent literary motif of sisterhood demolished by patriarchy in mythologies in the introduction of *Communities of Women: An Idea in Fiction* (1978) 3-32.

[237] Elizabeth Janeway, Man's World, *Woman's Place: A Study in Social Mythology* (New York: William Morrow & Co., 1975) 7. Here qtd. in Auerbach 12-15.

[238] 'True College for Women,' *Imperial Review* (1867): 8; quoted in *Duncan Crow, The Victorian Woman* (New York: Stein and Day, 1972) 199. Here qtd. in Auerbach 14.

[239] Auerbach 14.

[240] Wollstonecraft 194-5. Here qtd. in Auerbach 14-5.

[241] Auerbach 15.

[242] See Adrienne Rich, 'Compulsory Heterosexuality and Lesbian Existence,' *Feminisms: A Reader*, ed, Maggie Humm (London: Harvester Wheatsheaf, 1992) 177 and Susan Gubar, 'Feminist Misogyny: Mary Wollstonecraft and the Paradox of "It Takes One to Know One,"' *Feminist Studies* Vol.21 No.3 (Fall 1994): 461.

[243] The legalisation of civil partnership of gay couples in the UK in 2005, like some other European countries like Netherlands, Belgium and Spain, seems to indicate that same-sex relationships are more accepted (than in the previous centuries) in today's western Christian society.

[244] Downing 141.

[245] Estella Lauter and Carol Schreier Rupprecht, eds, *Feminist Archetypal Theory.* (Bnoxville: The University of Tennessee Press, 1985) 11.

文學小說類　PG2576　實踐大學 58

Women and Relationships in Contemporary Irish Women's Short Stories

作　　者 / 張婉麗
策　　劃 / 錢中媛
文字編輯 / 王雯珊
責任編輯 / 姚芳慈
圖文排版 / 蔡忠翰
封面設計 / 劉肇昇

發 行 人 / 宋政坤
法律顧問 / 毛國樑　律師
出版發行 / 秀威資訊科技股份有限公司
　　　　　114 台北市內湖區瑞光路 76 巷 65 號 1 樓
　　　　　電話：+886-2-2796-3638　傳真：+886-2-2796-1377
　　　　　http://www.showwe.com.tw
劃撥帳號 / 19563868　戶名：秀威資訊科技股份有限公司
　　　　　讀者服務信箱：service@showwe.com.tw
展售門市 / 國家書店（松江門市）
　　　　　104 台北市中山區松江路 209 號 1 樓
　　　　　電話：+886-2-2518-0207　傳真：+886-2-2518-0778
網路訂購 / 秀威網路書店：https://store.showwe.tw
　　　　　國家網路書店：https://www.govbooks.com.tw

2021 年 7 月　BOD 一版
定價：320 元
版權所有　翻印必究
本書如有缺頁、破損或裝訂錯誤，請寄回更換

讀者回函卡